MW01242111

Negotiations and Love Songs

Suzi Lindsay

Copyright © 2014 Suzi Lindsay

All rights reserved.

ISBN: 1496045297

ISBN-13: 978-1496045294

This is a work of fiction. Names, characters, dialogue, and incidents are products of the author's imagination or are used fictitiously. Any resemblance to actual events or persons, living or dead, is entirely coincidental.

ACKNOWLEDGMENTS

Writing can be a lonely job, but this book was a joy to write because of the enthusiastic support of my friends and family.

Marcy Holden was key in getting the book completed – never too busy to critique, plot, or keep characterization uniform, she once became so impatient with my ideas that she ripped a digital recorder from my hand and dictated notes for the next scene!

My daughter Connie contributed information on emergency medical response, Emergency Room procedures, and lampwork.

My beta readers, Doreen Wise, Lisa Guenthert, Trudy Kidwell, Jill Robey, Cyndi Bryant, Terri Mullins, Chris Johnson, and Jo Anne Roark of course told me I'm brilliant, but were also, thank goodness, brave enough to point out my errors. Sandra Carson, Mary Lou Carson, Damon Coronado, and Robert Tuck helped with technical problems.

Thank you all for your unflagging encouragement and help, and for making it so much fun.

CHAPTER ONE

Every time she had the nightmare about telling Park Palmer she'd stolen his sperm from the fertility clinic, Madison Templeton felt vaguely disturbed all day.

Aside from the fact that she could lose her nursing license and possibly have criminal charges placed against her, she worried that her child might be taken away. That the sperm was going to be discarded anyway didn't really seem to mitigate the crime, and she didn't think she could ever forgive herself for that insane act. It was almost as if the hand that put the syringe containing the sperm in her pocket was disconnected from her brain, which was screaming, "What are you doing?"

Since there was no reasonable remedy for the theft, she tried not to think about it, unfortunately without much success. Today she hoped a little yard work would at least distract her. She surveyed the results of an hour's work. She might as well forget checking leaf raking off her list of things to do today. As fast as she could rake a pile together, it was decimated by the payoff of her crime—her four-year-old son, Cameron—and her dog. Finally, she dropped her rake and plopped down in the leaves with them.

"Thanks a lot, Cam," she said. "I just bathed Dudley, and now he's filthy again." The little boy giggled and dropped the next armload of dusty leaves on Madison, instead of the dog. She grabbed him and spanked him playfully, then covered his face with kisses. Dudley popped up out of the leaves and jumped into her lap too, one leaf entangled in the black fur on top of his head.

Cam, a mini-me Park, brought her immeasurable joy. The thought of losing him were his paternity discovered was unbearable.

Madison shook off the dark thoughts. There was no reason to be afraid; no one could possibly figure out the secret of Cam's conception, and only her sister knew what had happened. Park Palmer had no reason to suspect that Cam even existed. Anyway, she knew she'd never see Park again. Wasn't that the way it had been all her life? The daughter of a traveling salesman who was constantly transferred from city to city, Madison had a long, painful history of losing people. Even when she was finally able to put down permanent roots, failed relationships had extended that pattern of loss. You love, you say goodbye. After her second divorce, she'd decided not to allow herself to love a man ever again. In fact, she didn't want anything she couldn't stand to lose. Well, except for her kids. Breaking that rule for Park Palmer had been one of the biggest mistakes of her life, because she'd lost him, just like all the rest. And she had never completely recovered.

Madison hugged Cam. At least she had a little piece of Park to soothe her soul. How she would love to tell Park about their child—to meet up with him again, looking her best, and present him with the son he'd always wanted. Unfortunately, she would never be able to do that.

"Mom, you're squashing me," Cam complained.

She released him, and he dived back into the leaves. As much as she regretted the impulsive decision to take the sperm, she adored her little boy. There just wasn't a way to reconcile the problem without injuring others, so Madison simply lived with the guilt and fear.

But Cam was worth it, she thought. Definitely worth it.

Besides that, after what Park had done to her, maybe he deserved what she'd done.

* * *

Park Palmer shivered in his thick, Irish-knit turtleneck as he drove slowly down Wayside Drive, looking for the street where there was a small house for rent. He turned the heat up a notch, eliciting a dirty look from his wife.

"I wish you would get your blood count checked," Claire said. "You're always freezing when your count is low, even when the weather's warm."

"Sorry," Park said. "I'll turn it off."

"Never mind." Claire struggled out of her sweater, tied it around her shoulders, and cracked her window. A strong odor of petroleum filled the car, and with a grimace of distaste, she rolled the window up again. "What a God-forsaken city. Are you sure we're in the right area? It looks like shantytown."

"According to the key map, it's right. There's no zoning in Houston, so people can build whatever they want on their property." They passed a boarded-up fish market and a pet shop painted hot pink, followed by a few single-family homes, a new video store, and a motel that appeared to be disappearing, one board at a time. "Sure makes it hard to tell which areas are safe, though. Maybe it's a sign."

"A sign of what?" Claire asked absently, once again absorbed in the Robb Report, the bible of connoisseurs of the luxury lifestyle. She was in the middle of an article about a New York boutique, convinced they would be interested in her jewelry designs. Which Park doubted.

He tried to squelch his irritation. Claire was a talented hot glass artist, and her work was slowly gaining a following on eBay and in one Dallas boutique, but it was a far cry from the fine jewelry featured in the Robb Report. He wished she would put the magazine down and help him watch for the street where he needed to turn. She didn't seem the least bit concerned about his urgent need to locate temporary housing in Houston.

"A sign that this is the wrong thing to do," he said.

"Well, what other choice do you have? We're broke. You haven't worked at all since you got sick. We've gone through our savings and retirement funds, and we're thousands of dollars in debt. Both of the houses are gone, and now, we're stuck in an apartment." Claire consulted her Tag Heuer watch, the last decent gift, she had recently pointed out, that he'd given her. "You're going to have to stop being so picky about your accommodations. I want to be back on the road to Dallas by four, and you need to have a plan."

Well, excuse the hell out of me for getting sick, Park thought, literally biting the tip of his tongue to keep from saying it aloud. "I guess if push comes to shove, I'll have to take an efficiency apartment in the medical center."

"Oh, that's smart. Use what little cash we have left on a ridiculously overpriced closet with a Bunsen burner for cooking and a Johnny-on the-Job for plumbing."

"I know it's not affordable. That's why I need you to stay one more day; I need help finding temporary quarters. If the hospital calls today with my test results, I may have to start treatment tomorrow. I'll never find a place to live, at this rate."

"You know good and well that I have classes tomorrow morning. You're just going to have to manage by yourself. One of us has to work, you know."

She didn't add, "and you promised when we married that it wouldn't be me," but Park knew she was counting on him, the shrink, to finish the sentence in his head. He usually forced himself to respond to her waspish remarks with a mild and reasonable comment, but today, it just took more energy than he could muster. "Oh, come down off your cross, Claire. Before I got sick, I didn't care whether you worked or not, although I've never understood why you bothered with a college education if you didn't want a career. Your degree was collecting dust, while you made jewelry."

"Well, finally the truth comes out. You consider making designer jewelry a hobby."

"That's pretty much what it is, unless you can sell your product."

"I am selling it."

"But not enough of it to pay the rent." He sighed. "I know this argument by heart, and I really don't feel like rehashing it. I've always covered our expenses, but right now, I really need you to return the favor. And if you can't do it with some grace, then I guess we don't have much of a marriage."

"You just might be right about the last part."

Park glanced at her in surprise. Claire was examining her French manicure, jaw set. He knew she thought their previously comfortable lifestyle had been permanently replaced with hardship, but it was the first time she'd implied that divorce was on her mind. A shiver of fear went through him. "Maybe it's time for us to get some marriage counseling."

"The almighty 50-minute-hour," she said. "Talk fixes everything, right?"

"No, but it's helped lots of people." Park turned into a neighborhood with houses that looked like they'd been built in the forties or fifties, each one different. The lawns were well tended, with an unusual combination of trees for Houston—live oaks, pines, palms, and a variety of old hardwoods. He knew a former patient of his, Madison Templeton, lived on this street, but he didn't have her house number with him. They had corresponded sporadically over the last few years, and when he'd seen the ad for a rental house on her street, he'd decided to look at it. The whole street was only two blocks long; with luck, he might run into her.

Park spotted the rental house and pulled into the driveway. It was a beautiful old neighborhood. Next door, a young woman raked up crimson and yellow leaves that had fallen from a huge oak, laughing as they were immediately scattered by a little boy and a black dog. Across the street in a well-tended park, a lively birthday party was in progress. The street dead-ended at a grassy area edged by a bayou resembling a small, curling river.

Their real estate agent, who was waiting inside, took them on a quick tour of the two-bedroom house. Sparsely furnished with nondescript furniture, it smelled moldy, and had a general feeling of neglect. Park looked despairingly at Claire. "This is hopeless."

"I don't see anything wrong with it. How fancy does a place have to be? All you're going to do is sleep and throw up for six months."

Park, stunned by this new level of insensitivity, said softly, "That's really nice, Claire. Thanks."

She turned and walked out the front door, flinging a barb over her shoulder: "Well, you wanted my opinion. Sorry if you don't like it."

* * *

Park followed Claire outside. As they reached their car, the dog in the yard next door started barking and ran toward them, followed by the little boy, who yelled, "Damn it, Dudley! Come back here!"

The woman sitting under the tree grabbed a red leash, jumped to her feet, and ran after them, clearly trying not to laugh at the child's language. Just as they reached Park and Claire, she caught the dog and snapped the leash on his collar.

"Sorry," she said, as she straightened up. He won't bite." When her eyes reached Park's, the color drained from her face. "Park," she said, her eyes and mouth round with surprise.

Claire's female intruder antenna shot up. The woman appeared to be in her early thirties; tall, broad shouldered, and long legged, she had long, shiny brunette hair, parted in the middle and secured behind her ears with barrettes. Her navy and green plaid flannel shirt was tucked into high-waisted navy corduroy jeans. She was covered with dust and a few dry leaves. Her eyes, fringed with dark lashes, were the color of stone-washed blue denim.

Park reached out and pulled a leaf from her hair. "Madison," he said, a note of tenderness in his voice, "how wonderful to see you! I knew you lived on this street, but not which house."

Park and Madison seemed paralyzed by each other, an awkward silence spinning out in the chilly air. It was totally unlike Park, always the gentleman, not to introduce Claire immediately.

The dog jerked Madison off balance, breaking the spell. She turned to Claire and offered her hand. "Hi. I'm Madison."

"Oh, yes," Park said, "This is my wife, Claire."

Claire ignored the extended hand, and squatted down to get a better look at the little boy. "And what's your name?"

"Cam," he said, dimpling at her. He had straight blonde hair, rosy cheeks and lips, and unusual light green eyes that twinkled behind round, wire-rimmed glasses.

In her entire life, Claire had only known one other person with eyes that exact shade of green—her husband. "Really," she said, archly. "Would that be short for Cameron, by any chance?"

"Yes Ma'am."

"And how old are you?"

"I'm four."

Claire stood and looked Park straight in the eye. "Fascinating. Park, how do you and Madison know each other?"

"She's a nurse," he said. "We worked in the same office building in Memphis."

Liar, Claire thought. She knew from snooping in Park's personal correspondence that Madison was a former patient of his. And maybe a little more than that—Madison would have been getting pregnant just about the time she and Park were moving to Dallas. She looked at her husband with fresh fury. Until this moment, as far as she knew, neither she nor Park had ever slept with anyone else; that was their special thing. Now, apparently, that was gone, along with everything else of value in their life.

"What are you doing in Houston, Park?" Madison asked.

Before Park could answer, Claire's cell phone rang. She squinted at the caller ID, tried to answer, then disconnected. "My battery just went dead. It's Anderson. We need to return the call immediately."

"You can use our phone," said Cam. He grabbed Claire's hand and pulled her toward the house. "C'mon."

"Is Cam your son?" Claire heard Park asked Madison.

"Yes."

"You never mentioned you'd had a baby, in your letters."

"Oh, surely I did," she said, her voice sounding high and thin to Claire. No you didn't, Claire thought, noting Madison's now scarlet face as she held the storm door open for her guests. Claire knew, because she had read every single letter Madison had written to her husband.

After Park had become ill and they'd moved to Dallas, Claire had combined his clinic and home offices. He'd had more complications with his medical treatment than anticipated, and had never started a new clinical practice, as planned.

One day, while organizing a file cabinet, she had unpacked a personal correspondence folder. It was worn and overstuffed, and when she picked it up, the bottom gave away, spilling cards and letters across the floor. More than half of them were signed by someone named Madison.

Claire had picked a letter at random. The ivory stationary had laser-cut lace edges and was written in beautiful Catholic school cursive, with peacock-blue ink. Although Madison hadn't said it directly, she was obviously in love with Park, and was agonized by his loss. Claire had sniffed the paper. At least the little witch had the grace not to perfume it.

The rest of the letters were more of the same, each written on a different type of stationary, with perfect penmanship, grammar, and composition, as if done by a professional writer. They should have been written in blood, as dripping with pain as they were.

Since Park was so ill, and they had left Memphis anyway, Claire had never mentioned her discovery. She was used to patients being attached to her husband, who was a wonderful therapist, but this relationship seemed different. Some of Madison's letters were responses to his letters, and there seemed to be an intense emotional struggle between them. Suspicion and fear had tainted Claire's feelings for Park from that day forward.

The floor plan of Madison's house was similar to the house next door, but the décor couldn't have been more different. The living room walls were painted deep lavender. Four sets of white ruffled curtains tied back with long-tailed bows stretched across the floor-to-ceiling front windows, which took up most of the wall. There was a candy-apple red daybed piled with royal blue and white pillows, appliquéd and quilted, too unique to be anything but handmade. A delicious smell wafted in from the kitchen, and oldies but goodies played softly in the background.

Claire mentally turned up her nose. Loving hands at home, she thought, much preferring the austerity of neutral colors, chrome and glass. And gourmet take-out meals.

Park stopped to take in the room as a whole. "Wow, this is really unusual. But what else would I expect?" He smiled at Madison. "I love the walls."

"Men always say that. Women never comment," Madison said, smiling back.

Claire stared at him. "I thought you liked neutral walls."

Park leaned over to examine a large, square coffee table. A mountain sunrise scene was carved into it, then painted in blues, purples, greens, and oranges. "I see you're over your Ethan Allen phase," he said to Madison.

"Oh, it's the same furniture. The house flooded a few years ago, and the tables were pretty much ruined. I decided to turn them into folk art, rather than throw them out. Please, have a seat. I'll fix some coffee. Claire, the phone is on that table."

Waiting until Madison had left the room, Claire picked up the phone, pretended to turn it on, then set it back in its charger. "This phone doesn't work either. Cam, does Mommy have another phone in her bedroom?"

"Yes Ma'am. Come on, I'll show you."

Park frowned at Claire. "Don't you think you should ask Madison if that's okay?"

"Oh, I'm sure she won't mind," Claire purred.

She followed the little boy to a back bedroom. It was painted robin's egg blue, with more lace-edged, ruffled white curtains. There was a queen-sized mahogany sleigh bed with a matching pie-crust table, from which Cam took a phone. He handed it to Claire, and she sat on the bed and dialed M. D. Anderson Hospital.

"This is Dr. Palmer's wife returning Dr. Bright's page." While she waited for the operator to connect her, she critiqued Madison's bedroom.

The theme of this room seemed to be a tea party, Claire thought distastefully. The bed was covered with a handmade quilt. The design and bright colors were interesting, however silly; the blocks were set on point, each with a different tea pot, one for each month of the year. Alternate blocks had tea recipes. Bubble tea was made with pearl tapioca and consumed through a fat straw; catnip tea, made with the obvious, was apparently for one's pets. In one corner of the room, two life-sized porcelain baby dolls, which Miss Loving-Hands-at-Home had probably also made, sat at doll-sized table, set for tea.

Oh, grow up, Claire thought. Madison seemed to be single, and no wonder. What man would want to live in a playhouse?

Dr. Bright finally answered. She informed Claire that Park had qualified for the anemia study, and was to start chemotherapy the next morning. Claire, whose attention was focused on a framed 8 x 10 picture on the pie-crust table, barely thanked her. She set the phone down, picked up the picture, and stared at it in disbelief.

It was a beautifully done, black and white study of Park. He sat at his desk in the Memphis clinic, head bent over his writing, glasses perched on the end of his nose. The room was lit only by his desk lamp, a vignette she had seen a thousand times, prototypically her husband. Claire had never seen this picture.

What she saw next put the last nail in the coffin of her marriage.

A miniature teacup and saucer sat by the picture. She picked it up and dumped the contents into her hand. It was a pair of cufflinks made of variegated green glass, shaped like barbells. And they were unmistakably Park's.

She should know. She'd made them.

* * *

Park believed you never really knew people until you had seen their homes. As he slowly took in Madison's living room, he thought it was an expression of personality like he had rarely seen. Most people picked out basic furniture and added knick-knacks. But every inch of Madison's home was decorated with handcrafted items, a showcase of her talents. He felt positively dipped in her essence.

A red leather recliner angled by the front windows, facing west; he remembered how nourishing it was to her soul to watch the sun set every day. Her end table was a smorgasbord of books. She was reading *Lying on the Couch*, a novel by renowned psychiatrist Irvin Yalom. Park smiled, imagining her critique of that work. There was a book on critical thinking; a biography of Hillary Clinton; a textbook on forensic nursing; some magazines— quilting, digital photography, crosswords, fiction writing—and Lee Strobel's new work, *The Case for a Creator*. As usual, Madison was multi-tasking both body and soul.

On a small laptop was a manuscript about 50 pages long that had been edited in pencil. Park tilted his head so he could read the first page without disturbing the papers.

NEGOTIATIONS AND LOVE SONGS
by Madison Templeton

CHAPTER ONE

"Weigh day! Weigh day! Everyone report to the lounge immediately!"

Reagan Steele, jarred from an uneasy sleep by the gravelly voice issuing from a speaker above her head, sat straight up and wildly scanned her surroundings: White room. White walls. White floor.

She was in a hospital bed. On the bedside table was a telephone with a one-foot cord. There were a couple of chairs. No drapes.

Then she remembered: She was in the funny farm. Reagan shivered and lay down again, rolling into fetal position and pulling her thin white blanket up to her chin.

Her door was shoved open, and a middle-aged woman said firmly, "Miz Steele, you need to get to the lounge to get weighed. Right now." The woman walked away, leaving the door open, violating the first rule Reagan had learned in nursing school: Always leave the door exactly as you found it.

She sat up, swung her legs over the side of the bed, and shuffled to the bathroom on leaden legs. Her back hurt so much she could barely walk, but there was no time to soak in a hot bath; apparently, it was urgent that she be weighed, as if they were charging her by the pound instead of the day.

"Come on. We're leaving."

Park looked up to find Claire standing over him, face red, eyes blazing. She clutched something in her left hand, her fingers curled so tightly around it that her knuckles were white.

"What's wrong?" he asked, but she ignored him, going silently out the front door.

Madison came out of the kitchen, drying her hands on a

towel. "What's going on?"

"I don't know, but something really upset Claire. Maybe we just got some bad news. I better go see what's up."

Madison followed him out the door. "But we haven't had time to talk."

"I'm really sorry. I'll be in touch."

Park hurried across the lawn, leaving Madison standing on the front porch. Claire was already in the car, staring stonily out the window. Park got in and buckled his seatbelt. "Is it bad news from Anderson? Didn't I qualify for the study?"

"Are you still having an affair with her?"

It took Park a moment to register the non sequitur. "What? *Still* having an affair? I never had an affair with her. Why on earth would you think that?"

"Oh, any number of things. Like a kid who is the spitting image of you?"

"That's ridiculous. Lots of kids with blonde hair and green eyes look like me. How does that add up to an affair?" He backed out of the driveway, and started the reverse route to their hotel.

"I'll send you some pictures of yourself at that age. You compare." She narrowed her eyes. "I know who she is, Park. And she isn't just a nurse who worked in your office building in Memphis. I read her letters when I consolidated your offices."

Park mentally cursed. He knew he shouldn't have kept Madison's letters. For this very reason, that they were so complicated to explain, and an incorrect conclusion could be drawn by an uninformed reader, like Claire. Still, she had no right to read material in his office, and she knew it.

"If you read confidential information," he said evenly, "then you know she was my patient. And I do not sleep with my patients. *Ever.* Or anyone else, for that matter. You are my one and only."

"Well, then, explain why your 'patient' wrote you love letters. I've been wondering for a long time."

"You've been married to a shrink long enough to know it's unethical for me to discuss a patient with you. And I wouldn't call them love letters."

"Well, what would you call them?"

Agony letters, he would call them. Never had he seen a person as devastated by a separation as Madison. She was in bad shape when she'd come to him for help, and she was in worse shape when he left.

And his agony had mirrored hers, not only because of the pain he'd caused her and the fear that she would harm herself, but because . . . well, because . . .

Park slammed on his brakes to avoid hitting a car that had pulled in front of them without warning. People in this town drove like maniacs. He needed to concentrate on driving right now, not on trying to convince his wife of his faithfulness. "Can we wait until we get back to the hotel to discuss this?"

"Why, so you can get your story together?"

"No, so I don't kill us."

"She's still in love with you."

"Claire, that poor girl had the worst case of transference I've ever seen. When a patient idealizes the therapist and has feelings for him, it's not an authentic type of love. You know that happens to a shrink. It's an occupational hazard."

"Authentic or inauthentic, it's love. Did you have the worst case of countertransference you've ever seen? And speaking of ethics, why were you still treating her, if she had such strong feelings for you?"

It was a question he'd asked himself many times.

"You didn't want me to go with you today, did you," Claire said, bitterly. "You knew the rental house was next door to hers. You wanted to see her."

"That's not true. You said you were tired. I was just trying to be considerate. I admit I wanted to see my former patient, but I certainly didn't expect it to happen like this." It was the truth, but not the whole truth, and he hated himself for lying by omission.

"I don't believe you. In all the years I've lived with you, I've never known you to go to a patient's house. Especially one whose décor you're familiar with."

"When she was in therapy, she told me she'd bought new furniture. I've never been to her house."

"Really. Then why were these on her bedside table?" Claire held out her hand and opened it.

Park pulled into the valet area of the hotel and turned off the car, then looked at what she held. Nestled in her palm was a pair of cufflinks he had lost several years ago. He took them from her, surprised they had reappeared. "Madison had these?"

Claire got out and slammed the door so hard, the car rocked. By the time Park got to their room, she had her suitcase out and was cramming her clothes inside.

"Claire, please don't jump to conclusions. I don't know how she got the cufflinks. I don't even remember when I saw them last."

Claire gave him an "I am so sure" look.

"Let me talk to Madison," Park said, "and with her permission, I'll explain the whole thing. You're making assumptions that just aren't true."

"You're in love with her," Claire said. "She's beautiful, and young, and obviously talented, even if her taste in decorating is pathetic."

"Well, she wasn't beautiful when I was treating her. She was quite obese, and wore thick glasses. And FYI, she's the same age as I am."

"That makes it even worse! There's something so special about her that you fell in love, even when she physically repulsed you. Now you can have the best of everything."

"Claire, look at me. I am not in love with her."

"Liar. I saw the way you two looked at each other. Or rather, tried not to look at each other." She zipped the suitcase and picked up her purse. "By the way, you qualified for the study. You start chemo tomorrow at eight a.m. I guess you'll get a cure this time, with a bone marrow donation from your son."

At the door, she added sweetly, "Oh, would you ask Madison if I can have a copy of that 8 x 10 of you that she keeps at her bedside? Have a nice life."

Park was still absorbing the information about the picture as she slammed the door. The comment about his 'son,' he ignored.

Because he knew that simply couldn't be true.

CHAPTER TWO

When Park and Claire were out of sight, Madison closed the front door and leaned against it. Flooded with adrenalin, her heart pounded and her hands shook. Dear God, why was Park in Houston, on her street, looking at a rental house? What had happened that made them leave so precipitously? Had they figured out what she'd done so many years ago? And what had Claire meant when she'd said, "It's Anderson"? Did she mean M.D. Anderson, the cancer hospital? Did Park have cancer? If he did, it was a rare kind, because he could get ordinary cancer treatment at home in Dallas.

"Mom," Cam said, "Why is Claire mad?"

"What do you mean? When did she get mad?"

"When she looked at Park's picture."

"She was in my bedroom?"

Cam nodded. "She said the phone was broken, and could she use the one in your bedroom. So I showed her."

"Did Park go back there too?" Say no, she thought. Say no, say no, say NO.

"No, just me 'n Claire. And she looked at Park's picture and her face got all red. Then they left."

Madison felt her blood drain to her toes. Park's picture was on her bedside table, along with his cufflinks. She heard her dead mother's voice in her head: Your little Park-shrine might be your undoing and it serves you right, Missy.

Shut up, Mom, Madison thought. She settled Cam in front of the TV with a video, and on watery legs, went to her bedroom.

The picture was exactly where it belonged on her bedside table. But the teacup, a souvenir her British friend had brought her from "Will Shakespeare's" house in England, sat in the middle of the table, empty. The cufflinks were gone.

Madison grabbed the phone and shakily punched in her sister's number in Memphis. Messed it up, tried again.

"Come on, Bree, be home, I need you," she whispered as the phone rang several times. Finally, her sister answered.

"Bree," Madison said, "you will never guess who just left my house."

"Uh, let's see. Elvis? No, I just saw him at the mall. One of your exes, who lives in Texas?"

"Park and Claire Palmer."

"You're kidding. What were they doing there?"

"Looking at the rental house next door."

"Why? That is too weird."

"I've no idea. I only got to talk to them for a couple of minutes. Maybe they're moving to Houston. But why would they rent a house, and why in this neighborhood? They're more the River Oaks type. This is way too low rent for them."

"Not to mention that the odds of them looking at a house right next to you are astronomical."

Madison broke out in a sweat. "I know. I'm really scared. Do you think it could have anything to do with Cam?"

"I didn't think Park knew about Cam."

"He doesn't. Or didn't. I guess I'm just paranoid. The problem is, he might figure it out now. Park couldn't lose that kid in a crowd, he looks just like him. You should see them side by side. I think Claire is suspicious." Madison didn't mention the picture Claire had seen, or the cufflinks. "Do you think I should tell him about Cam? I mean, what if he figures it out? Wouldn't that be worse?"

"It depends on how you look at it. What's the worst that can happen if you tell him? What's the worst if you don't?"

Would he hate her? Would he try to get custody? Would he even have claim to a child who had been created with his sperm—sperm that was, for all practical purposes, trash? Did he retain rights to discarded genetic material? Would he even want Cam?

"I don't know," Madison said. Oddly enough, I was just sitting outside, wishing I could tell him about Cam. I guess I just didn't factor his wife into the equation."

"Yeah, that would have been a good thing to think about before you stole the sperm."

"I didn't exactly steal it."

"Yes you did."

"Well, maybe so, but anyway, it was supposed to be thrown away. And you know the state I was in when that happened. There wasn't much thinking involved."

"If you had thought he and his wife would find out about Cam, would you still have done it?"

Madison thought back to the day when the lab technician at the clinic had asked her to discard a couple of sperm samples that were possibly contaminated with soap, and therefore unusable. To her surprise, one of the samples belonged to none other than Park. Park, who was abandoning her, moving on to a better job. Leaving her shattered, with only a handful of mementos to prove that he'd been there: His business card, a sticky note with a list of chores in his nearly illegible handwriting, the end of a roll of antacid tablets, a pair of cufflinks. A pathetic collection of his belongings she had picked up—well, okay, she amended—snitched— as if they were body parts she could use to make a Park clone after he left.

But now, she had something way better than that little pile of junk. She had his sperm, and she could make a baby. All she had to do was a simple insemination. It was exactly the right time in her cycle, and although the sperm was prepared for a different type of procedure and wasn't optimal for an insemination, it might work. Assuming the soap residue hadn't killed the sperm. That was easy enough to find out. All she needed was a tiny drop of the sample. She could check it under the microscope at the clinic tomorrow morning.

Madison, once described as a person whose biggest problem was that she wanted to be an angel, had to make a decision. The pain of losing Park was unbearable, and to her shame, she was also angry at him for leaving her. The perfect revenge had been handed to her. Let him go; she would still have a piece of him. It seemed destined, somehow; after all, what were the odds of this happening? And what would be the harm? He would never know.

Later the doubt would creep in, the guilt. She knew it was selfish and unfair to be so angry. Furthermore, she didn't even know why he was having sperm frozen. He didn't have any children; he was probably preparing for infertility treatment. But if he couldn't use the sperm, was it wrong for her to use it?

"Madi, are you there?" Bree asked.

"Yeah, just thinking."

"Look, I know your brain wasn't in gear when you did it. Sounds to me like you might need some legal advice. Are you okay? How did it feel, seeing him after all this time?"

"I'm confused. Do you remember when I had to go to that convention in Toronto, when I was just three months sober? I was sitting at the bulkhead of the plane, right behind first class. Just before we landed, the flight attendant whipped back the curtain, and there was a duty-free liquor cart with a huge bottle of Kahlua. It was like seeing one of my exes—I didn't know if I wanted to hug it or punch it in the nose. Right this minute, it feels kind of like that."

"You're not going to drink, are you?"

"Of course not. I'm going to smoke and OD on sugar."

"Oh well, that's acceptable. How does Park look, five years later?"

"Very thin, and kind of tired."

"What's his wife like?"

Madison's reaction to Claire was simple and clear: Instant jealousy. "Very striking, although not at all what I thought he would choose. Tall, gaunt, haughty. White-blonde hair skinned back in a bun, pale, piercing blue eyes, long nose with a bump in the middle, like it had been broken. Prada heels, designer jeans. She wore some beautiful jewelry, though. Very unusual lampwork beads."

"That's the hot glass thing you want to do, where you have to melt different kinds of glass with a torch to make the beads?"

Madison sighed. "Yeah. Guess that will have to wait. I'd better save every penny, in case I have to lawyer-up. Damn it. I just don't want to deal with this."

After she hung up, Madison made dinner for Cam. She couldn't eat; her guts were tied in knots. She paced, couldn't settle down. Tried to call her AA sponsor; no answer. Pictured the bottle of Kahlua on the airplane cart; right now, she wanted to hug it. A triple White Russian sounded like heaven. A good slug of booze would settle her right down.

Damn it, now she had to go to a meeting. It was an inflexible rule she'd set for herself in early sobriety: If she had a serious thought about drinking, she went to an AA meeting immediately. She looked at the clock. The Sunday night meeting at her home group started in thirty minutes.

Luckily, her teenage babysitter was able to come straight over, and Madison headed for Pasadena, praying that one of the regulars who had some quality sobriety would be at the meeting.

* * *

Park didn't know what to worry about first. His immediate and most pressing concern was to make a decision about where to live for the next six months.

The events of the last two hours ran through his head like a movie on a continuous loop. In particular, he replayed Claire's sudden blow up. What did she mean by "Have a nice life"? Was she leaving him?

How he wished he could turn back the clock. Yes, he had wanted to see Madison, but he could have done that later. Now he was in a disaster of epic proportions. Aside from losing Claire physically, which he couldn't even contemplate right now, she was his sole support. Park had a separate checking account with a little over a thousand bucks in it, which wouldn't last long. It was imperative to be as frugal as possible.

There was no time to look further for cheap accommodations; he would have to lease the house next door to Madison. And it would serve Claire right, said a nasty little voice in his head. She had abandoned him. She could have stayed with him in Houston and taught art history courses by internet this semester, but she had refused. And now it looked like she might be gone for good.

He hated himself for thinking things like that. But he knew that if he traced his feelings all the way to baseline, he would find fear.

No, terror. Terror of dying, alone and miserable while it was happening. The doctors never had figured out what caused his bone marrow to stop producing new cells, a condition called aplastic anemia. His first round of treatment with chemotherapy and a bone marrow transplant had failed, and he had been sent to Houston to see if he qualified for experimental treatment with a promising new drug. It had been hard enough when Claire was there to help him . . . the thought of facing it alone was unbearable. Also, a new bone marrow donor had to be found; that in itself caused overwhelming worry.

He tried to push down the memory of Madison sitting in his Memphis office, saying, "You have helped me so much—I owe you. If you ever need help, just dial M," but it surfaced anyway, because not only did he need help—he needed help from someone who cared about him. And then the shrink in him took over, worried that his behavior was totally inappropriate, and potentially harmful to Madison.

Which brought him to the problem of the cufflinks. He knew patients sometimes took personal belongings of therapists if they had an opportunity, even though it had never happened to him before; but he couldn't imagine how Madison had acquired his cufflinks. He seldom used them, because he wore shirts with French cuffs only on dress occasions.

Then he remembered the last time he'd worn the cufflinks—it was right before he and Claire had left Memphis, when they had attended a black tie fundraiser for the Junior League. But still—how did Madison get the cufflinks? She'd never been in his home.

The picture of him, he could explain; it was probably the one she had taken in his office one evening, after a therapy session. The little boy who looked like him and was named after him, he could not explain. That had to be total coincidence.

It was nearly 6 p.m., and Park needed to get organized, but he just stared into space, allowing pain to overwhelm him. Everything was wrong. In the last five years, he had lost his home, his livelihood, his health, and maybe his wife. He flashed back on Madison when she was in treatment, her face tear-streaked, saying, "Why does every damn thing you love have to be taken away from you?" as he sat there smugly in his good health and tailor-made suit.

Finally, with leaden limbs, he called the real estate agent and arranged to deliver a check, sign the lease on the house, and pick up the keys. He simply did not have the energy to look for anyplace else to live. He packed and checked out of the hotel.

After meeting the agent, he stopped at Super Target for supplies.

Park was totally unprepared to stay in Houston. He had thought if he were accepted in the study, he'd have time to go home, at least for a few days, before starting treatment. He had only the bare necessities with him—his laptop, some reading material, some clothes and toiletries. He wandered up and down the aisles of the store, trying to focus on what he needed, listlessly throwing things in his basket—a set of sheets, a blanket, a pillow. Soap, towels, and washcloths. In the grocery section, he stood in front of a freezer for a while, blankly staring at frozen dinners, then randomly chose ten. Added some bottled water and a few apples to the basket, and plenty of designer beer. Checked out, knowing he didn't have everything he needed. That was Claire's department. She took care of him so thoroughly that he was hopeless at taking care of himself.

Retracing his earlier route, Park got back to the rental house at 9 p.m. The lights were still on at Madison's. He heard a swing creaking, and realized she was sitting in the dark on the front porch, illuminated only by stripes of light that spilled through the front window blinds. He walked across the yard, his eyes gradually adjusting to the dim light.

Madison sat with one foot propped on the seat of the porch swing, pushing herself with the other. Her head rested on the back cushion, long hair hanging down behind her. She was wrapped tightly in a long turquoise quilted robe, decorated with red, yellow, and green dinosaurs. He recognized it as the one she'd worn in the hospital, years ago.

"Hi there," Park said. "Whatcha doin'?"

"Thinkin'," she replied, as if they were having an ordinary conversation.

"About?"

"Well, let's see. About what you're doing in Houston, generally, and what you're doing at my house, specifically, and what the hell happened this afternoon, microscopically."

Park sat down on the edge of the porch, and leaned back against one of the posts. "You're angry."

"Well, how would you feel if you were sitting in your front yard, fat, dumb, and happy, and your past dropped in on you, like a Kansas house on a witch? And then disappeared just as suddenly?"

Park was silent, giving her time to throw it all up.

"It's your turn," Madison said. "I'm not your patient anymore, so save your psychotherapeutic techniques."

Park couldn't help himself—he chuckled quietly. It was a perfect example of why he had found her such a delightful patient: Every session, she had given him one hell of a run for his money.

"Some things never change," he said, then sobered, groping for the words to explain his sudden reappearance in her life. He dreaded breaking his medical condition to her, this woman whom he had once grievously injured with his selfishness and poor judgment.

He took a deep breath and blew it out. "I'm in Houston for about six months, for medical treatment. I rented the house next door."

She sat up, the swing screeching in protest. "That's what the phone call to 'Anderson' was about! You're here for cancer treatment!"

"No. I have aplastic anemia. They're not sure of the cause, but it's not cancer, although it's sometimes treated with cancer drugs. Madison," he said softly, "I'm sorry I just appeared in your life, out of the blue. If you can't handle it, I can find someplace else to live while I'm here."

"Park Palmer, don't you dare give me therapy when you're the one in trouble now!"

"I just don't want to hurt you again, and I don't want you to relapse. Assuming you're still sober."

"I'm not going to drink. I can overindulge in these if I get desperate." She held up a pack cigarettes and a bag of Hershey's kisses, tossed the candy in his lap. "Here, have some. Everybody knows chocolate regenerates bone marrow."

"I wish. What's with the cigarettes? I thought you'd quit."

She caressed the unopened pack like it was a precious child. "I did, when I got—when I started working in the in vitro fertilization department. You know, IVF, the test tube baby thing. Cigarette smoke is embryo toxic, and I promised my boss I would quit for good."

"Was it hard?"

"Compared to other things I've given up—no. Anyway, powerful mojo woman that I am, I just knew if one of the patients didn't get pregnant and I had smoked a single cigarette, it would have been my fault. But we digress. Tell me more about your anemia. When were you diagnosed? What's your prognosis?"

"Madi," Park said, gently redirecting her, "tell me how you are, really."

"I'm okay. I'm off antidepressants, and I gave up my identity as a psych patient last year. I didn't even have to be surgically removed from my therapist. Isn't that good?"

He smiled. "Lucky therapist." Early in therapy, Madison had jokingly told him he'd better have a few units of his blood frozen for future use, because when therapy was over, she would have to be surgically excised from him. His heart twisted with pain at the memory of the day he'd told her he was leaving. Arrogant ass that he was, he'd assumed her reaction to separation, which she'd described early in therapy, was exaggerated. Well, he was wrong. And, as she had predicted, it was bloody. For months, he'd been afraid she would kill herself.

When she'd confessed she was in love with him, he probably should have sent her to another therapist. He didn't, telling himself that she would experience that as rejection. Besides, he had successfully treated other patients who thought they were in love with him; eventually, they realized it was only transference, a displaced sort of love, like you would feel for the father you wished you had.

But deep down, he knew he'd kept her as a patient because he enjoyed her company so much. She was the most unusual woman he had ever known. As her therapist, he could not admit to her, and had flatly refused to admit to himself, how he felt about her. Even now, after five years, the old magic was in the air, and he felt the old temptation to touch her. He tucked the hand closest to her under his hip.

"And now," she continued, "here you are, unburdened by ethics and treatment modalities, so while you're getting well, we can get to know each other as real people. You can finally tell me about yourself, information which you previously refused to share, if you remember."

"The 'therapeutic plum,' I believe you called it, with which I escaped."

"My, my, did you memorize all my letters?"

"No, but certain phrases stuck." He paused, searching for a delicate way to introduce the next subject, his curiosity about who had fathered her child. "You can fill me in on what's happened since I last saw you."

She shrugged. "What more could you possibly need to know about me?"

"Well, for instance, you seem to have omitted a small detail in your letters, like the fact that you had a baby. Judging from his age, you must have gotten pregnant just before we left Memphis. Why didn't you tell me you were in a new relationship?"

"Because I wasn't in a new relationship." She stood, indicating the conversation was over. "I should get to bed. I have to get up early." She walked toward her front door and opened it, warm light spilling over her. "Goodnight," she said.

"Madi, wait. We have to talk about the cufflinks."

"Cam told me Claire found them. I am really sorry about that. I just wanted something of yours to remember you by," she said in a small voice. "One day, when you went out of the office to take an emergency phone call, I took them off your desk."

"Claire made those cufflinks for me, and I was very careful with them. I only used them on special occasions. They wouldn't have been in the office. In fact, the last time I saw them, they were on the dresser in my bedroom. So how did they get from my bedroom to yours, is what my wife wants to know."

Madison clutched her robe tightly around her and hung her head. "Did you know," she said softly, that love screws up your brain chemistry to the point where you'll do things that later seem so bizarre, it makes you sick?"

"Of course I know that."

"Things that you can't undo. Like pushing medicine into an IV. You can't get it back."

Park hated the pain in her voice.

"I have never loved a man like I loved you. Never. And because our relationship was so schizophrenic—me turning myself inside out like a dirty sock, you sitting there in your Brooks Brothers suit, polishing your halo and refusing to tell me who you really were—and between us this—this feeling that you denied—my curiosity about you became unbearable.

"One Sunday afternoon, when your home in Memphis was on the market, there was an open house. I went in. I can't believe I did that. I was terrified that you'd come home and find me there. But I wanted to know the real you, the you that was withheld from me. I just wanted to know something very personal about you, to hold in my heart. Like what kind of furniture you have. Where you sit to watch T.V. What you read before you go to sleep. Anything."

Her expression begged him to understand. "Your cufflinks were on the dresser, and on impulse, I took them."

Had Park thought the situation through, he would have realized this was the only possible explanation. But it never occurred to him that a patient would invade his home. He felt violated to the core. Not that he wouldn't have been happy, in time, to have her in his home, given the opportunity to choose how to present himself. But not like this, with her free to discover intensely private things.

Park held his temper, tried to frame his reply in a therapeutic manner. It was inappropriate to get angry at a patient. On the other hand, Madison was no longer his patient, and the day had completely sapped his tolerance. "Do you have any idea what you've done? My wife thinks we had an affair."

Madison fired back. "Well, if I'd known your wife was going to ramble around my bedroom today, I'd have put the cufflinks away."

"You wouldn't even have the cufflinks if you hadn't been rambling around *my* bedroom. And stolen them, I might add. Have you stolen anything else of mine?"

"I think you better go now," she said tightly.

Park tossed the bag of candy on the swing, stalked back across the yard, and started unloading the car. He dumped everything on the foyer floor in the house, finishing in three trips.

The house was dark and cold, and his footsteps echoed on the ceramic tile floor. He turned on the single living room lamp and the heat, then started putting things away.

In the kitchen, he opened a beer and chugged half of it. Screw sobriety, he thought, wiping his mouth on his sleeve. Now Madison would know she wasn't the only one with a drinking problem. He pitched the frozen dinners, now soft, in the freezer. Drained his beer, snagged another one. Stuck the apples, water, and the rest of the beer in the fridge.

Pathetic. He was pathetically unprepared for the rest of his life. And now he was at odds with the one person who would probably be willing to help him.

Madi was right, their relationship had been schizophrenic. From time to time she had requested personal information about him, which he'd withheld. Not that it was inappropriate for a therapist to share some personal information with a patient. It was just that Park, her almighty and omniscient therapist, was in fact a clay-footed mortal who was afraid she wouldn't like the real him.

He was embarrassed when he thought about what she could have found out about him, sneaking around in his home. Did she find out that, contrary to her belief, he was not a brilliant thinker who spent his life in search of the ultimate truth? That all he wanted after a full day of psychotherapy was brain candy? A daytime idealist, was Park Palmer, and a nighttime Austin Powers fan.

She probably expected to find some psychology tome on his bedside table. Most likely, she found copies of *Sports Illustrated* and some warped psychology humor, like *Dr. Mezmer's World of Bad Psychology*.

Park carried the rest of his purchases to the bedroom. He opened the stiff sheets, snapping them viciously in the air as he made the bed. You wanted her to admire you, he lectured himself. You liked the fact that she loved you. You puffed up your ego and played come here/go away with her. Bright girl that she is, she had a pretty good idea you were doing that, too. But you denied it. To her, to yourself. And now to your wife.

And then he'd left Madison in confusion, the very reason she had come to him in the first place—confusion over whether or not other "Gods" in her life loved her.

He hung up his clothes, took his toiletries to the bathroom, finished his beer, got another one. Good, now he would have a hangover on top of everything else. That suited his mood perfectly. Hell, he'd probably be nauseated after chemo tomorrow anyway.

He wanted to talk to Claire, to make sure she'd made it home okay, explain about the cufflinks, make it all go away. But he didn't have a phone yet, or even an internet connection to e-mail her. There wasn't a TV or even a radio in the house. Or an alarm clock, for that matter. They had only one cell phone, and Claire had it.

Crappy as it was, the house was still a good enough place to sleep and throw up in for six months, he thought bitterly.

In the bedroom, Park stripped down to his shorts, and

settled between his scratchy new sheets. He set his watch alarm for six a.m., praying that he would hear it. He had to be at Anderson by eight.

Then the beer hit his brain, and he fell into an uneasy sleep.

CHAPTER THREE

Madison closed the front blinds and sat down on the edge of the recliner, clutching her robe around her. Her heart was pounding so hard that she could feel each beat in her chest, and she was hyperventilating, a sure precursor of a panic attack. Even the thought of a panic attack notched her pulse up.

She leaned back in the chair, willing her breathing to slow. If she didn't calm down, her heart would kick into the irregular rhythm that plagued her periodically. It wasn't lethal, but once it started, it often lasted a whole day, leaving her short of breath and exhausted.

Madison had long dreamed of a reunion with Park, one that was poignant and bittersweet with the love she was convinced was mutual, love they had both sacrificed to maintain honor. But she had never *really* expected to see him again, much less have him show up at her house with his wife. Why on earth had he done that?

And now that he had seen Cam, he would surely connect the dots. Madison's heart skipped a beat, then another, then settled into the dreaded arrhythmia that would probably last all night, keeping her awake and gasping for breath.

She rushed to the kitchen, filled a glass with water, and

took out her heart medication. Her hands shook so hard, she couldn't get the child-proof cap off the bottle, and when she finally did, tiny pink pills spilled out across the counter in a thousand different directions, like a disturbed ants' nest.

As she collected the pills, she realized she'd picked up her blood pressure medication, which she had already taken that morning. She steadied herself against the counter, closed her eyes, and took a deep breath. Taking out the correct bottle, she read the label twice before downing the pill.

Madison let Dudley out in the back yard, wondering if Park could possibly have figured out that Cam was his child, even though they'd never had a physical relationship. They had worked in the same building in Memphis; Park had maintained a private psychology practice, aside from his university teaching work; Madison was the coordinator of an infertility clinic.

The clinic processed semen for various reasons—analysis, infertility treatments, long-term storage, research. She had assumed, since Park had no children, that he was having sperm stored for infertility treatment. Now she realized he had probably known about his aplastic anemia, and intended to store his sperm before he had chemotherapy, which destroyed sperm production, often permanently. If, after his chemotherapy, he ever wanted children, the sperm could be used for artificial insemination or in vitro fertilization.

Adding another layer of guilt to what she had done, Madison wondered if she would have taken the sperm if the specimen hadn't been contaminated. With the sperm gone, Park's fertility might have been lost forever. The shame of that day was burned into her soul, and no amount of therapy or twelve-step work would ever erase it.

Did her feelings for Park mitigate her actions? She had lived for her psychotherapy appointments with him. The way she had prepared, you'd have thought she was going on a date—her hair freshly washed, her nails manicured, her nicest clothes, her topic prepared and rehearsed. She saw him after she finished work, and was usually his last patient for the day. Madison loved sitting in his office high above the city, wrapped in the cocoon of his gentle voice, watching the lights come on below, night settling down like a blue velvet blanket. He never rushed her, never cut off a session, no matter how long it took. In fact, she had often ended sessions herself when they ran over, out of consideration for him. Tucked away in her subconscious was a catalog of ways she believed he showed he cared about her, and his willingness not to end a therapy session abruptly because the fifty minutes was up, like most therapists did, was first on the list.

The evening he'd told her he was leaving, she had started the session by telling him about a curious dream, one that was, in retrospect, oddly prophetic: She was moving, packing her belongings, and she couldn't take much, so she was discarding things—old hats, mementos, junk left behind by other people, and a dress pattern, which she had pressed between her mattress and box springs.

"Interesting that you were hiding a pattern," Park said.

"I don't think I deliberately hide patterns from myself. The problem is being able—or willing—to change them. For instance," she said, picking at a hangnail, "maybe I subconsciously keep myself from getting well, so I don't have to leave you."

She glanced at him obliquely, then looked away, anticipating rejection. She couldn't stay in psychotherapy forever, and her inevitable separation from him was always floating around the room, like a poltergeist. Park had once hinted that they might be friends after her therapy was over, which had thrilled Madison; but later, he'd waffled. They'd already had one huge disagreement about it, and she was desperate for a firm commitment from him. That night, for some reason, her need for reassurance was especially strong.

Park evaded the issue. "Has that been a pattern in your life? Being needy, holding on to someone who takes care of you?"

That's right, hide behind your Freudian beard, you coward, she thought. "You side-stepped the question."

"I'm sorry, was there a question in there for me?"

"You know what the question is."

Shrinkly silence, observation. Waiting. Shame transforming into fury, she stubbornly answered silence with silence.

He cracked first. "We'll stay in touch."

The coldness and distance of his comment was so unlike him. "No we won't," she said. "I'll walk out of this room and never see you again. Just like a thousand other people in my life."

Ordinarily, Park sat very still during therapy, except for alternately jiggling his feet, and never took his eyes off of her face; but that night, he kept shifting in his chair, frowning and stroking his beard. In a barely audible voice, he said, "Madi, this is a very difficult situation. I understand your separation issues. But sometimes, separation simply can't be helped. Things change. I'm trying to find a way to tell you—to tell you—that I'm leaving."

Madison stared at him in complete shock, barely breathing, holding herself together so tightly that she felt like she was turning to stone. As if from a long distance, she heard his disclaimers— private practice wasn't lucrative enough to pay the bills . . . applied for a job in Dallas, never expected to get it . . . last chance to excel and use his education before slowing down . . .

After he wound down, they sat in silence. Lights came on in the city below, people getting on with their lives. Madison's life had frozen, a clock with its pendulum stopped on the upswing. She simply could not absorb the enormity of it. After five long minutes she said, "I'm sorry. I can't even react to this." She gathered her belongings and walked numbly down the long hall to the elevators with him trailing behind, talking to her back.

"I'll be out of town for two days, but they know how to get me. Call if you want to talk."

It was the worst day of her life. Madison went straight to Joe's Liquors, where she was greeted like an old friend. She used to stop by Joe's daily to get her ration of booze, because it never lasted in her house; whatever was there, she drank. The guys at Joe's said they could set their watches by her. Five o'clock, on the dot, Madison was there for her fix.

Feeling like lightning might strike her at any moment, she bought a gallon each of Kahlua and 100-proof vodka, and a carton of cigarettes. Just like they said, cunning, baffling, and powerful was alcohol; in seconds, Madison had rejected everything she'd learned in recovery. All she could think about was the electric chocolate-coffee taste of a White Russian, its icy progress to her stomach, the knowledge that pain relief, albeit a Trojan-horse cure, was on the way to her central nervous system.

On the way home, she went by Park's house. He lived on the riverfront, near the community where Madison lived. Beyond caring who saw her, she parked across the street and opened the vodka, unwieldy as a jug of moonshine, and took several gulps, spilling some down the front of her shirt. When it had stopped burning her throat, she did it again. And again.

The realtor's sign in his front yard attested to the fact that Park had known for a while that he was moving. She'd known that he might be changing jobs, but he'd assured her he was not leaving Memphis. Liar. The type of plans he'd made didn't happen overnight. That had made her furious, but in fairness to him, she pushed the feeling down. It was his life. She had no right to be angry. And it might not even be true; he could have accepted the job yesterday, for all she knew. What was he supposed to do? Call her and tell her?

Madison lit a cigarette, inhaled deeply, sat back and waited for her drugs of choice to perform their magic. Hurry, hurry, hurry, she thought, feeling the pain coming for her. She stared bleakly at his house, trying to imagine a life without him, even if all she'd ever had was an hour a week with him, for which she had to pay.

At home, she sat in the dark, tears streaming steadily down her face, pouring liquor into a body that had been dry for a year and a half. Combined with the cigarettes, it hit her hard and fast. All night, she relived the incident, his voice echoing in her mind: I'm trying to tell you I'm leaving . . . I'm leaving . . .

Madison came back to the present, the pain of that memory making her chest ache. She brushed her teeth, checked Cam to make sure he hadn't kicked his covers off, and set the house alarm. In her bedroom, she hid Park's picture in her dresser, then crawled into bed and pulled the quilt up to her chin. Her mind turned to the day Cam had been conceived.

It was Park's last day in Memphis, a cold, rainy Friday afternoon. Madison was waiting to do an insemination, which required her to inject sperm directly into her patient's uterus through a tiny catheter. It seemed to be taking forever to get the sperm ready, and finally, she went to the andrology lab to see what the problem was. Tired and hung over, all she could think of was going home to drown her sorrows some more.

Rachel, the andrologist, was on the phone. She hung up when she saw Madison. "I was just paging you."

Madison tried to keep the irritation out of her voice. "What's taking so long?"

Rachel's face was white. "The semen samples are contaminated."

"Contaminated? With what?"

"I don't know. Soap, maybe. Normally, I give the guys disposable plastic cups to collect their specimens in, but we're out of them, so I had to give them the glass jars we use for IVF. Maybe there was some kind of residue from the sterilizer in the jars, or maybe they weren't rinsed adequately after they were washed. I thought all the particles would be gone by the time I washed the sperm and let it swim up, but there were still some left. Do you think we should use it?"

"Gosh, I don't know. What if it gave the patient an infection, or some kind of toxic reaction? Did you call Dr. Bascomb?"

"She's out of town. I left a message at her hotel."

"Well, personally, I'm not willing to risk my nursing license on an elective procedure, and by the time we hear from her, the sperm will be compromised. I say we cancel all procedures."

"Executive decision accepted." From the warmer, Rachel took two bags containing syringes loaded with concentrated sperm. "Darn, I had this sperm all washed, rinsed, and fluff dried. What a waste of time." She handed two bags to Madison. "My biohazard container is full. Would you discard these for me?"

"Sure." Madison slipped the bags into her lab coat pocket. With heavy heart, she went to the exam room where Lila Smythe, one of her favorite patients, waited for her insemination.

Lila turned toward Madison with an expectant smile that changed to tears when she learned her insemination was canceled. Every cycle was precious to couples who dealt with infertility; every delay lessened their prospects for parenthood. Madison let her cry.

"Was Rob's count good this time?" Lila asked, between sobs.

Madison took the bags out of her pocket and laid them on the counter. She opened the first bag and took the syringe out, unable to believe her eyes. "Yikes," she whispered. "Olympic sperm." The count was so high it had to be a mistake; it was rare for an infertile man to have a count that high. She turned the label over to read the patient's name. Palmer, Park C.

Park? Madison could not believe her eyes. Why would he have a semen specimen here? Were he and Claire infertility patients? She knew they didn't have any children, but she didn't know why.

"Madison?" Lila said.

Refusing to think about what she was contemplating, Madison slid the syringe into the bag and put it back in her pocket, then took the syringe out of the other bag and read the name and the sperm count.

"Only one million this time, Lila," she said. "Rob has had better counts. Maybe this is a good thing, after all. You only get four free inseminations in this study. I bet next time his count will be up, and you'll have a better chance of getting pregnant."

"It only takes one sperm," Lila said.

"Well—it's a bit more complicated than that. Come on, sweetheart, get dressed. Go home; call me when your cycle starts. In the meantime, you guys try to have some fun. It's gonna be all right."

Madison walked out of the clinic with Park's sperm still in her pocket, just knowing at any minute she was going to be stopped at the door, like when she was a kid and tried to leave K-Mart without paying for some candy she'd eaten. She absolutely refused to think about her intentions, because if she did, she knew she'd turn around and do the right thing—discard the sperm.

At home, she took out the report and the syringe, checking the name again, and the date of birth. She knew the month and year Park was born, but not the day. The month and year were right; it had to be his sperm.

Feeling equal parts of anger, love, and revenge, Madison did a fast calculation of her cycle date. Day 13. Sperm lived 48 hours. If she ovulated the next day, she had a chance of conceiving.

The insemination only took seconds. It was ridiculous to hope it would work, because the sperm had been prepared for a different procedure, and there was the question of whether or not the contaminant had damaged the sperm; but Park had Klingon sperm, and she was a fertility goddess who had conceived twice when she was trying *not* to get pregnant, so there was at least a chance of pregnancy.

Then reality set in.

For a long time after that, Madison tortured herself. With one insane action, she had violated the moral, ethical, and legal foundation of both her personal and professional lives. But the worst thing was, way down deep, she believed that if she were put in that situation again, she would do the same thing.

Now she turned over in bed and punched her pillow into shape. Would a normal person suspect someone of doing something so bizarre? Most people didn't even know how artificial insemination was done. Surely what she had done would never occur to Park. Even though he'd figured out she was pregnant around the time he left Memphis, he had said earlier that he didn't know she had a kid. So it couldn't be that he'd come to Houston hoping he had a child to donate bone marrow, if bone marrow transplant was part of his treatment regimen. Maybe he just wanted to see her, or just needed help during his treatment, which his precious wife obviously wasn't interested in providing.

Which brought her to the issue she'd been repressing, Park's aplastic anemia. He had glossed it over when he'd told her, and redirected her attention to his concern for her. A shrinkly ploy. Madison knew next to nothing about aplastic anemia, except that it was a serious disease. She felt her heart rate increase, and checked her pulse. Her heart was still beating irregularly, at twice the normal rate. There would be little sleep for her tonight.

She got up and booted the computer in the front bedroom that served as an office/studio, spent an hour printing information on aplastic anemia and its treatment, then padded back to the living room and sat down to read.

In aplastic anemia, the bone marrow stopped producing red blood cells, white blood cells, and platelets. Causes included malfunctions of the immune system, certain diseases, and adverse reactions to drugs.

"Oh, my God," she said aloud, alarmed at the mortality rates. The statistics were grim. There was only a 25% cure rate, although it increased to 75% with a successful bone marrow transplant. The problem was, many patients died while waiting for a compatible donor.

Shit, shit, shit, she was going to have to tell him about

Cam. She could not let Park die. She had to help him. But the thought of telling him he was Cam's father made her physically ill. And putting Cam through a bone marrow aspiration was simply not an option.

Then she remembered something that might keep Cam safe. After his birth, she had banked his umbilical cord blood. Even better than bone marrow, she could provide Park with Cam's stem cells from the cord blood! That would at least spare Cam from the bone marrow aspiration.

Maybe if she could save his life, Park would forgive her. At the very least, she was sure he would stay in her life if she told him about Cam. A commitment, even if forced.

Guilt for such a thought kicked in immediately. Get thee behind me, Satan, she thought. She had often told Park that if she could write the script for the future, making their relationship come out any way she wanted, she didn't know what she would do. It couldn't be anything that would hurt anyone. The newly reconstructed Madison tried to be careful about hurting other people. Still, a tiny flame of hope glowed deep in the recesses of her heart. It sounded like Claire was mad at him; someday, he might be single . . . if she could only have him, at long last, her life would be perfect.

That is, if she didn't go to jail for Grand Theft Sperm, or have a custody battle over Cam.

And if Park recovered from his illness.

* * *

Park was ripped from sleep by a window-rattling shriek. He looked around wildly, disoriented, then fought his way out of his covers and ran outside. The noise was a security alarm, coming from Madison's house, and he flew across the cold, wet grass and banged on her front door. It was still dark, and he had no idea what time it was.

The alarm stopped, leaving a ringing silence, and Cam

opened the door, crying hysterically. He held his arms up and Park picked him up. "Cam, what's wrong?"

"I don't know," the little boy wailed. "I think it's a boogaler."

Park stepped into the house. Through the dining room archway, he could see a corner of the kitchen; the back door was open. Holding Cam tightly, he advanced cautiously across the living and dining rooms, until he could see into the kitchen.

He almost laughed when he saw Madison sitting in the middle of the kitchen floor, legs splayed, in Mickey Mouse pajamas. In her arms she held her wet, shivering black dog, wrapped in a bubble gum-pink towel.

"Oh, Dud, I'm so sorry!" she said, kissing him on the top of his wet head. Dudley looked up at her adoringly and licked her cheek.

"Madi, what on earth is going on?" Park asked.

She rubbed the dog vigorously with the towel. "I forgot to let him back in last night. Stupid dog never will bark when he wants in. It rained, and he's soaked, and he's freezing. Do you think he'll get pneumonia?"

The dog squirmed out of her arms and shook himself, showering Madison with water, then padded over to his dog dishes, lapped up some water, and started eating.

"I don't like to wake up like this, Mom," Cam said, rubbing one eye with his fist.

"Me either," said Park.

"I'm sorry, guys," she said. "I was so upset when I realized I'd left him out in the rain, I forgot to turn the alarm off before I opened the door."

Park saw Madison give him a quick head to toe scan, suddenly aware that he was standing in her kitchen in yesterday's T-shirt and boxers.

"Well," he said uncomfortably, "I'm glad you're okay. And I'm sure Dudley will be fine." He set Cam down and made a fast exit.

Back in the rental house, Park drank a beer as he showered and dressed. He had a hangover, and he felt inexplicably frightened about his upcoming treatment. He needed Claire badly. She had taken him to all his treatments the first time, and the thought of walking into that hospital alone made him physically ill. The pain of her abandonment added to his misery, and he scoured his brain for a solution. He could try explaining how Madi had acquired the cufflinks, but he didn't think Claire would believe him. She had picked up the electricity zinging between him and Madi; combined with the circumstantial evidence, the case against him was probably closed.

Park put off leaving until the very last second. He sat in his car, looking at Madison's house, wishing she could go with him, knowing without a doubt that she would if he asked. With her new-found sobriety, if she ever needed chemo, she'd probably sail through it bravely; he admired her for learning to tolerate discomfort without drinking. He couldn't even tolerate discomfort *with* drinking.

Even in the short period of time he'd been around her in Houston, he could see she had grown so far beyond where his skills as a therapist could have taken her, that sometimes, he didn't know which one of them was the shrink, which one the patient.

* * *

Madison decided to call the vet later, rather than take Dudley in to see him. She had to get to work; her IVF case had to be set up and the patient ready by 7:30, no ifs, ands, or buts, and she was already running late.

She had slept only a couple of hours. Her damn heart was still beating erratically. A cup of high-octane coffee might make her arrhythmia worse, but she had to wake up.

The stinging spray of a hot shower did little to stimulate her. It would be a long, miserable day, and all she wanted to do was get in her bed and sleep until her life returned to the simple pleasure of sitting under her big tree, playing with her son and her dog.

It was seven by the time she got to work, and she needed to move fast. Her patient, Sara, stood in the dark hallway outside the office, leaning against her husband, Boris.

"Hi guys," Madison said. "Have you been here very long?"

Sara licked her dry lips. "About thirty minutes. We didn't want to take a chance getting caught in traffic."

"Starting out early is always a good plan in Houston." Madison led them down the hall to the Recovery Room, where she would prepare Sara for her egg aspiration. While Sara changed into a hospital gown, Madison set up her paperwork and drugs, chatting with Boris as she worked.

When Sara came out, she climbed in bed and covered up with a sigh. She looked tired and drawn.

"Did you sleep any last night?" Madison asked, as she took Sara's vital signs and started an IV.

"I tried to go to sleep, but I just couldn't. I just kept going over everything. How much this costs, how it's the only IVF cycle we can afford, how many eggs will they get, is it going to hurt, will Boris be able to collect his specimen without me to help, blah, blah, blah . . ."

"Would you like me to give you something to take the edge off your anxiety?"

"That would be great."

Madison had Versed, a powerful sedative, prepared to use during the procedure, and she gave Sara a milligram in her IV. "This will hit you real fast, so don't be scared. It will make the room go around for a minute or so. I want you to take some deep breaths and relax."

She dimmed the overhead light, then got a warm blanket and covered Sara. "We're going to take very good care of you," Madison said quietly. "I'll be right there with you the whole time, and I'll tell you everything that's going to happen, so there won't be any surprises."

Sara groped blindly for her husband's hand, and smiled bravely. "Thank you, Madison," she whispered.

In the cold, dim procedure room, Mari Kumar, the other IVF nurse, expertly assembled the complicated tubing system required for the egg aspiration.

"Thank God it's your turn to scrub," Madison said, as she set up her monitoring equipment. "All that tubing looks like a pile of spaghetti to me today. I'd never get everything hooked up right."

"Are you sick?" Mari asked.

"No, I just didn't sleep much."

"How many eggs does Sara have?"

"Looks like there are about six."

"Maybe you can go home early. Dr. Bascomb will have six measly eggs out faster than a lizard can catch a fly."

Madison snickered at the imagery." True, she does everything fast. I guarantee you a fly never landed on her in her entire life."

Madison brought Sara in, asking her questions to distract her as she was prepared for her procedure. When Dr. Bascomb came in, the pace of the room picked up. Within minutes, Sara was prepped and draped, and an ultrasound probe was inserted into her vagina. Madison gave Sara another milligram of Versed and a milligram of morphine. Mari handed Dr. Bascomb what seemed like a yard-long needle, which she slid through a guide on the probe.

Madison sat at the patient's side, holding her hand. "Okay, Sara, we're ready to do the 'big stick.' Take a deep breath . . . hold it . . ."

With a quick jab, Dr. Bascomb passed the needle through Sara's vaginal wall, into her ovary. Sara screamed.

"Okay, sweetheart," Madison said. "That was the worst. It will get better now. Breathe, in through your nose, out through your mouth."

Sara continued to squirm and cry out as Dr. Bascomb moved the needle from one area of the ovary to another, aspirating eggs.

"Give her another milligram of Versed," Dr. Bascomb said, her eyes never leaving the ultrasound screen.

More like ten of morphine and ten of Versed, Madison thought sourly. She peeled her hand away from Sara's and administered the medicine, sneaking in an extra milligram of morphine. Pain control was an ongoing battle between Madison and Dr. Bascomb, who insisted patients had more anxiety than pain. Maybe so, but Madison always held her patients' hands during procedures, and when her own hand was crushed to the point that she couldn't tolerate the pain, that, in her opinion, was an indication that her patient needed more pain medication. Sometimes Madison woke up in the middle of the night with her hands aching.

Twenty minutes later, Sara was back in the recovery room, with six eggs in the lab, waiting for her husband's sperm.

While Mari cleaned the procedure room and sterilized instruments, Madison monitored Sara's vital signs and prepared charts for clinic. There were several new patients, and most of the charts didn't have previous medical records, which was bad. The patients were supposed to have their records sent to the office before their first visit, so there was time to evaluate prior treatment and consolidate the information; but sometimes, they brought the records with them. In that case, Madison would never get home, as Dr. Bascomb insisted that the records be summarized immediately, which required extra time. Madison was tired, and needed more down time to process yesterday's events.

All day, in her head she carried the image of Park standing in her kitchen in his T-shirt and boxers, hair sticking up on one side of his head, eyes bloodshot. Though she hadn't been real close to him, she thought she smelled beer. The problem of Cam notwithstanding, she was thrilled to have Park back in her life, but as much as she thought she wanted to know the real Park, Madison began to realize that she might not like what she found.

She supposed that was one of the many reasons therapists were secretive—their patients might lose respect for them. Madison knew that she'd idealized him, but she never thought she had done so to the extreme. Now she wondered . . .

She couldn't tell if he was still mad at her. He had come charging into the house to help her, then left abruptly. Well, she supposed it would have been awkward to invite him for coffee. After all, she had been inappropriately dressed as well, in her Mickey Mouse pajamas. God, how embarrassing. But if he was living next door, she supposed it would be impossible to look her best all the time.

Sara was fully awake and ready for discharge at noon. Madison took her charts back to the office, and grabbed a packet of peanut butter crackers and a diet drink for lunch. Her heart rhythm still had not returned to normal. The arrhythmia had never lasted for twelve hours straight, and she was getting frightened. She made an appointment with her cardiologist for late afternoon. She also called the vet, who reassured her that Dudley did not need to be admitted to the doggie ICU.

Promptly at one o'clock, the first patient arrived for clinic, demanding a pregnancy test before her procedure, which was a biopsy of the lining of her uterus. Madison couldn't think of a reason to object, other than that it would delay clinic, so she sent the patient to the lab.

Dr. Bascomb breezed in a couple of minutes later, surprised to find Madison in the nurses' office, instead of down the hall in the clinic area. "No patients yet?"

"I had to send the first one for a pregnancy test."

"Why? Isn't it just an endometrial biopsy? All I'm going to do is slide a tube in the uterus and suction off a piece of the lining."

"I explained that to her, but she just *knows* she's pregnant this time, so what could I say?"

"You could say there's an infinitesimal chance of disturbing a pregnancy with this procedure."

"It would be my luck that she's pregnant, and would spontaneously abort and blame it on us."

"Won't happen. We don't instrument a pregnant uterus."

"Right, therefore we should probably do a pregnancy test before every biopsy."

"Don't need to. The biopsy won't disturb a pregnancy."

Madison thought she was the only other person in the world who hated to lose a debate worse than Dr. Bascomb. She looked at Basc, as she was affectionately called, and laughed. "That's a circular argument, and you know it. But I'm too tired to try to bust you."

Caroline Bascomb was a tall, thin woman with jet black, cropped hair. Her eye color was so vivid that it looked like it had come straight from a tube of cerulean blue paint. She was a brilliant, hardworking woman with a fiery temper and a will of steel. Her sense of responsibility in all aspects of her life, and her conviction that she was always right, led to controlling behavior and micromanagement that drove Madison crazy.

But Basc loved Madison, and had helped her through some very hard times. And Madison loved her back, although when they fought, things could get pretty ugly. Their arguments always reminded Madison of a scene in the movie *Michael*, when the archangel had spotted a bull in a field and they charged at each other, butting heads and nearly knocking each other out.

"You're so cute," Basc said.

"Yeah, I'm precious." Madison took a handful of M&Ms from a bowl on her desk, picked out the blue ones, and dropped them back in the bowl.

"Why are you doing that?"

"The blue ones are bitter."

"That's ridiculous," Basc said scornfully.

"No, it's not."

"I don't believe you can really tell the difference," Basc said, taking a handful of candy. "Let's put it to the test. Close your eyes. I'll feed you three pieces, and you tell me which one is blue."

"Fine." Madison closed her eyes, and Basc fed her three candies, one at a time.

"Very funny," Madison said.

"What?" said Basc, innocently.

"None of them were blue."

"Guilty. Okay, let's try it again." She fed Madison three more.

"Very funny," said Madison. "All of them were blue."

"Wow, that's truly amazing. We should write you up for the genetics journal. I bet your siblings can do the same thing." She took the bowl away, setting it on Mari's desk. "No more candy for you. It will only make you more tired. Why are you tired, anyway?"

Madison propped her head on one hand. "I just couldn't sleep, worrying about Park. And then this morning, I thought I would die of embarrassment. I opened the back door without turning off the house alarm, and he came running over in his boxers and T-shirt to see what was wrong. And there I was, in my Mickey Mouse pajamas."

"Park? Surely you don't mean that Memphis psychologist." She studied Madison. "You *do* mean that Memphis psychologist! You didn't mean to tell me he's here, did you? Why can't he just leave you alone?"

Madison could have kicked herself for her careless remark. "He didn't come here to see me. He's being treated at M. D. Anderson."

"For what?"

"Aplastic anemia."

"Bad stuff," said Basc. "Why was he at your house in his

underwear? I don't understand."

"He rented the house next door for a while."

"He and his wife?"

"No," Madison said in a small voice. "Just him."

"That's unconscionable! You're his patient!"

"No I'm not. Not any more."

The secretary stuck her head in the door. "Madison, your next patient is here."

"I'll be right there." Madison grabbed the chart. "It's a new patient. I'll call you after I've taken the history."

"I'm not through with you," Basc called after her.

Madison could hardly blame Basc for her reaction; in fact, she could have predicted it. Madison was working for Basc in Memphis at the time Park left. She had spent many an hour comforting Madison. When Basc planned to move to Houston, she'd asked Madison to come with her, not only because Madison was an excellent nurse, but also because she needed to leave the memories of Park behind. It was a huge step for Madison, who had lived most of her adult life in Memphis; and, although geographic cures in general were a poor idea, it had turned out to be a good change.

Madison put her own troubles out of her mind and focused on her new patient.

Jana Thompson was a 40-year-old, chunky blonde who taught kindergarten. Madison had special compassion for teachers who suffered from infertility, especially elementary school teachers. For an infertile woman to spend every day nurturing other people's children seemed especially cruel.

Although this was Jana's first visit to the clinic, Madison had met her husband, Brett, a month earlier. Brett, a photojournalist, was going to Iraq on assignment for three months, and he'd had sperm stored, so Jana could do a treatment cycle while he was gone. Brett had related that it was a first marriage for him and Jana, and that they had tried to start a family immediately;

but after three years, there had been no pregnancy.

Madison smiled warmly at Jana, shook her hand, and introduced herself. "I met your husband last month. He seems like a good guy. You're lucky." Jana's chin quivered, and for a moment, Madison thought she was going to cry. "Are you okay?"

Jana nodded, but Madison still felt uneasy. "We have the results of Brett's semen analysis; he has about two million sperm, not the greatest count in the world, but enough for us to work with. I see you haven't had any testing done, and I'm wondering why you chose to come straight to IVF. Usually, a workup is done, and people try conservative treatment first."

Jana silently looked down at the table.

"Jana," Madison said, "most people who walk through these doors have pretty much been through the wringer emotionally, physically, and financially. We know that, and we're going to make it as easy for you as possible. It's okay to cry; it's a wonder we haven't floated away on our patients' tears."

"Brett's dead," Jana said woodenly.

Madison was so stunned, she couldn't even respond.

"He went to Iraq three weeks ago," Jana continued. "He was embedded with the military, and spent his days crammed in the back of a Hummer. About a week ago, he complained about pain behind his knee. He thought it was because of the position he sat in most of the day, but then his calf started hurting."

Madison could picture it. Dehydration from excessive sweating caused his blood to thicken; sitting in a cramped position for a prolonged period caused blood to pool in his lower extremities; the combination had probably caused a clot to form in one of his deep veins.

"They said he might have a blood clot in his leg, and they gave him aspirin and sent him back to work."

Madison struggled to keep her facial expression neutral, but she was outraged. "Why didn't they put him on bed rest and a blood thinner?"

"They said it was a soft diagnosis. At first, there wasn't any objective evidence, other than the pain. Then his leg started to swell, and he got dizzy and couldn't breathe. He started coughing up blood."

"Pulmonary embolus," Madison said.

Jana nodded, tears gathering in her eyes. "A piece of the clot in his leg had broken off and traveled to his lungs. He died the next day."

"I am so very sorry." Madison handed Jana a handful of tissues, and sat quietly while she composed herself.

"You'll probably think I'm crazy, but I want to do my IVF cycle anyway. I want our baby."

How well Madison understood her feelings. "No, I don't think you're crazy. Let's finish your history, then you and Dr. Bascomb can discuss your options."

Ten minutes later, Madison was back in the nurses' office, summarizing Jana's history for Dr. Bascomb. "Basically, Jana's had no testing, no treatment, and now, she has no husband. But we do have frozen sperm. She wants to do an IVF cycle."

"Statistically, at age 40, she has a better chance of pregnancy with inseminations," Dr. Bascomb said.

"Insemination," Madison corrected. "We only have one semen specimen, and with a poor sperm count."

"Then I'll suggest an egg donor and IVF. That's probably what I would have done in the first place."

"You can't do that, she'll freak! I don't even know if there's been a funeral for her husband yet. She's not in any condition to deal with the process of accepting egg donation. Besides, it defeats the purpose. The baby is only special because it's her egg, his sperm, *their* baby. Something to remember him by."

Dr. Bascomb thought for a moment. "Do we have any idea if she ovulates?"

"No, but chances are she doesn't. She's overweight, and

she has long cycles."

"Bad all around. Well, let's stall for time. She needs a standard workup anyway, which will give us a couple of months. Then we'll reconsider."

As Basc exited the office, the secretary walked in and handed Madison the first patient's pregnancy test.

She read the results and grinned. "Well, I guess we won't be instrumenting this uterus," she said, and went off to tell the patient she was pregnant, reflecting that the patients weren't the only ones who rode the infertility emotional rollercoaster.

Basc was taking a long time with Jana, so while Madison waited, she slipped into the nurses' station and sat down at the microscope. She donned a pair of gloves and slid her hand into the plastic bag in her lab coat pocket, removing the syringe she had used for her insemination. She had to know if there was any live sperm. If there wasn't, she didn't have to worry about being pregnant. She touched the tip of the syringe to a slide, put a cover slip over it, and set the slide on the microscope stage. To her horror, when she adjusted the focus, hundreds of live sperm came into view, their long tails whipping, moving them quickly forward. She had the feeling she was already pregnant.

At three, Mari relieved Madison, who went up to the 25th floor to see her cardiologist. She changed into a hospital gown and a technician did an EKG. Dr. Fische, an appropriate name for someone who always gave his patient a limp handshake with his cold, clammy hands, came in after a few minutes. He sat down and started reading her chart.

"So, how has the arrhythmia changed?"

"It's more frequent," Madison replied. "I've tried to eliminate the things that trigger it. One thing that really bothers me is my thyroid medicine. If I take it, I have arrhythmia almost every day. I've been cutting it down, but I finally stopped it—"

He interrupted her. "You can't stop taking your thyroid medicine! That in itself affects you heart. There's no correlation between the thyroid medicine and arrhythmia," he said scornfully, "unless you're taking too much."

Well, that's not what the Physician's Desk Reference says, Madison thought, but she said nothing.

"Are you taking an aspirin a day?"

"No," she said. "You didn't tell me to do that."

"What about your cholesterol medicine?"

"I stopped taking it because I had muscle pain. I still have pain in my arms."

Fische pitched her chart on the desk. "That's ridiculous. The medication was out of your body in a week. Now I don't know if it was the medicine or something else that caused the problem."

It was the second time in one day a doctor had told her she was ridiculous. She wanted to tell him to go to hell, but that sort of behavior with men usually backfired on her. "All I know is that my muscles hurt so much I could barely hold my head up, and I felt like hell."

He ignored her comment and addressed the arrhythmia problem. "There are several things we can do. One, there are five medicines for arrhythmia, and we can try them one at a time until we find something that helps and you can tolerate. Two, we can do an ablation, which is an invasive procedure. There is only a 75% chance it will work. Three, we can do nothing."

Or four, Madison thought furiously, I can fire you and get another doctor. Never would this jerk stand over her with a sharp object in his hand. She could just imagine trying to tell him he was hurting her. "I guess I'll try another medication, for now."

He took her blood pressure and said, "Is your blood pressure always this high?"

You gotta be kidding, Madison thought. Typical doctor, thought it was his right to be abusive; it probably didn't even occur to him that he made people mad when he was nasty. "No," she said, and finished the thought silently. Only when I want to kill an arrogant cardiologist.

He wrote out a new prescription, ordered her to get a thyroid test done before she left the office, gave her another fish handshake, and left the room.

Madison fumed all the way home. How dare he speak to her like that? She thought when her mother died, no one would ever treat her like she was a retarded child again.

"Wrong," she said aloud, veering around an old lady poking down the street at 20 miles an hour. What made her madder than anything was that she had chosen Dr. Fische not only because he had an excellent reputation, but also because she'd been told he really listened to his patients, and worked with them to find solutions.

"And wrong again." Damn it. Time to find another cardiologist.

By seven p.m., she had Cam fed and bathed. She could put him to bed in an hour. For now, he seemed content with an activity book, and Madison sank into her recliner, hoping to write for a while. Writing forced her to focus on what was troubling her, organize her thoughts, and see what she could fix and what she just had to accept. A word she despised. Accept.

But before she even picked up her laptop, the doorbell rang. She peeked through the blinds to see Park, one hand propped on the house as if to hold him up. When she opened the door he looked up, his face ashen. "Madi," he said, closing his eyes and weaving slightly, "I need help."

"What's wrong?"

He wobbled into the living room, and she helped him to the daybed, where he immediately lay down on his side. She took his pulse, which was fast and weak, and scanned him quickly, expecting to find him bleeding somewhere, but he wasn't.

Park swallowed hard, several times. "I started chemo this morning. I'm sorry to bother you, they said the side effects are mild and usually don't even start until the next day. But I got dizzy and nauseated on the way home, and I've been vomiting ever since. The whole room seems to be moving."

"Didn't they pre-treat you for nausea, just in case?"

"No, they just gave me a prescription. I didn't get it filled. I barely made it home."

"Where is the prescription?"

"On my coffee table, I think. Or maybe in the bedroom."

"I'll get it filled for you. Give me your keys."

He handed them to her. She instructed Cam to stay with Park.

Even in her haste and concern for Park, Madison could not suppress the tight anticipation that always came when she had an opportunity to find out something new about him. A nasty thought, but he was the one who cloaked himself in secrecy.

She opened the door to the rental, which she hadn't been in since her elderly neighbor, Tom, had died a year earlier. The living room was exactly the same. After his house had flooded during tropical storm Allison, Tom had bought only a few pieces of cheap furniture, as if he knew he wouldn't need it for long. And he hadn't; he'd only lived for six more months. That flood had taken years off everyone, including herself.

Park's laptop, some books, and a stack of files were on the coffee table, but Madison didn't see a prescription. She wondered why he was re-reading *Every Day Gets a Little Closer*. The book, written by Irvin Yalom, was about a psychiatrist and his special patient, Ginny, with whom he baldly admitted he was "a little in love." They had both written their versions of her therapy sessions, which made for fascinating reading.

Madison and Park had discussed the book, and she thought both of them had toyed with the idea of writing a similar one. He had once asked her, "Do you think what we get from these sessions is as different as Yalom and Ginny?" Mischievously, she'd replied, "Well, I don't know what you get out of them. Why don't you let me read your notes?" To which she'd received his typical, non-committal smile.

Madison opened the top file, thinking it might contain the paperwork from M.D. Anderson. There should at least be a copy of the consent form for Park's research study. But the document appeared to be a book proposal, ready to send to a publisher. The writer in Madison, ever curious for details, and the sleuth in Madison, ever insatiable for details about the man she loved, wanted to read the entire proposal; the new and improved Madison wouldn't think of such a thing. The in-a-hurry Madison won. She put the file down and opened the next one, which contained medical papers, but no prescription.

She walked back to the bedroom. The bed was unmade, and clothes were thrown on the floor. A beer bottle sat on the bedside table, along with the consent form and several prescriptions. It looked like they had prepared Park for a variety of side effects, with medications for pain, heartburn, diarrhea, and nausea. Phenergan was ordered for nausea, to be given by mouth, but it wouldn't help him right now. He would never keep it down.

She went back home and called in prescriptions for Phenergan by injection as well as by mouth, and syringes and needles, giving Basc's name as the ordering physician. Phenergan was actually one of the standing orders the nurses were allowed to call in without speaking to her, so Madison didn't think Basc would mind if she ordered it for Park in an emergency.

Cam had dragged the quilt off his bed and covered Park, who was now shivering. "Mom, he's so sick." Cam said, his face creased with concern.

"I know, sweetheart. We're going to get him some medicine. Put your shoes on."

"But I'm in my jammies," Cam wailed.

"You can leave him with me," Park said, teeth chattering.

"No, it will be fine. Cam, get your jacket."

Park smiled wanly. "Don't trust me?"

"Not right this minute," Madison said. In the car, she wondered if it were true; would she trust Park with Cam, if Park were well enough to supervise the child properly? After all, Park was Cam's father.

The prescriptions weren't ready when Madison and Cam got to the store, so they wandered around for a while. She picked up a couple of liters of Seven-Up; Cam begged for a Spiderman book. But when they got to the check out, Madison looked at him in surprise; instead of the book he'd asked for, he put two cans of chicken noodle soup and a box of mini-peanut butter crackers on the counter. She had been so preoccupied, she hadn't even noticed the switch.

"This is the good stuff to eat when your tummy's upset. We already have Hershey's Kisses," he informed her solemnly.

Oh, dear God, Madison thought, he's going be a nurse. She applauded his special diet for Park, with the exception of the Hershey's Kisses; she suspected that was more for the little nurse than for the patient.

Back at home, she drew up the Phenergan and ordered Park to roll over and bare his derriere.

"Just put it in my arm," he said.

"No way," Madison said. "This stuff burns. Roll it, Buster."

Madison won. Injection given, she went to the kitchen to dispose of the syringe and alcohol sponge, and to fix Park a glass of Seven-Up to settle his stomach a little.

When she came back to the living room, Cam had turned on the freestanding electric heater, its fake flames flickering cozily. Geez, it made her crazy when he did things like that. She lectured him about safety once more, and tried to put him to bed; but he so loudly insisted on making sure Park was okay that she gave in. She turned off the TV and all but one light, and gave Cam permission to stay up and read for a while.

Cam settled in the rocker and opened his book, but his eyes were on Park, who continued to shiver and shake. Madison sat down to read Park's post-chemo instructions and the consent form, which explained his treatment in detail.

She had a difficult time understanding his treatment. Consent forms were supposed to be written in seventh-grade English, with simplified definitions of medical words, but this one wasn't. She wondered how it had gotten approval by the hospital's Institutional Review Board. If a medical person could not understand it, how on earth could a lay person?

Last night, she had visited the M.D. Anderson research website, trying to guess which study Park might be in, but the list was endless. Treatments ranged from medications that suppressed the immune system to the most heavy-duty chemotherapy agents. Park was getting a new medication with a long chemical name that meant nothing to Madison.

He was right, the consent said the side effects of the medication were supposed to be mild, and usually didn't start, if they did at all, until the second day. But all of his symptoms were listed, so she didn't think they needed to call his doctor, unless he spiked a fever.

Dudley jumped up on the daybed and Cam climbed up after him, both of them curling up at Park's feet. "Cam, get down," Madison said. "Park needs to rest."

"Actually," Park said, "they're helping me warm up. I've never been so cold in my life. I feel like I'm frozen clear to the bone."

Madison went over and put her hand on his forehead. He was cool and clammy, which was better than having a fever. Apparently, direct heat was what he needed, and if two small warm bodies were helping some, one large warm body would help a lot. She slid off her shoes, climbed over him, and snuggled up to him under the quilt, not caring a whit if he objected. Which he didn't.

The moment she touched him, Madison felt the old euphoria, and knew she was still in trouble. As she drifted off to sleep, she whispered to herself, "Damn it, I thought I was over you, but I still love you."

After twenty minutes, his shivering decreased, and all four of them fell into an exhausted sleep.

CHAPTER FOUR

When Park woke again, it was 5:00 a.m.; to his surprise, he had slept through the night. It was dark, but the electric fire lit the room with flickering orange light. Cam and the dog were still curled at his feet; Madison slept on her side in the crook of his arm, head on his shoulder, one arm flung across his chest. With his index finger, Park swept away the hair that had fallen across her face, then allowed his hand to trail lightly down the long, silky fall of hair that reached halfway to her waist. Everything about her—hair, clothing, even the pillow she had given him—smelled freshly washed. In contrast to Claire, whose haute couture looks and aura of imported-cigarette smoke and expensive perfume brought a Dior model to mind, Madison evoked a Norman Rockwell painting: Clean sheets flapping in the wind on a cold, sunny day, the smell of freshly-baked bread wafting through an open window, a solid feeling of all being right in the world.

It was like being part of a family, a feeling Park had known only briefly in his life. The only child of an attentive but not particularly demonstrative single parent, Park had had a lonely childhood. And his marriage, while perhaps appearing ideal to the casual observer, was sustained primarily by duty. He lived his life on the surface of love, not deep within it.

Park's feelings about Madison were a mixture of joy and despair. His relationship with her had been problematic from the very beginning. They had connected on a deep level the first time they'd met, and although he had spent a lot of time thinking about her, he'd never been able to adequately analyze his feelings for her. Of course there was the therapeutic transference and countertransference, a concept that infuriated Madison, because she thought it implied that the flow of feelings between therapist and patient was inauthentic; but it went far beyond that. Madison had a fascinating mind; what interested him the most was the combination of her obsession with understanding and feeling the essence of God, and her formidable intelligence, which prevented her from believing in God without proof. She was driven to find that proof and read incessantly, her choices an eclectic mixture of religion, medicine, psychology, literature, physics, and philosophy.

He had looked forward to her appointments, ever curious about what she had read and how she had assimilated it. The walls of his office were lined with bookcases crammed with psychology tomes and self-help books, and during therapy sessions, he often caught her eyes mining the shelves for new ideas. Sometimes he would lend her books, happily anticipating her feedback.

He'd once told her he hoped when she found the answer to life, it would be underlined for her, and she'd responded tartly, "Not to worry, I'll underline it myself." He smiled at the memory. A typical Madison response, forged by equal portions of right- and left-brain thinking. She was so funny, totally unable to understand why people sometimes found talking to her intimidating.

Their attraction was so powerful that throughout therapy, they had both felt the unspoken need not to do or say anything that could even remotely be construed as inappropriate, which created an unacknowledged tension that occasionally erupted into disagreement. A conversation about the sort of relationship, if any, they would have after Madison's treatment was complete almost always left them both jarred. How could they remain friends, without the appearance that something more was going on? Which was ridiculous; they were so emotionally intimate, a physical relationship wouldn't have added much anyway. Or so he told himself, his hand resting on the flat of her back, feeling the warmth of her skin through her clothing.

She had once asked him how in the world you could walk around with yourself all day and convince yourself that red was really green, rain was really snow, love was only transference. Like hello, are there two people in your head? One to tell the lie, and one to believe it? Park, confused about his feelings, ethically prohibited from revealing them, and unwilling to act on them, had given a rambling, evasive response, which he knew made her angry. He had hurt her and created a situation similar to why she'd had her meltdown in the first place, but he didn't know what else to do.

Worst of all, she had paid him for this treatment.

How odd that pain once again linked them, this time his pain. Although things were a bit awkward, he felt as connected to her as if they had never been separated. He'd heard patients describe that experience with their siblings: A sense of shared history, of knowing each other so well that they merged seamlessly after long separations. Siblings were the ones who knew you the best—who knew that you cheated at Monopoly, walked in your sleep, stole five dollars from Mom's purse.

Despite the fact that Madison had welcomed him into her home, things had happened so fast that he felt like he was taking advantage of her, even though it was unintentional. At least he told himself that, although deep down he knew he had engineered the situation, knowing Claire was abandoning him in Houston. He needed Madison now like she had needed him when she was sick. It seemed unfair to her, because no matter what, she would be mortally wounded again when he finished his treatment and went home. If, that is, she still had intense feelings for him. And if he still had a home.

Madison stirred and looked up at him, sleepily studying his face. "You're going to be just fine," she whispered, as if she had read his mind. "We're going to take good care of you."

A lump formed in his throat, and his arm tightened around her. He looked at her sweet mouth, her beautiful, straight white teeth, her cheeks flushed from sleep, and came within an inch of kissing her.

* * *

The comforting sounds of Madison getting herself and Cam ready for the day lulled Park off to sleep again. He awoke again to her cool hand on his forehead.

"Still no fever," she said. "Are you sick to your stomach?"

"Extremely. It's worse than last night. I don't understand; they told me it wouldn't be as bad as the last time."

"It's impossible to know how any drug affects a patient until it's administered. You can give three people penicillin, and have three different reactions: It will cure the first one, kill the second one, and do nothing at all to the third one. Shall I give you another shot, or do you think you can keep a pill down?"

"Shot, I guess."

After Madison gave him the injection, she said, "You'd better call your doctor this morning. She may want to pre-treat you for nausea before your next chemo."

"Okay."

"You're welcome to stay, as long as you want." She picked up his watch and moved it to the center of the coffee table. "Don't leave your stuff on the edge of the table, though. Dudley's a klepto."

Dudley, at Madison's feet, barked once.

Park laughed, despite his misery. "He's partial to jewelry?"

"He's partial to 'bling-bling,' I think. Last time I cleaned out his stash, he had Cam's watch, a piece of foil, and a spool of gold metallic thread."

She set Park's nausea pills and the telephone on the coffee table, and wrote down her work and cell phone numbers. "I left some chicken soup on the counter for you. When the medicine settles your stomach, try to eat some; hot salty stuff will help. If you keep that down, take a pill at ten, then every six hours. If you take it regularly, maybe it will prevent or at least reduce the nausea. There are cold soft drinks, and, of course, you have an array of snacks right here." Madison smiled widely and made a Vanna White gesture at the crackers and Hershey's Kisses that Cam insisted were the cure for nausea. "There's a set of scrubs and a toothbrush in the bathroom, if you want to get cleaned up. I should be back by four or so, but call if you need me."

"Mom, I can stay here and take care of him," Cam said.

"I think he'll be okay. See how much better he looks this morning?"

"But he'll be lonely."

"Dudley will keep him company. Come on, sweetheart, we're late." She took Cam by the hand and practically dragged him out of the room, his head twisted and his eyes on Park until he rounded the corner.

"I should be back by four or so, too," Park heard him say from the kitchen, just before the door closed.

The injection put Park back to sleep, and when he woke again, it was noon. He sat up, feeling like he had a hangover. He should probably go home; there were things he needed to do. But he felt completely innervated, and more than anything, he did not want to go back to the drab, silent rental house. He decided to get cleaned up, then make a decision about what to do.

He took a shower, dried off with one of Madison's soft, sweet-smelling pink towels. He had neither razor nor energy to shave, and decided just to let his beard grow, even though he would look scruffy for a while.

In the mirror, he tried to see himself as Madison would see him. His straight blonde hair had come back after his first round of chemo, and he had lots of laugh lines around his eyes. But it was his expression, not the wrinkles, that made him look older than his 42 years. The corners of his mouth turned down, his eyes were dull, and he looked tired. He stood up straight and practiced smiling, feeling as goofy as if he were looking into one of a psychiatric hospital's one-way mirrors, with an observer on the other side. Now he just looked tired and silly.

He put on the worn green scrubs Madison had left for him, then gave himself a tour of her house, deriving a great deal of satisfaction from invading her privacy, exactly as she had invaded his. He took his time, inspecting her space closely.

The house looked like something out of a magazine, every inch decorated with hand-crafted work of various kinds. When Madison was in therapy, he had tried to live in her world through her descriptions, but his imagination paled compared to the real thing. The colors were vivid and it was not a restful place, but it was interesting and quite unusual.

Cam's room was startling, painted the color of a Granny Smith apple. There was a desktop computer built to look like a dragon, and a Spongebob Squarepants table lamp. In one corner, pajamas spilled out of an apple-green alligator clothes hamper. Two bookcases were crammed with books, and little-boy educational toys littered the room. Apparently, Madison allowed happy chaos to reign here, in sharp contrast to the rest of the house.

The front bedroom, which doubled as Madison's workroom, was full of sewing paraphernalia and art supplies. Two desks were painted with folk art scenes, on one a clothesline with a quilt hanging on it. Painted underneath, in two-inch cursive letters, was "Quilting is better than therapy . . . Freud," and beneath that, "Quilting is cheaper than therapy . . . Jung." Park burst into laughter. Of course, judging by the three computerized sewing machines, piles of fabric, and huge pegboard hung with tools, quilting didn't look cheaper.

The back bedroom was less dramatic than the other rooms.

He could imagine her relaxing there before she went to sleep, reading one of the books on her bedside table—*Alcoholics Anonymous* and *Conversations with God*, which he had attempted to read twice, and found completely unintelligible. He would bet she understood it, though.

There wasn't a picture of him on the table, as Claire had said, but there was a pair of earrings, and for a moment, he thought about filching them and letting her blame it on her klepto dog, who was following him around the house. Park leaned over and scratched the dog behind one ear. "You hungry, dude? I mean Dud?" The dog panted, turned in a circle, and barked. "Okay then, let's eat."

In the kitchen, Park heated a bowl of chicken soup for each of them, and carried the bowls into the living room. He got his pillow, Cam's quilt, and the Hershey's Kisses, then opened the front blinds and settled in Madison's recliner by the window. She was right, the hot, salty soup felt good in his queasy stomach. He took his pill as instructed, then covered up with the quilt, leaned back in the recliner, and unwrapped a few Kisses. Dudley, now enamored with someone who had shared a meal, was also ready for dessert. He jumped up beside Park and settled against his legs, following every move as Park ate the candy.

"Oh, all right," Park said, giving him a Kiss. "But just one. And don't you tell on me."

He turned on the TV and channel-surfed for a while, but when the most interesting program was Oprah interviewing Brad Pitt, he switched to a music channel playing elevator music.

Madi's manuscript, still on the table next to him, beckoned like forbidden fruit. He lost the struggle with his conscience within seconds, picked up a handful of the pages, and started reading. The font was small, and he didn't have his reading glasses, but there was a pair on the table that worked just fine. He picked up where he'd left off yesterday, the day her character woke up in the psychiatric unit.

After a horrified glance in the mirror, Reagan tried not to look at herself again. Her face was pale and bloated, her eyes like golf balls, from crying. Starch from the hospital sheets had dulled her long hair. Her double chin was the same, however, even though she had lost some weight since she'd stopped drinking.

Just the word drinking made her start crying again. Although she'd been sober for three and a half months, she knew she wasn't going to make it this time, either. Knew it. Because nothing filled that big empty space in her. Nothing. Not her children, not her work, not her home, not her hobbies. Booze gave her a few hours of respite each day, and it was one sneaky, seductive master. Yes, master. Coming, master.

Reagan shuffled down the long, green-tiled hall, looking for the lounge. She felt spacey, unreal. It was 6:45 a.m., and she should be across the street at the hospital where she worked, setting up her room for the open heart procedure she was assigned to today. Instead, here she was in the Ha-Ha Hotel. Well, that was a place she had always wanted to be. Plucked out of her miserable life, plunked down in a place where she could get some help. Time out for Reagan.

She joined a line of what she assumed was patients. The staff wore street clothes in this unit, and she couldn't distinguish them from the patients, most of whom looked pretty ordinary. Reagan's turn came. Vital signs, weight. To her surprise, she had lost a few more pounds.

She took her breakfast tray back to her room and sat on the bed, listlessly picking at rubbery scrambled eggs while she tried to decipher the schedule that had been left for her. Activity after activity after activity. As much as she wanted help, she didn't know how she could do all that. She had been running on empty for so long. All she wanted to do was go to sleep. Permanently.

But doctors' rounds were at eight, and she would meet the psychiatrist assigned to her. Christ, what a way to pick a doctor. You crawl into a cuckoo's nest, and they send some stranger to fix you.

Park smiled, reeled back five years. "Some stranger" had turned out to be his colleague, Colleen Mary O'Hara, M.D., all six-foot one abrasive black Irish inches of her. She had instantly alienated Madison and earned, fairly in his opinion, a new name: "The Psychiatrist from Hell." And Madison didn't use that title only behind Colleen's back, either.

"Well, my gosh, what does she expect?" Madi had said. "I tried to describe a day in a psychiatric hospital from a patient's point of view, which one would think a psychiatrist would find of interest. This is all I said, see if you find this objectionable: 'I know what this treatment is. It's aversion therapy. This is how your day goes: First you talk to the medical student and tell her your whole miserable story. Then you tell the story to the nurse. Then you repeat it to the social worker. Then the psychologist comes in, but in the middle of the session with the psychologist the psychiatrist comes in, so the psychologist leaves so you can talk to the psychiatrist. Then you go to group therapy, in the middle of which you get an urgent message to call the Director of Nursing from the hospital where you work, who threatens to fire you because you didn't call her personally and tell her you had lost your mind. A message was not good enough. Then you find your case manager to let her know the outcome of the call, and during the conversation, the head nurse says, 'Why aren't you at stress management?' Uprooting great wads of hair, you scream, 'Stress management? Oh my God, why would I need stress management?' And after a day of all this, you decide isolation at home wasn't so bad."

Labeled histrionic by Colleen, Madi had subsequently greeted her in the morning by dramatically presenting what she called "The Question of the Day," the topic of which ran the gamut from the interesting to the merely disgusting, such as "Quick, what's a synonym for thesaurus?" to "Why did God make cockroaches?" Park found her imagination and presentation amusing, but it infuriated Colleen, who added the label of bipolar disorder, and threatened to put Madi on Lithium.

"She and what army will put me on that shit," was Madi's

75

response. "I'm just restless. Christ on a crutch, I haven't had a chance to sit down since I was fifteen, and the lack of activity is making me crazy."

"Crazier," she amended.

Park continued reading, suspicious that Colleen had also prompted other scathing passages in Madi's book, although the hospital personnel were also capable of such insensitivity.

One of the great no-no's at the Ha-Ha Hotel was a type of behavior labeled "codependency." No one seemed to know the exact definition of the word, but it had something to do with your career and any kindness to another person. For instance, if you try to keep a patient from fracturing his skull during a seizure—that's codependent behavior. For nurses, that's "being a nurse." For housewives, that's "being a mother." Codependency apparently encompasses all helpful behavior, including but not limited to passing the salt at dinner, holding the door open for the person following you, and suggesting to a fellow inmate that slathering himself with Ben Gay from head to toe is somewhat offensive to others.

Park skipped ahead, looking for the first meeting of the characters he presumed were based on himself and Madison.

There was a free hour between six and seven p.m., and Reagan lay propped on her elbows on her bed, reading Sartre and eating Butterfingers. Her room was freezing. She wore her robe, one she had made out of dinosaur kiddy fabric, over her jeans and sweatshirt. Her ensemble was completed by slippers made of loopy royal blue cotton yarn that made them look like a pair of dust mops.

In walked a sloe-eyed centerfold straight from Gentleman's Quarterly. She froze, Butterfinger halfway in her mouth, taking in his perfectly tailored suit, straight blonde hair, green eyes.

"Reagan? I'm Wesley Brandon, one of the psychologists. Dr. O'Hara asked me to see you." He tipped the book with one finger and looked at the cover. One eyebrow cocked, he said mildly, "Existentialism is on the approved reading list?"

"I'm reasonably sure it's not," she said, hastily standing and jamming book and Butterfingers in the drawer of her bedside stand, doubly enamored with a man who was drop-dead gorgeous and philosophically informed. But how could he take her seriously, considering her attire? She wrapped her dinosaurs tightly across her chest, wishing she could disappear.

He took a seat by the windows, holding her chart in his lap. "So, life is meaningless, and God is dead?"

"Perhaps, Dr. Nietzsche," Reagan said, smiling. She sat in the chair across from him. "Of course, to believe God is dead begs the question that God was ever alive."

"Well, Dr. Darwin," he rebutted, crossing his legs and settling into the quid pro quo, "I see that you believe man accidentally created himself, evolving from the primordial ooze. But what if God created ooze as the mechanism of evolution?"

"A possibility," she conceded. "But that's not proof that God exists."

"Proof is important to you?"

She looked at him like he was the one who was crazy. "Of course it is. Otherwise, religion is just another form of government, enforced by superstition and indoctrination. I was in kindergarten the first time I challenged a Catholic nun about something that made no sense to me. She whacked me on the head with a ruler and said, 'Reagan Marie, you must take this on faith.'"

"What did you ask her?"

"Oh, I don't know. Probably why I would go to hell for eating a hot dog on Friday. I was a very literal child, and I took the idea of burning for eternity very seriously. Of course, I also believed hot dogs were actually meat."

Wesley smiled. "And after Vatican II in the 70s, the rules changed. Eating meat – or hot dogs – on Friday was okay."

"I just hope everyone who was sent to hell for that got grandfathered into heaven."

Wesley laughed.

"You mentioned Vatican II—are you a Catholic?" Reagan asked.

"I am no longer a practicing Catholic. But let's focus on you. Why is belief in God so important to you?"

"Because the world is too damn scary and painful otherwise. Because life seems pointless. I want to believe in God. I believe in lots of things I can't see: Electricity, microorganisms, oxygen, radio waves. I can't prove their existence, but I can see their effects. Flip a switch, a light comes on. Ingest microorganisms, get sick. Hold your breath, turn purple. So why can't I believe in God?"

"You don't see any effects you can attribute to God?"

"Sometimes if I pray, I feel better. And I can find some serendipity in life that might be engineered by God. But how do I know that's not just magical thinking? Why can't I just let go and believe like everyone else?"

"Everyone, Reagan?"

"Except thee and me."

Wesley ignored that comment. "Perhaps your medical training has gotten in your way."

"Au contraire, mon frère. I don't believe the human body emerged because a bunch of molecules randomly stuck together. The body is far too complex. Statistically speaking, the earth hasn't even existed long enough for that to happen. No, the problem is that I can't feel God like other people seem to, and I'm just not able to suspend disbelief long enough to accept God's existence on faith. And I have a problem with appearing and disappearing people."

"What do you mean?"

"Oh, I mean things like the comings and goings of Christ after the crucifixion, and so forth. The closest I can come to believing in God is the theory of relativity. Think about the composition of an atom, how each component gets smaller and smaller. Smaller than an electron, smaller than a quark. God becomes so small He transforms into pure energy, and is invisible to the naked eye."

"You mean like string theory?"

"Exactly! Particles smaller than a quark vibrate at different frequencies, and make different things. Kind of like vibrating piano strings make different tones. When you die, your body doesn't fall apart, so some strings must still be vibrating. And as matter changes into energy, you slowly disappear. Bingo! I have solved the greatest metaphysical puzzle of the universe, appearing

and disappearing people."

"Or disappearing people, anyway."

"So there must be something that makes people appear in the first place," Reagan said.

"The argument of 'first cause?'"

"That's correct, St. Thomas. But here's the real question: If matter and energy are interchangeable, how come you don't collect energy as you decompose, and blow the lid off your coffin? Maybe that's why graveyards are always filled with fog."

Wesley smiled. "I sense there's someone in a lot of pain behind that big, funny fence you've constructed around yourself."

Reagan's eyes suddenly filled with tears. No one else had ever figured that out. They all thought she was the jolly fat girl.

Park stared out the front window. Sunlight glittered through trees riffled by gusts of wind; leaves floated through the air and collected in red and yellow drifts. It was around this time of year when Madi had been admitted to the psych unit for depression, a time of year always tinged with sadness for Park, since he had lost his son to sudden infant death syndrome on Thanksgiving many years earlier. He remembered his delight in Madi, a welcome distraction clothed in a dinosaur robe, dust-mop slippers, and existential angst. No ordinary psych patient, this . . . how could anyone not love her.

* * *

Madison was finally able to leave the office at six p.m., two and a half hours later than she had intended. She could hardly wait to get home, to see if Park was still there. But her patients had conspired against her, with one crisis after another.

In preparation for their IVF cycles, sixteen patients were on Lupron, a drug that shut down their estrogen production and put them in a temporary menopause, which made them *and* their nurses irritable, unreasonable, and sometimes irrational. The normal load of phone calls always doubled when a new round of cycles started. One message from a patient could turn into five calls for Madison, between tracking down doctors for orders, calling in medications, scheduling tests, calling the patient back with instructions, and playing telephone tag with the lot of them. Just for fun, while a patient had her on hold, she had counted her message slips: 53 today. 53 x 5 = 265. Was that physically possible? Even cut down by a conservative 50%, it was still insane.

Madison despised telephones. By the time she picked Cam up and made a quick stop at the grocery store, she had dealt with two more emergencies. Or rather, what the patients considered emergencies: One set of stuck windshield wipers, one IVF cycle that stubbornly refused to coordinate with a Caribbean vacation.

She heard her dead mother's voice in her head: You're the one who needs a vacation, when your attitude gets like this.

Yes, I do, she thought back. Preferably, in a place with no phones.

When she pulled into her driveway, it was dark. The living room blinds were open, and light spilled out across the front porch. Park was still there! Madison's spirits lifted.

All day, she'd savored the feeling of awakening in the arms of the man she had loved for years, even knowing there was no hope of ever being part of his life. Up to last night, she had never even touched him, except for a couple of A-frame hugs when she was in therapy. Although his current presence in her life probably meant nothing except that he needed help, she'd kept her mental arms around him all day.

A dangerous place for you to be, Missy, said Mom, who would not stay dead.

Madison waited impatiently for the garage door to go up, then pulled inside. While Cam gathered his backpack and project of the day, she walked across the front porch to get the mail, and peeked in the front window.

The scene in her living room was so comical, she almost burst out laughing. Park was stretched out in her recliner, sound asleep under Cam's quilt, her red-flowered reading glasses resting on the end of his nose. Dudley stood on the recliner footrest, grinning at her and wagging his tail.

A handful of her manuscript pages lay face-down on Park's chest. Madison loved it. She was going to ask him to edit her book anyway, but reading personal stuff without permission was tantamount to spying, and if he couldn't resist spying on her any more than she could resist spying on him, it meant he was interested in her.

Smiling, she went back to the car and collected her purse and groceries, and she and Cam went in through kitchen door. "We have to be very quiet," she cautioned. "Park is asleep."

"Okay," Cam said in a stage whisper. "But he has to wake up pretty soon and see the turkey I made for him." Cam disappeared around the corner.

"Cam! Come back here." Madison dropped purse, keys, and groceries on the counter. She tried to catch him, but he was already in the living room. Oh well, it was a wonder Park was still asleep anyway, with the racket the garage door had made.

Cam leaned over the recliner arm peered into Park's face. Dudley licked Cam's cheek, and he shoved him away. "Stop it, Dudley! You got bad breath."

Dudley barked his objection to the insult, and Park woke with a start, sat up, and jerked Madison's glasses off. Paper went everywhere.

"Mom, he's awake!" said Cam. "Can I talk to him now?" He crawled into Park's lap.

Madison picked up the papers, knowing Park was squirming. He smiled sheepishly and said, "Busted."

"I guess we're even now." She felt not a smidgeon of remorse for torturing him. "This is even worse than peeking in someone's underwear drawer."

"You peeked in my underwear drawer?"

Madison laughed. "No, of course not, dummy. You never could tell when I'm exaggerating."

"I made this for you," Cam interrupted, presenting Park with a margarine tub and construction paper turkey.

"Why, thank you." Park gave it a serious examination. "That's excellent work. Fine feathers."

Cam basked in the praise. "Yeah. You can put some gummy bears in it."

"How are you feeling?" Madison asked.

"A little better, thanks. The soup-soda-sugar combo did the trick."

"I see you've made a friend," she said, indicating the dog. There were two empty soup bowls, one on the end table, one on the floor. "Dudley Anne, you are shameless. You know better than to eat in the living room."

"Dudley Anne?"

"Yeah, the vet at the doggy orphanage cut off his stuff. He's psychosexually confused."

Park looked from Madison to Cam and back, as if to ask if her language were appropriate in front of a small child.

"It's okay," Madison said. "He's the son of a GYN nurse. He knows what 'stuff' is."

Cam giggled, Park shook his head, and Dudley barked twice. Cam pushed him off the chair. "Get down, you trundle tail, you hurt my ear. And you're not allowed on the furniture, anyway."

Park looked back at Madison. "What's a trundle tail?"

She shrugged. "I don't know. Ask him."

Cam said, "It's a mutt. Everybody knows that."

The trundle tail jumped back up on the chair.

"Everybody who has a book of funny old words, you mean," Madison said. "What do you guys want for dinner?"

"A hambooger and some earthapples," Cam said. When Madison just looked at him, he added, "I mean French fries."

"Park? Are you hungry?"

"Yeah, actually I am. Hamboogers and earthapples sound

good to me."

Madison left them to entertain each other, eavesdropping on their conversation as she put groceries away and started cooking.

"How do you like my quilt?" Cam asked.

"It's very warm. And colorful. Did you make it?"

"Mom made it. But I helped."

"What part did you do?"

"I drew the pictures, and Mom painted them on the material. It's a map of all the places we've been. See, here's the Butterfly Museum, it's in Houston. There's a whole bunch of butterflies loose in there. One landed on my hand. It was just a regular old Monarch, though. Not a good butterfly. They got a bug zoo, too. We're going to the Santa movie at the IMAX. Do you want to go? It's only seven dollars, Mom will take you too."

"I'd love to go. What's this?"

"That's the Space Center. We saw the moon buggy, I could make one as good as theirs with 'luminum foil and duck tape."

In the kitchen, Madison smiled. The moon buggy did, in fact, look like something a child had constructed with aluminum foil and duct tape, and about that sturdy.

"This is where Emma and Dane live, in Memphis," Cam continued. "That's my big brother and sister. They're all grown up."

"Do you get to see them often?"

"No," Cam said, scornfully. "They live way far away."

"That's too bad," said Park.

"Yep. This is Graceland. It's Elvis's house. He's a singer but he's dead. He's buried in his back yard."

"With his hamster, no doubt," said Park, chuckling. "Do you know any Elvis songs?"

"No," Cam said, "you gotta be old to know those songs. But Mom knows a lot of them."

"I see. What's this?"

"That's the Pyramid, they play basketball there. It's on Mud Island, where Mom lived when she got me."

The hamburger Madison was flipping slipped off the spatula and fell into hot grease, splattering it on her hand. She grabbed a wet rag and wiped it off, mentally willing Cam to shut up as she rushed for the living room to distract him before he gave something away. He was telling Park his whole life story; how long would it be before he revealed that he was conceived by insemination?

"I don't have a dad like regular kids," Cam continued. "I got a 'nominous donor. That means Mom got a cell from a nice man and put it with hers. Then she grew the rest of me. Did you ever live on Mud Island?"

Madison mentally groaned.

"No, I lived further downriver, on the bluff," said Park. "Right about here."

"That's close to where Mom lived. Maybe you're my donor. You got a bump on your hand, just like me. Did you have six fingers when you were born? I did. They just tied a string around the extra one, and it fell off. But it left the bump. It's called hexa— hexa—"

"Dactyly," Park finished, faintly. "Hexadactyly."

Madison barreled into the living room. Park was staring at the small white bump on Cam's right hand as if it were a poisonous spider. She saw an identical bump in exactly the same place on Park's right hand. God, of all the things for Cam to notice.

Park's eyes met hers. If he knew the word hexadactyly, he probably knew it was a common and usually innocuous birth defect. Still, it added to the list of things that might lead him to believe that Cam was his son. But surely it would never occur to him that she would steal his sperm. Would it?

I wouldn't be too sure, said Mom, in her head. After all, you were pretty whacked at the time.

Shut up, Mom, Madison thought. Her heart skipped several

beats. She needed to get her new prescription filled.

"And your eyes are the same color as mine," Cam rattled on innocently.

"Yes, they are," Park said. "Exactly the same color."

"Okay, guys, dinner's almost ready," Madison said, her voice so cheerful that sounded phony, even to her. "Cam, come help me for a few minutes."

"But Mom, I'm not through talking to Park."

She took his hand and pulled him off Park's lap. "Now, son. I need you to wash your hands and set the table."

"I don't know how to set the table," he whined, reluctantly following her into the kitchen. "Mom, do you think Park is my donor? He's got murfles on his nose, like me."

"What the devil are murfles?" Madison asked, helping Cam wash his grubby hands at the sink. Right this minute, she didn't find his odd vocabulary charming.

"Freckles. Wouldn't it be good, Mom? I could have a dad like the other kids. Even Emma and Dane got a dad. Park and me could do stuff. You think worms are icky, but I bet Park likes them, and he could take me fishing in the bayou."

Madison dried his hands. "We don't fish in the bayou. It's dirty."

"Then how come there's fish in there? Are the fish dirty? How do you tell if a fish is dirty? Can't you give a fish a bath?"

"Cameron," she said evenly, "we are not going to fish in the bayou. Period." She handed him three placemats. "Put these on the table, one by each chair, then come back and get the silverware and napkins."

"And you know what else, Mom?" Cam said from the dining room. "Park's got a dent in his chin, just like me."

Was she going to have to do a laryngectomy to get him to shut up? Speaking of fish, her heart was flopping around like one. She took her heart medication from the cabinet, and took an extra dose.

Cam came back for the silverware. "Mom, how can we find out if Park is my dad?"

Madison sat at her small kitchen desk, so she and Cam were at eye level. "Honey, your donor cell came from California, a long, long way from where we live. We can talk about this more later, but we don't talk about it around other people. Remember?"

"But I want a dad."

He looked so sad, Madison wanted to cry. She hugged him and kissed his cheek. "I know, love. Now go get Park. Dinner is ready."

The phone rang.

"Howdy, Ma'am," said her best friend, David.

"Howdy," she said with pleasure. "How's the weather in the Beehive State?"

Park came into the kitchen to wash his hands, Cam and Dudley trailing close behind.

"Utah is abysmal. Fortunately, I'm in the Lone Star State."

"You're in Houston? Got all the loose ends tied up, or is this just a quick trip?"

"It took forever to get things straightened out after Dad died, but I finally found someone to manage the business, and I'm back for good."

"I know Basc will be happy. She's sorely missed her partner. She's been on call for six months straight."

"Well, I kind of hoped you'd be happy, too," David said.

"Oh, my dear, rapture is a much better description of my feelings." Phone cradled between shoulder and chin, she assembled hamburgers, dished out fries, and got Cam and Park settled at the table. "Will I see you at work tomorrow?"

"Yeah, I'm doing the embryo transfer. But I have a present for Cam. Mind if I stop by for a minute?"

Madison wanted to spend the evening alone with Park, but she couldn't think of an excuse fast enough. "Uh—well, I have company, but sure, come on over."

David ignored the hint. "I'll be there in five minutes."

She plastered mayonnaise on Cam's burger, cut it in four pieces, and set a pickle on the side. With his index finger, Cam pushed the pickle over so it didn't touch anything else.

"Mom," he said, "is David back?"

"Yes."

"Who's David?" Park asked.

"He's Dr. Bascomb's partner. We've been friends for years, since he was a medical student in Memphis. He's been out of town for quite a while, and wants to stop by for a minute."

"Oh, yes, I remember you talking about him in therapy."

I bet he remembers me talking about you, too, Madison thought. And he won't like you one bit.

"David's dad got sick," Cam said. "He's been gone to Utah a long time. I miss him. He teaches me to be a critical thinker, so I can be a doctor like him when I grow up."

"How does he teach you to be a critical thinker?" Park asked.

Cam took a huge bite of his hamburger, then talked around it. "We got a book. I have to read a sentence, then write a word to finish it."

Park looked at Madison in astonishment. "He reads and writes?"

"Believe it or not, he taught himself. Looked at a tuna can one day, and said, 'Mom, does that say fat free?' I said yes, and he said, 'I'm gonna write it.' Darned if he didn't come back with a paper that said, 'fat free.' He didn't even look at the can to write it."

"Amazing," Park said. "Kids who read and write this early usually have genius IQs. He must have good genes." He held Madison's eyes a little longer than necessary.

"I got Levi's," Cam said proudly.

Madison's stomach was in knots, and her heart was flipping around so much, she was short of breath. She needed some quiet time to think things through. Park was inching toward the truth. If he figured it out by himself, he would never believe she'd intended to tell him. He would think she had been willing to let him die to hide her crime.

The doorbell rang, and Cam and Dudley ran to answer it, with Madison trailing behind. David came in, arms loaded with packages and a six-pack of Mickey malt ale. Cam fired off questions.

"David, did it snow in Utah? Did you get to ski? Did you bring me a present? Is it skis?"

"Whoa, Spike, let me get in the door." David set everything down and gave Cam a bear hug, then handed him a big FAO Schwartz bag. "No skis, but maybe you'll find something you like in here."

David had put on a few pounds, and it looked good on him. His thick, wavy brown hair was longer than usual, brushed straight back from his face. Despite the fact that he had a five o'clock shadow and was a bit rumpled from traveling all day, he still managed to look casually elegant in jeans, white shirt, and Italian loafers. No socks, as usual.

"I see your mother fed you well," Madison said.

"Mother never misses an opportunity to stuff me with roast grizzly bear and porcupine fricassee." He shucked off his leather bomber jacket and tossed it on the recliner. Madison saw him look over her shoulder into the dining room. Then, to her surprise, he wrapped his arms around her and pulled her tightly against him.

"Hi there, Florence Nightingale," he said in her ear. "Mmm. You smell good. How's the baby business?"

"Booming."

"I had no idea I would miss you so much. How could I not know that?"

This was all very un-David-like. Madison leaned back and smiled uneasily at him. "We missed you too."

Then he kissed her.

Madison was stunned. Their relationship was as ambiguous as it had ever been; she had never known exactly where she stood with him. In fact, for the last few years, they had been nothing more than friends. For him to kiss her in front of a stranger, who could be Madison's date for all David knew, was bizarre. Cheeks burning, she pushed him away.

Cam squealed. "Mom, look, a Robopet!" Madison walked around David to look at the toy while composing herself. It was a remote-controlled bulldog that did tricks, barked, and growled.

"Well, Santa can take that off the list," she said. "Honestly, David. You spoil him."

"Why not? I'm loaded. Just consider it an early Christmas present. We'll write a new letter to Santa." He sat in the recliner and offered to help Cam with batteries, but Cam picked up the toy and took it to show Park, climbing in his lap.

David opened a Mickey ale and took a long slug.

"Come meet my friend," Madison said.

David shot a hostile look in Park's direction. "In a minute. Sit down, I have something for you, too."

Madison perched on the edge of the coffee table, and David handed her a large package. She opened it quickly, increasingly uncomfortable that Park was excluded from the conversation, and took out a powder blue cable-knit sweater. "Thank you. It's beautiful."

"Made by maidenly Mormon ladies, especially for you. And here's something to decorate the sweater." David took a box from the bottom of the bag and opened it, revealing two necklaces.

They were made of long strings of handmade glass beads, and Madison instantly recognized them as the work of a hot glass artist she admired. The first one had brightly colored hearts with contrasting diagonal rows of braille dots, starting with yellow and continuing through all the colors in the spectrum. The second was totally different, meant to make you smile, with black and white hearts made to look like a side view of chickens, with a red comb on the right dome of the heart, a blue eye beneath, and an orange beak on the side. She slipped both necklaces around her neck. "Thank you, David. I love them."

"We saw them in that boutique in Dallas, remember? I picked up a business card and ordered them off the internet while I was in Utah."

Next he handed her a bottle of Cabernet Sauvignon. "New from the Thorpe vineyard. Dealcoholized wine, made especially for you by grape-stomping Mormon monks."

Madison laughed. "Mormon monks?" She took the bottle from him, holding it as if it were a rattlesnake. "Thanks. For all the lovely gifts."

David leaned over and kissed her again. "My pleasure." He picked up the ale and they walked into the dining room.

"Park," Madison said, "this is my friend, David Thorpe. David, Park Palmer, an old friend from Memphis."

Park set Cam on his feet and stood, offering his hand. The two men sized each up. Madison could almost smell sulfur in the air, as if two devils were in the room. She half expected their hands to sizzle when they touched.

Park looked at Madison's necklaces, then at David. "Chicken Hearted, Schizophrenic."

David's jaw dropped. "What'd you call me?"

"Not you," said Park, "it's the name of the necklaces. Chicken Hearted, for obvious reasons, and Schizophrenic, for less obvious reasons."

"How do you know that?" asked Madison.

"That's my wife's work. She makes jewelry, I name it."

"You're kidding," said Madison.

"Nope. Look at the clasps. There should be silver tags with the initials CP. Claire Palmer."

Madison took the necklaces off. Sure enough, the tags were there. "Claire made these? Wow, she's really good. My daughter, Emma, has mentioned her work. I never knew the artist's last name, so I didn't connect her with you."

"What a coincidence," said David, clearly dismissing it as inconsequential. "Have a Mickey?"

Park looked at the beer, then the bottle of wine Madison held.

"Oh, it doesn't bother her if we're drunks," said David.

"Really," said Park, making no attempt to disguise his disapproval. Still, he accepted the ale.

"Madison, I'm starved," David said. "Got an extra burger?

"Sure, I'll fix you a plate."

David followed her into the kitchen. "Park Palmer? An unusual name. Isn't that the shrink who screwed you up so bad?"

"That is Park," Madison said evenly, "and he is the psychologist who treated me a long time ago."

David finished the ale and opened another one, while she nuked his burger and fries.

"What in God's name is he doing here?"

"He's in Houston for medical treatment."

"What's wrong with him? How long is he going to be here?"

"I'm not at liberty to reveal his medical history. New government privacy regulations, you know? Not that it's any of your business."

Park's medication bottle was on the counter. David picked it up and read the label. "Palmer, Park. Phenergan 25 mg. Take as directed. Physician: Bascomb, Caroline. Well, maybe it is my business, after all. Does Caroline know she's treating him?"

"She wouldn't mind."

"The hell she wouldn't."

"Keep your voice down. What are you, the Phenergan police? I have a standing order."

"You have a standing order for our patients only."

"David Thorpe, don't you dare pull rank on me."

"What's Park doing at your house? Is he staying here?"

"No," she said thinly, realizing how odd it looked, "he rented the house next door."

"This is totally inappropriate, and totally unprofessional. He ought to be reported to the board."

Madison's eyes shot fire. "Back off, David." She shoved his plate at him. "Go in there and make nice."

"This isn't over," he said. She heard his plate hit the table with a thunk.

Madison nuked her burger, then leaned against the counter, willing her heart to slow down. She had to get David out of the house as soon as she could; he was liable to say anything.

When she had calmed down enough to join them, Cam was sitting in David's lap. David hadn't eaten much, but his second ale was gone. Now he wore a gray cashmere sweater, one he had left at her house the previous winter; he had obviously gotten it from her bedroom closet. She narrowed her eyes at him. Let's show Park we know our way around Madison's house, she wanted to say. Damn it, he was going to ruin everything. Her heart was flopping around like a fish, and she took a deep breath.

David reached over and put two fingers on her wrist, checking her pulse. She jerked her arm away.

"Quit taking your meds again?"

"I take my medications as prescribed."

"Then they're not working."

"If you don't mind, I already have a cardiologist who makes my life miserable, and I don't need additional help."

David withdrew his hand. He pushed Cam off his lap and said, "Be a good bloke and get me and Park a couple more brewskies."

Cam trotted off, then returned with the ale. Madison glared at David, who smiled innocently her. She hated it when he used Cam like a St. Bernard, packing his booze around.

"You been a good boy, Cam?" David asked.

"Yes sir, I go to school every day. And I learned some

commandments when I went to church with my friend. You can give me a test."

"Okey dokey, what's the first commandment?"

"The first commandment was when Eve told Adam to eat the apple."

They all laughed, and the tension eased a little. Cam stuck out his bottom lip. "I don't like it when people laugh at me."

David ruffled his hair. "We're not laughing at you, Spike. We're just tickled cause you're so smart." David pointed to his eye. "Tell Park what this is."

Cam rolled his eyes. "Eye."

David pointed to his mouth.

"Mouth," said Cam, bored.

David pointed to his nose.

"Vomer," said Cam. Impatient with the game, he pointed to David's forearm, knee, and leg in rapid succession, saying, "Radius, patella, femur."

"Tell Park what a normal heart sounds like."

"Lub-dub. 'cept Park's heart. It goes lub-dub-click. Why does it do that?"

"That means he has an artificial heart valve. Good pick-up, Spike. Are you working on your journal?"

Cam nodded. "Mom and I write every night, 'cept for last night, 'cause we had to sleep with Park to keep him warm. He had the gwenders."

David's head swiveled from Madison to Park, and back again. A dark flush started up his neck. Madison rearranged her French fries.

"David," said Cam, crawling up in his lap again, "Will you get me a Harry Potter watch?"

"Sure. Anything you want."

"And one for Dudley, too? He can wear it around his neck."

"Why does Dudley need a watch?"

"So he won't get mine." He handed David the Robopet control, and showed him how to make the toy dog sit up and beg. Dudley circled it nervously.

"Park, you wanna see Dudley go bonkers?" asked Cam, grinning. "All I have to do is press this button."

"Cameron, no!" said Madison.

Cam gave her an impish look, pressed a button on the remote control, and leaned over and said to Dudley, "Basil Rathbone!" Dudley barked, turned in a circle, and started running frantically back and forth between the dining room and the bedrooms.

"Yowzer," said David. "I didn't know you could control a real dog with that thing."

"What's wrong with him?" Park asked, as Dudley streaked by again.

"I don't know why he does that," said Madison. "One night, we were watching a movie, and someone asked the name of an actor. I said 'Basil Rathbone,' and Dudley took off running."

"Some deep-seated doggy psychosis, no doubt," said David. "Park, you can shrink his head while you're hangin' out. Maybe Basc will prescribe some doggie Prozac." He looked at Madison. "Or do you have a standing order for that, too?"

"David, if you can't be civil, perhaps you should leave."

"That's okay," Park, said, standing. "I really need to go."

Madison trailed after him as he collected his clothing from the bathroom, and stopped in the living room to put on his shoes. "Please don't leave."

"Don't worry. I'm better, and I have some things to take care of anyway. I hope you're not in trouble for getting the medicine for me."

"I'm not in trouble. He's just being an ass."

Park collected his wallet, watch, and keys from the coffee table. "Can I read some more of your book?"

"Only if you promise a brutally honest critique." She

94

handed the papers to him. "This is only the prologue and the first three chapters."

"I'm hardly a fiction editor," he said, "but I'll do my best."

Madison walked him to the door. "Well, you're eminently qualified to assess the character of the psychologist. It's hard for me to think like a shrink, because I have no idea what a shrink thinks."

Park laughed. "I'm afraid that sometimes they don't know what to think."

"Any thoughts on the story, so far?"

"I feel like I'm right back in that hospital room with you. How can you remember all those details?"

She looked into his eyes. "Some things are just etched in my memory forever. Other things come from my journals."

"I hope your fictional shrink does the right thing."

"What's the right thing?"

"I'll tell you when I figure it out." They stepped out on the porch. "Madi, thanks for everything. My next treatment is Thursday, and hopefully I'll be better prepared."

"Don't you dare stay over there in that dungeon by yourself. You don't even have a TV, for God's sake."

"Well, we'll see." He hesitated for a moment, searching her face. "Madi, that's the guy who had you so screwed up when you were in the hospital in Memphis, right?"

Madison sighed. "Yes."

"I thought you made a clean break from him when you moved to Houston."

"I did. But he moved here after he finished his fellowship."

"Was that a surprise?"

"Yeah, because he had already been offered a position at the University of Tennessee in Memphis."

"What made him change his mind?"

"Basc offered him a partnership in her practice."

"I see. Well. Be careful with your heart, Madi. Good

night."

Very good advice, especially coming from *him*, her mother said.

* * *

The first thing Park saw when he stepped outside was the car in Madison's driveway, a Mercedes Benz roadster convertible, top down, gleaming like black patent leather under the street light. A silver Benz touring bike was haphazardly jammed behind the seats, front wheel dangling over the passenger side, which was crammed with a suitcases. Park had priced that bike a couple of years ago, and knew it was worth over $3,000; God knew what the car was worth. It all sat there unprotected, as if having it stolen were of absolutely no consequence. Even at the zenith of his career, Park had never had enough money to be that casual with his possessions.

He looked back through the living room window. David was roughhousing with Cam; Madi stood over them, hands on her hips in exasperation, trying to make herself heard over Cam's shrieks of laughter.

Park hadn't known she still had a relationship with David. She'd spent hours in therapy talking about how much David's refusal to commit had hurt her. Madison had never mentioned him in her letters after she'd moved to Houston, and Park had assumed David was out of her life. Of course, she had never mentioned Cam either.

The night had turned cold; thick fog hung low over the bayou, and was ghosting slowly around the bases of the trees in the park across the street. Feeling irrationally creeped out, Park had to force himself to walk across the yard to the rental, opening the door to pitch black and a breath of musty air.

Light dispelled some of his uneasiness, but he was restless. It was only 7:30, too early to go to bed. He tried to read more of Madison's manuscript, but his mind kept drifting back next door, to the little boy who looked so much like him. Was Claire right? Could Cam possibly be his son?

When Cam had pointed out the hexadactyly they shared and said he was conceived by sperm donation, Park's mind had reeled back to Memphis. Knowing he was about to undergo chemotherapy that would likely cause permanent damage to his reproductive capabilities, he'd planned to have sperm frozen for long-term storage at the clinic where Madi worked. But he'd been told that his specimen had accidentally been contaminated, and had been discarded.

He wondered if Madi had access to that specimen. Nah, that was a crazy idea; she wouldn't do that—would she? Considering the fact that she was bold enough to invade his home and take a souvenir, confiscating discarded sperm might seem like a minor infraction to her. It could hardly be called theft.

But what if the specimen hadn't really been contaminated? What if she had taken it, and the clinic had made up a story to cover themselves?

Half of him was outraged at the idea. But the other half wanted it to be true, wanted that bright, engaging little boy to be his so much that he could forgive Madi anything.

Park paced from the living room to the kitchen, his mind racing. If Cam were his son, Claire would have the painful issue of their barren marriage shoved in her face. After they had lost their baby to sudden infant death syndrome, Claire had flatly refused to have more children. Should Cam prove to be Park's child, he did not think Claire could bear it. And she would never believe Park had not slept with Madi.

Another thought lurked in the back of his mind: Cam might be a bone marrow match. But how could he ask a four-year-old to donate bone marrow? And how could he not? If Cam were his child, why hadn't Madi disclosed the information? Would she let him die to protect her secret?

Of course, he could be way off base. Maybe David was

Cam's father. But if that were so, why would Madi pretend she had used donor sperm? Wouldn't she want Cam to know his father?

How the hell had he gotten into this mess? Two days ago, the biggest problem he'd had was a relapse of his anemia. Now, his wife thought he was having an affair, he might have a child, and he had once again been mesmerized by Madi, instead of dealing with his life. Hell, he hadn't even called Claire to make sure she'd gotten home okay. He needed to do that without delay.

Park drove to the closest "Stop 'n Rob," as Madi called Houston convenience stores, and called Claire from the phone kiosk outside. She answered on the first ring.

"Hi, it's me," he said inanely.

"About time you called," she said.

"I'm sorry. You know I'm hopelessly disorganized without you. I still don't have a phone."

"You could have gotten a cell phone."

"I'm going to. I just didn't think about it Sunday night, and I've been sick since Monday."

"I thought this drug wasn't supposed to make you as sick as the first one."

"It's not, but by the time I got home from the first treatment, I was so sick, I could barely stand up."

"Speaking of home, have you found a place to live?"

Park hesitated. It was the question he'd dreaded, and one of the reasons he hadn't called her from Madi's that morning. "I had to rent the house we looked at." His voice came out small, and he knew it would convey his fear of her reaction.

"Oh, how odd," she said. "In a city with a few million places to live, you had no choice but the house next door to Madison. Funny things worked out that way."

Park sighed. "Claire, I had no idea it would turn out like this. After you left, I just felt kind of—helpless. And I only had a few hours to get organized."

"You could have taken one of the efficiencies in the

medical center."

"Well, you already nixed that idea." Park tried to think what he would say if he were counseling a couple. Above all, he would encourage them to be honest, and to take responsibility for their actions. "I know you think I planned this and I'm trying to pass it off as accidental. I didn't, and I regret how it evolved, but I can't undo it."

"Yes you can. You can move somewhere else."

"That's just not practical. I had to sign a six-month lease, and we'd lose the deposit and first and last month's rent, and then we'd have to come up with the same, for a more expensive place."

"Well, then, I guess you've got it covered."

Park sighed. "You should know me well enough to know that if I wanted to end our marriage, which I don't, cheating on you is not the way I would do it. I'd earn my way out of it, in a civil manner."

"Oh, please! We haven't had a marriage for years. Our marriage ended the day you let Nathan die."

If she'd reached through the phone and thrown ice water in his face, Park couldn't have been more shocked. "What do you mean, I let Nathan die?"

"I told you to get him up while I was gone to the store, but you just sat there and watched the football game. If you'd done what I asked, he wouldn't have stopped breathing."

Park couldn't believe that for all these years, she had secretly harbored the thought that he was to blame for Nathan's death. No wonder their marriage had disintegrated. No wonder he had never been able to help her. "That's an unbelievably vicious thing to say."

"Truth hurts," she replied, her voice cold.

"The Medical Examiner said it would have happened sooner or later. It had nothing to do with what I did or didn't do."

"The Medical Examiner couldn't know that."

"Why didn't you tell me you felt like this, so we could

work through it?"

"You think talk is the solution to everything, but it can't bring our son back, and it can't fix us. When life was fun, I could bury the feelings. But now, I can't. I want a divorce."

Even if they didn't have a storybook marriage, she was still his wife, his partner. He did not want to lose her, would never sacrifice her for a dream of romantic love with someone else, however tempting it was.

"Claire, don't you see, this is good, this is a breakthrough. Things will get better financially. We'll get some counseling, and we'll get our life back."

"I don't know why you want to fight this. Do you think you can have me and your girlfriend too? Not going to happen. So have a nice life with your new family."

"*Please* don't do this. We need talk face to face. This is no conversation to have on the phone." Park got a dial tone in response.

This could not happen. He could not, would not accept it. He started the car and headed north, toward Dallas. He had to talk to Claire. Tonight.

* * *

Madison wanted to kill David. He had ruined her evening. She sent Cam, protesting loudly, to put the robot away and pick up his mess in the living room, while she cleared the table.

David picked up napkins and glasses, and followed her into the kitchen. "So how was your day?"

Oh, right, she thought, rinsing plates and jamming them in the dishwasher. Let's make small talk and pretend the last hour didn't happen. "I have twelve patients on Lupron. How do you think my day was?"

David put condiments away and started wiping the counters. "Just tell them they'll get better when we start stimulating their ovaries with estrogen."

"Hello, then they swing the other direction, with too much estrogen. One of them called me a bitch. *Me*, Nurse Jane Fuzzy Wuzzy."

David made a ward-off-the-evil-spirit cross with his index fingers. "Who are you, and what have they done with my Madison? This isn't a bit like you. You're the patient advocate, the Ralph Nader of patient care."

She gave him a dirty look. "You think I'm a bitch? Well, you try living in estrogen-more / estrogen-less hell."

"Uh—I sorta do," David said carefully.

"Ha ha," Madison said, then took off in a different direction. "Then there's just the regular old day-to-day stuff to deal with. This morning, a patient accidentally took her dog's antibiotic, instead of her own. A new patient found out she wouldn't be having her husband's biological child because he used to be a woman, don't ask me how he hid that, and another one has frozen embryos that she wants to transfer at a time when she couldn't possibly get pregnant, because she's decided she wants a divorce instead of a baby, and she doesn't want to discard the embryos or donate them to some other poor desperate woman."

"Well, they're her embryos, she can do what she wants with them."

Madison put the last plate in the dishwasher and slammed the door. "The good news is, after my cardiologist bitched me out for discontinuing my thyroid medication and bug-tussled me to the floor to draw a thyroid level before I left the office, he didn't even have the decency to call and apologize when it came back normal. His nurse called just as I was merging onto the freeway. I laughed so hard, I nearly had a wreck."

"Doctors," David said with disgust.

Madison ran hot water into the frying pan and added dishwashing detergent. She had to bite her lip to keep from laughing. But she wasn't going to forgive David's despicable behavior without an apology.

David picked up the coffee pot and stood by the sink, waiting to fill it. They always had coffee and conversation after dinner, normally a pleasant prospect, but she couldn't believe he expected that tonight, after he had barged in and behaved like a cuckolded husband.

"David, I really don't have time to chit-chat tonight. I need to get Cam to bed, and I have some other things to do."

"Okay," he said, looking wounded. He replaced the coffee pot. "Do you have any new pages for me to read?"

"No."

"You gave Park three chapters."

The last thing she wanted David to read, albeit "fiction," was what had happened between her and Park. "That's something new," she said evasively, "and it's very rough. He's just helping me develop a particular character."

"Fine," he said. "Enjoy your new writing partner."

"Oh, so now you're not going to write with me because you're jealous? When did I become your exclusive property?"

"I guess when you have a kid with someone, you feel a little ownership."

"What are you talking about?"

"Well, you got pregnant right before you left Memphis, when we were together."

Madison's jaw dropped. "You think Cam is your kid? He was conceived with donor sperm from California Cryo, and you know that!"

"If that's true, it's easy enough to verify. We'll just call Memphis, get them to send your chart, and look at the paperwork."

"Do you really think I would do an insemination at *our* clinic?"

"Why not?"

"Maybe I didn't want everyone in the world to know?"

"Or maybe it's not true? You always said you didn't want any more kids, so why would you plan an insemination? The pregnancy had to be an accident."

Madison scrubbed the pan viciously. "Cam was certainly not an accident."

"Oh, so he was an 'on purpose?'"

"David, back off. It's really none of your business. And if you think Cam is yours, why didn't you ever say anything?"

"I've been waiting for you to tell me. And if he's mine, it's very much my business."

That explained a lot—why David had tried to rekindle their relationship after he moved to Houston, why he helped her so much, why he spent so much time with Cam and showered him with ridiculously expensive gifts. Stalling for time, Madison rinsed the pan under scalding water and turned it upside down on the counter. The issue was something she had shoved out of her mind, because she had wanted Cam to be Park's child. But for the first time, she admitted the possibility that David might be his father, too. After all, it would be somewhat of a miracle if the insemination had worked. But she wasn't ready to admit it to David.

"Cam doesn't even look like you," she said, knowing the comment was ridiculous.

"You know that doesn't matter. Do your siblings all look like your parents?"

"You've met them, you tell me."

"Well, let's see. Black, brunette, and blonde hair. Blue and brown eyes, as I recall. Which one looks exactly like one of your parents? Not a single one."

"Well, each of us has at least one of our parents' features."

"Fine," David said, exasperated. "So your only possible parent is one with a similar feature. Okay, maybe Cam's hair will darken to brunette as he gets older. Right now, he looks a lot like Park. Maybe Park is his—"

David stopped in mid-sentence, realization slowly showing on his face, as if someone were turning up a rheostat. "Oh, I see.

Now we've really got a problem. You were sleeping with both of us."

"I was *not!*" Madison said hotly. "And I will not discuss this with you any further, especially when Cam is within earshot. I think it's time for you to leave."

"Don't make me get a court order for a paternity test, Madison," David said, his voice steel. "If he's mine, I want to know."

"Don't you dare threaten me, David Thorpe."

"I'm not threatening you. I'm telling you that I intend to find out if he is my child. With or without your cooperation."

She followed him to the living room, and stood fuming as he put on his jacket and said goodbye to Cam. He roared away in a Benz convertible she'd never seen, top down despite the cold.

Just what she needed. Another dilemma. Deep down, Madison knew she would tell Park about Cam, but if, in fact, Cam was not Park's child, she would be confessing her crime unnecessarily. More importantly, if Cam were David's child, he could not help Park. She didn't know which to hope for.

Madison locked up and put Cam in the tub. She chewed over the evening as she shampooed his hair.

"Mom, that hurts," he said, pushing her hands away. "Are you mad at me?"

Madison realized she had been scrubbing his head as if it were a frying pan. "No, of course not. Why do you think I'm mad at you?"

"Because of what I said to Dudley. I'm sorry. I know you don't like us to run in the house."

Madison rinsed his hair and soaped a washcloth for him. "It's not about running in the house, sweetheart. It's just that I don't know what Dud expects to happen when we say you-know-what to him."

"What do you mean?"

How to explain a Pavlovian response to a child. "Well,

maybe you'll understand if I tell you a story about a man named Pavlov. He did an experiment. Every time he rang a bell, he fed his dog. Pretty soon, when he rang the bell, the dog thought it was going to be fed. But what if Mr. Pavlov had rung the bell, then kicked the dog? Then, every time he rang the bell, the dog would think he was going to be kicked. Do you understand?"

"You mean Dud might be running away because he thinks I'm gonna kick him?"

"Something like that. That's why I don't like you to do it."

"Oh." Cam looked at Dudley, who stood beside Madison, chin on the edge of the bathtub. Cam patted Dudley's head with a soapy hand. "I'm sorry, Dud. I won't say it again."

Madison tucked Cam in and let him read her a bedtime story. She sank gratefully into her own bed at 10 p.m. But sleep did not come easily. For there, in the deep silence of the night, she had to confront what she had repressed so long.

Red was not green, transference was not true love, and she really did not know who Cam's father was, Park or David.

Madison the agnostic, the recovering Catholic, picked up the rosary she kept on her bedside table for desperate circumstances, and began the litany of generic prayer, an all-purpose cry for help.

CHAPTER FIVE

By eleven, Park had Dallas in sight, and at 11:20, he pulled into his apartment complex. The light was still on in Claire's bedroom. He took the stairs two at a time and opened the front door, calling her name so he wouldn't frighten her, but she didn't answer. Feeling awkward in his own home, as if they were already divorced, he went to her bedroom.

Even in a cheap apartment, Claire had managed to create a feeling of simple elegance. Her bedroom walls were pale pink. There was a white floral comforter with a black and white striped dust ruffle on the bed; Degas ballerina prints were hung on the walls. Claire, in a black silk chemise, was propped up on several pillows, smoking one of her Kool mocha taboo cigarettes and writing a letter.

Park approached her as if she were a rattlesnake coiled to strike, and sat beside her.

She pulled the comforter up to her neck, and looked away. "What are you doing here? I don't want you here. Go back to Houston."

He looked at her helplessly, deserted by the healing words that came so easily when he was working with a patient. He'd never been able to penetrate her psychological armor, which he'd assumed she wore because she'd never healed from the unexpected loss of their baby. It had never occurred to him that her hardness was anger at him. "We need to work through this face to face," he said gently.

She stubbed out her cigarette and crossed her arms over her chest, refusing to look at him. "What good will it do?"

"It will help us get closure, Claire. What we've always needed."

"I don't want closure. I don't want to forget Nathan. And I don't want a replacement child!"

As if he could ever forget Nathan. The pain of losing him was like wearing a pair of gray contact lenses that permanently dimmed the world.

"Forgetting is one thing," he said. "Coping is another. And I never asked you to provide a 'replacement child.' You know that as much as I want children, I understand and accept your feelings about not having more." The last words nearly stuck in his throat, though. He'd grown up an only child with no father, and he had always wanted a family.

"So you just sleep around, and have your children with someone else."

At some point, he would have to stop playing therapist and just be a husband, letting his anger out, and he was nearly at that point now. But he knew that Claire was fragile beneath the hard veneer, so he caged his feelings and said, "How can I convince you that I did not sleep with Madi?"

She laughed bitterly. "You sound suspiciously Clintonesque. 'I-did-not-have-sexual-relations-with-that-woman.'"

"I *didn't* have sexual relations with her."

"Okay, then, here's how you can convince me. Get a paternity test."

Park sighed and looked at the floor. She was right; a paternity test would answer all the questions, but he could hardly demand it. If he wanted to save his marriage, he would have to tell her what he suspected about Cam's conception. There was no way around it. Which meant he would have to confess he'd tried to store sperm, knowing it would never be used for Claire to conceive a child, and he would have to explain why he'd done that—something he'd never even explained to himself.

"There's something I need to tell you," he started, but Claire interrupted him.

"Yeah, I bet."

"Just hold on. You don't know what I'm going to say." He took a deep breath and plunged in. "Right before we left Memphis, the doctors suggested I bank some sperm. So I took a semen sample to the clinic in my building."

He looked at Claire. She was rigid, breathing so shallowly her chest was barely moving. "What for? You knew another pregnancy wasn't an option for me, so what were you planning to do with the sperm?"

Park was silent, grasping for words adequate to explain his fear of permanently losing his reproductive capacity, his identity as a man.

Then Claire's face changed to the expression of someone who had opened a jewelry box and found a black widow spider instead of a diamond ring. "Oh, my God, you gave the sperm to Madison. You didn't sleep with her, but you might as well have!"

"No! The sperm was to be frozen. Nothing more."

"Fine," she said, her eyes glittering. "Then the sperm is still at the clinic. That's easy enough to verify."

He looked at her miserably. Now was the time to tell her his suspicions about Madi, but the words would just not come out. "The specimen was contaminated, and they discarded it," he said hollowly.

Upper lip curled in contempt, she pushed him away, got up and put on her robe, jerking the sash so tight he thought she would cut herself in half. "That does it. I'm through talking. I'm filing for divorce."

"Claire, please. This is ridiculous. Don't you think some marriage counseling is a better idea? I don't want a divorce."

"I bet you don't. At least until you've finished your current round of treatment and don't need me to support you anymore. Well, I won't let you use me."

"You'd abandon me in the middle of my treatment to punish me for some imagined crime?"

She held her hands palms up. "You're the one who made the choice."

His heart started pounding as he thought about the consequences of her decision. "What am I going to do for income? What will I do for health insurance? My treatment will be interrupted. Claire, don't you care if I die?"

"You can get Cobra coverage. How you pay for it is your problem. Now pack up whatever you want and get out."

The last shreds of their marriage disintegrated like rotting fabric turning to dust. Before him stood the real Claire, the one he had refused to acknowledge. The one he had pampered and endured, for whom he had sacrificed a life of happiness and warmth and support. At last, outrage overtook the therapist in him. "Fine," he said tightly. "Have it your way. But I'll leave when I please."

In the kitchen, Park poured himself a stiff drink and took it to the smaller bedroom where she had moved him when he first became sick, because he disturbed her at night. She had not bothered to decorate it. Boxes that hadn't been unpacked after their move from Memphis filled at least half of the room, and the other half was crammed with file cabinets, bookcases, a single bed, and his desk, which was buried under stacks of papers and neglected professional journals.

Somewhere in the mess was a spiral notebook with a list of jobs he could do at home during his treatment. Emotion aside, the critical issue was income. His rent was paid for a month, and if the nausea from his treatments kept up, he wouldn't be eating much.

But after that, he was in trouble. He needed to find a source of income immediately. He'd already been looking for months, and the prospects were dismal.

Things could be worse, he'd once said to Madi when she was in a similar situation—suffering unfairly because of someone else's actions. She'd just stared at him like he was an idiot, not even bothering to change her expression, until shame had crept up his neck all the way to his hairline. Life had a funny way of teaching compassion, by making you experience the same thing you had made someone else experience.

Park found a suitcase and started packing the essentials. Claire could have the rest. All he wanted was to get home. Home to Houston.

Home to Madi.

* * *

At ten o' clock Wednesday morning, Park abruptly surfaced from a nightmare that Claire had filed for divorce, leaving him sick, jobless, and broke. Then he realized it wasn't just a nightmare. He was still in their Dallas apartment, surrounded by half-packed boxes. Exhausted and overwhelmed by the situation, he'd started drinking, and passed out in the middle of the job. He sat up on the edge of the bed and rubbed his face with both hands. He was nauseated, but he'd left his medication in Houston, at Madi's house. Maybe a beer would fix him up.

He shuffled to the kitchen, groaning when he found the countertops littered with food wrappers and containers, and a half-empty—or half-full, depending on your perspective, or both half empty and half full, as Madi would say—bottle of scotch. Damn it, he was sleep-eating again. Claire had left the mess for him to clean up.

He pitched two empty chili cans, a head of cabbage with several bites taken out of it, and some sticky, raw refrigerator biscuits into the garbage. He had absolutely no memory of eating these things. There were cigarette filters and shreds of tobacco all over the place. In sleep-eating mode, he'd eaten all sorts of strange things—several tablespoons of Crisco, a frozen chicken breast, an entire jar of chopped garlic. But never, to his recollection, had he eaten a pack of cigarettes.

He grabbed the scotch and went back to his bedroom, holding his stomach. The little nocturnal foray in the kitchen had set off his peptic ulcer, and he needed his medication. The medicine bottle was open on the nightstand; apparently he had taken some during the night. He took so much of the stuff that years ago he'd started ordering it on the internet. He could get 500 pills for $52.78, cheaper than insurance. And the online doctor even wrote the prescription.

Park took a couple more pills for good measure, washing them down with a slug of scotch, and sat there cradling his bottle and staring into space, like a good alcoholic. With no income, he would have to make his pills last a long time. Guess he'd have to panhandle for booze, hope he met some good souls who didn't know the concept of curbside enablement.

This was all David's fault. If it hadn't been for David, Park would still be at Madi's, he wouldn't have eaten all that junk, and his peptic ulcer wouldn't have kicked up again.

What a stupid ass that guy was. David couldn't know Madi very well if he thought a bottle of wine was an appropriate gift for her. That was like bringing five pounds of Godiva chocolates to a diabetic. He couldn't believe she'd let David back into her life. And he couldn't believe he'd let David shove him out.

Park took another swig of scotch and laughed. Claire was right. He was as bad as any patient he had treated. He wanted both Claire and Madi in his life. He leaned back and waited for the Scotch to do its magic before he started packing again.

* * *

Wednesday promised to be a light day for Madison, and she planned to leave work a couple of hours early. She was worried that something had happened to Park during the night; his car hadn't been in the driveway this morning when she left.

She looked at her watch for the tenth time in as many minutes. An embryo transfer was scheduled for noon, and it was already 12:30. The patient was ready, her husband was restless, and the andrologist, who was babysitting the embryos, had already asked Madison twice what the holdup was. David was late, like he was for every procedure, a passive-aggressive effort to get Basc to change inflexible scheduling rules. Madison wished he would just grow up. When he became director of the department, perish the thought, he could make the rules.

At 12:45, she went to David's office to see what was keeping him. He sat with his feet up on the desk, casually eating an apple. She stuck her hands on her hips and glared at him. The least he could do was look like he was late because he was dealing with an emergent situation. "I wish you wouldn't do this," she said.

"Do what?" he asked innocently.

"You know what. FYI, you're not making a point with Basc because she doesn't even know what you're doing. I don't run down the hall and tattle on you. This doesn't do anything but punish Cam. For every minute you're late, that's one more minute you keep me from doing my work, one more minute I have to stay late, one more minute before I can pick up Cam, one less minute I can spend with him. And it pisses off the people in the lab and the patients, who also have other things to do. So come on, dammit, and let's get this done."

David finished his apple, tossed the core in the trash, and wiped his hands on his scrub pants. "Put the patient on the table," he said. "I'll be there in five minutes." He picked up the phone, punched in a number, and leaned back in his chair, staring her down.

Fifteen minutes later, he finally arrived, and by the time

they finished the embryo transfer, Madison was more than an hour behind. She grabbed some peanut butter crackers and a diet Coke, and picked up her messages. Only ten this morning, but four of them were pregnancy test results that she would have to call to patients who would be devastated by the news. Three tests were negative and one was equivocal, which meant weeks of uncertainty that would probably end in a miscarriage for that patient.

Madison put her head down on her desk and closed her eyes for a moment. She didn't know how much longer she could take this job. It just hurt too much.

Basc came in, pulled up a chair, and sat beside her. "Are you okay? David said there was a problem during the embryo transfer."

"He reported me?"

"Well, not really—he just seemed concerned."

"I made a mistake. When he injected the embryos and was ready for me to lower the patient's head, I accidentally hit the button to lower the foot of the bed. You know it happens once in a while. The room is dark, the buttons are right beside each other, and they're hard to see. You know I would never do that deliberately."

"Of course you wouldn't, that's why I'm worried. You seem distracted, and you asked for a day off."

"I'm just tired. I had one free hour that I wanted to use to knock out some chores before my teaching visit, but David wasted that hour for me. And now the patients for the teaching visit are late. I don't like them anyway, there's something off about them, so I'm doubly irritated."

Just then, the secretary came in with a cookie bouquet. "Your patients are here. And look what they brought you."

Greatest Nurse on Earth! proclaimed the center cookie, shaped like an old-fashioned nurse's cap.

Madison groaned. "I hate myself," she said. "Here I am talking about them like they're dogs, and they bring me cookies."

Basc smiled. "That's the real definition of professionalism—when you don't like the patients, and they have absolutely no idea."

Madison laughed. "Nice try. Thanks anyway."

"Now tell me what's really wrong," Basc said.

Oh, how Madison wished she could tell her the whole story. Basc loved and mothered her, and was often Madison's soft place to fall. But if Basc found out one of her nurses had misappropriated sperm, discarded or otherwise, she would certainly fire her, and maybe even prosecute. It would end their friendship, and Madison might even lose her nursing license. Truth told, she probably should, anyway. Just for stupidity, if nothing else. "It's just the thing with David," Madison said, evasively.

"I never have understood why you two haven't gotten married."

"I understand," Madison said. "He's never asked me. He's never even told me how he feels about me."

Basc looked surprised. "Really? He's told me."

"What did he tell you?"

"That he loves you."

"And therein lies the problem. It's the story of my life, you know. I seem to attract men who love me but are incapable of saying so."

"Obviously, with the exception of David, you pick the wrong men."

Madison laughed. "It's not like I've had a huge selection."

"You limit yourself too much. I mean, look at what's happening right now. You're getting involved with that unprofessional, immoral shrink again."

"That's not true. Park is sick. He just needs some help right now. He helped me. I owe him."

"You owe him nothing. You paid him for his services. Don't you see how inappropriate this is?"

"Why? I'm not his patient anymore. I hadn't even seen him

for five years."

"Because it is never appropriate for a shrink to be involved with a patient, past or present."

"I'm not involved with him."

"Not physically, maybe. But he's been having an emotional affair with you for years. He's way out of bounds. Haven't you learned anything from this?"

"What do you mean?"

"You keep falling in love with impossible men. First there was that surgery resident who was married, then there was that guy who couldn't decide if he was straight or gay, then Park, who is the worst of all. He's not available, and stringing you along keeps you from finding a viable relationship."

There was truth in what Basc said, but Madison didn't want to hear it. "I still love him as a friend, Basc, but don't think I can fall in love with him again."

"I don't think you ever fell out of love with him. Madison, you have to give up the idea of a romance with this shrink. Don't you know what happens to your brain in romantic love? A hundred billion neurons are firing all day long, and your brain changes; it's saturated with the chemicals that control pleasure, and depleted of those that control common sense."

Madison thought about how it felt to wake up in Park's arms, feel his hand trail down the length of her hair, see the expression on his face when she thought he was going to kiss her. It was true, she had responded to him, but deep inside, there was a barrier of distrust.

"And what happens to your brain when your trust is betrayed?" Madison asked. "I'll never have a pure feeling of love for Park again. I was in the middle of some gut-wrenching emotional work when he left. I already felt like I'd climbed to the top of a skyscraper and couldn't get down, but then, when he left, it felt like he'd pushed me off. That was unforgivable, even though he had every right to do whatever he wanted with his life and had no legal commitment to me."

"And that's exactly why his level of emotional involvement is unconscionable—because he does have the right to walk away at any time. And worst of all, he has a very serious illness, one he might not survive."

"That's not true! He's going to be fine. He's going to recover and go back to work and have a wonderful life."

"Statistics say otherwise," Basc said, with her usual bluntness. "Survival rates after a relapse of aplastic anemia are very low. But let's say he gets well. Then what? He goes home to his wife?"

"Maybe, maybe not. They're having problems."

"Why am I not surprised? He's using you, Madison, and I'm worried that you'll get so upset that you'll go back to alcohol for comfort. I don't want to see you get hurt again because of him."

"I have five years of solid sobriety under my belt, and I've learned to tolerate discomfort. You don't need to worry." She stood, gathered her medications and supplies for her teaching visit. At the door, she turned and said, "But thank you for caring so much."

Madison could barely concentrate on her teaching. All her brain wanted to do was process what Basc had implied: That David was in love with her. The information hovered at the edge of her consciousness, making it hard to focus.

Once again, her effort to get out of the office was thwarted by "emergency" phone calls, and it was five by the time she was ready to leave. On her way out, she stopped by David's office; he was back from his Wednesday afternoon clinic at Ben Taub, the county hospital. Although he wore a dress shirt and tie under his lab coat, and had even shaved, she would bet her paycheck that his desk concealed a pair of jeans and loafers. David had standards about just how conservative he was willing to be.

Madison shut the door and sat down. "Thanks a lot for

reporting me," she said.

"I didn't report you. I was just frustrated, and I needed to talk to a friend."

"Basc may be a friend to both of us, but don't forget, she's still my boss. If I'd thought I had made a mistake that adversely affected the patient, I'd have told her myself. I apologized to you, and I certainly didn't expect it to go any further."

"I'm sorry," he said defensively. "I didn't mean to get you in trouble."

"Yes you did."

David was silent.

"If we're going to continue to work together, we're going to have to clear the air about some things," Madison said.

"Like what?"

Unable to think of a clever way to ask the question that had been burning her up for hours, Madison looked him directly in the eye and said bluntly, "David, have you ever been in love with me?"

David froze. He stared at her, unblinking, for a full minute before he answered. "Yes."

Madison could not believe her ears. "Why didn't you ever tell me?"

"I was going to. But then you got all tangled up with Park, and I was glad I hadn't."

"Things might have been different if you'd told me."

"Are you saying you love me, Madison?"

"I did. But I don't know how I feel now."

"Why didn't *you* tell *me*?"

"I was afraid. I was confused. I couldn't tell how you felt about me. It seems like every man in my life gives me mixed signals. First it's come here, then it's go away. Finally, I just gave up."

"No you didn't. You just switched to someone else. What's he got that I don't have, anyway?"

"Only one thing. He's able to talk to me."

"I talk to you."

"About medicine, about what movie I want to see, about where to go to dinner, about how far you rode your bike."

"What else is there to talk about?"

"My gosh, David, you're a doctor! I've heard you talk to patients about their needs, their wants, their goals, their pain. People need to talk about those things outside the office, too."

"Okay, I can do that."

Madison rolled her eyes. "Park talks to me about feelings. He's interested in what goes on in my head. He helps me sort things out. He likes me, he likes my ideas, the things I read, what's important to me."

Madison could see a flush creeping up under David's collar, a muscle in his jaw jumping.

"I may not have the gift of gab," he said evenly. "But I was there when you were hospitalized for depression. I was there when Cam was born. I've been there for you through a hundred other crises. I thought that meant something."

"It did, David. It does. I'm talking about something different—a kind of intimacy, a sharing of someone else's inner world that makes you feel close."

"I want to be like that, Madison, but it's not something that comes easily to me."

"It's a wall you can take down, a wall that keeps people separate from you."

"I'll work on it," he said.

"No matter what happens, you are too embedded in my life for us to be at war with each other. Above all else, we're friends. I want to make peace."

"Me too. Where do we start?"

Madison felt a tremendous sense of relief. "Obviously, part of the dilemma is Cam's paternity. We could do that mouth swab test on the two of you. That would rule you in or out."

David shook his head. "We need a blood test."

"Why? Cam is terrified of needles. I tried to give him a tetanus shot once. I had to chase him around the house and drag him by one foot, out from under his bed."

"There's another issue. I assume Park is slated for a bone marrow transplant."

"If they can find a decent match."

David nailed her with his eyes. "Madison, is there even the remotest possibility that Park is Cam's father? Because if there is, Cam has to be tested as a donor."

Madison felt as if all her blood had drained to her feet. There was no way around it. She would have to let David think she had slept with Park. David was Basc's partner. She must not let either of them know she had mishandled sperm. "Yes, there is a possibility," she said in a small voice.

"Then I suggest that you, Cam, and I volunteer to be tested as donors for Park," David said. "That will give us all the answers we need."

"How?"

"Our immune systems use markers, or alleles, to recognize which cells belong to our bodies, and which don't. You inherit half of your alleles from your mother, and half from your father. That's why siblings, who have alleles from both parents, are usually the best donor match. But children can be close matches, too. If Cam has alleles from you and me, we know he's mine. If he has alleles from you and Park, we'll know he's Park's. And either way, we'll rule him in or out as a donor."

Panic inched its way through Madison's chest, and her heart skipped a beat. She stood suddenly and went to the door. It was too soon, she didn't want to know, she couldn't deal with it. "I have to think about this."

David followed her, put his hands on her shoulders and turned her around. "Madison, we have to do this. We can't let Park die. And Cam deserves to know his father, whomever that may be, and his father to know him."

She looked at him in wonder, touched by his concern for Park and Cam. David was a wealthy man who was generous with money, a behavior Basc attributed to a need to buy his friends; but Madison knew he was motivated by generosity. He was one of the truly unselfish people in the world. Her spiteful thoughts the night before were just that—spite—because she knew he would have done all the things he'd done for her since Cam's birth, no matter who the father was.

"I know I messed up," he continued. "I hope you'll give me a chance to get it right."

He took her face in his hands and kissed her, sweetly and gently, and to her surprise, a hundred billion neurons fired, straight down the center of her body. Madison was speechless, her brain reduced to a soggy neurochemical mess. Her relationship with David after she got pregnant with Cam had not been physically intimate, and she was shocked by her reaction.

He opened the door and they walked down the hall together; Madison was sure everyone in the building could tell she had been thoroughly kissed, all the way to her toes. As she opened the door to her office, he said, "We'll talk later."

She fervently hoped her brain had regenerated by then.

CHAPTER SIX

By the time Park had slept off his hangover, packed, and driven back to Houston, it was sunset. He'd just started to unload the car when Madison got home.

Cam ran across the lawn, waving a piece of white construction paper, looking like miniature prep in his button-down shirt, khakis, and penny loafers. He wore a brown leather bomber jacket, a gift from David, Park would bet; it matched the one David had worn last night. Anything you want, David had told Cam. Park wondered why he was so indulgent with the child.

"Hey, Park! Look what I made for you," Cam yelled.

Park squatted and accepted Cam's creation. A line drawing done in crayon, it was a study of the quadrangle of Cam's life, depicting his mother, David, and Park, with Cam positioned between the two men, holding their hands.

"It's our family," Cam said, wounded when the expected praise was not forthcoming.

"That's fine work," Park said, thickly. Madi was crossing the lawn now, and he stood and composed himself.

"Howdy, neighbor," she said. "I'm glad to see you. I was worried when your car was gone this morning." She glanced inside the car, jammed with sports equipment, boxes, and clothes. "Been shopping?"

"Sort of. I just got back from Dallas."

"Dallas! When did you go to Dallas?"

"Last night. I called Claire, and we had a conversation that I thought we should finish in person." He smiled grimly. "She's filing for divorce. Looks like Houston may become my new home."

He watched emotions pass across Madi's face, shock followed by happiness, he thought, then guilt. He knew her so well; she would think she was to blame, and certainly her little home invasion antics had contributed to the demise of his marriage, but it was probably in its death throes, anyway.

"Don't blame yourself," he said. "It's a complex situation."

Cam pulled a fishing pole out of the car. "Wow, look at this! Park, will you take me fishing? I can put on a worm all by myself. Mom won't do it. She thinks they're icky. We can't fish in the bayou, the fish are dirty—"

"Cam, why don't you take that into the house for Park?" Madison said.

"Okay, I can help Park take everything in. I'll be right back." He trotted off with the fishing pole.

"And so he will," Madison said ruefully. "Are you okay? You look tired."

"I am tired. World-weary."

He unloaded some boxes from the trunk, then poked around until he came up with a small, beat-up red plastic box. When Cam came back, Park handed it to him. "I brought this for you. It was my tackle box when I was a little boy."

Cam hugged the box to his chest. "Thank you," he said, his eyes glowing. He sat down on the grass and opened it, exclaiming over colorful lures and floats. Madison watched him, frowning.

"Don't worry," Park said. "I removed the fish hooks." He smiled. "I wish I had his enthusiasm for life."

"You'll get your enthusiasm back. Are you going to be

okay tomorrow? I know you had trouble driving home after your treatment on Monday."

"To tell you the truth, I don't know if I'm even going to continue treatment."

"Why? You can't quit. You have to have treatment."

"With Claire cutting off my income, I may not be able to afford it. And honestly, I just don't know if I can go through this again."

"Well, that's just not acceptable. We'll figure out a way to keep you in treatment." She studied his face for a moment. "I'm taking a mental health day tomorrow. Do you want me to go with you? I don't have anything special planned."

Park weighed the offer for a moment, hating to take her day off, but needing her. "I'd love to have you with me. I have to be at Anderson at eight. Is that a problem?"

"No. I'll drive; come on over at 7:15, so we'll have plenty of time to drop Cam off at school. Would you like to have dinner with us tonight?"

"We're having bumbo and lullibubs," Cam volunteered.

"I think I'll pass," Park said. "Doesn't sound too appetizing. Thank you anyway."

"Okay. See ya in the morning. Come on, Cam, you need to let the 'trundle tail' out and feed him."

Cam closed his box and clutched it to his chest, his voice trailing behind as he followed his mother home.

"Mom, how do fish get in the bayou? Do they swim up the bayou from the ocean? If they swim up from the ocean, are they dirty? Are there ocean fish and bayou fish? How can you tell an ocean fish from a bayou fish? . . ."

Madison shot Park a murderous look over her shoulder.

* * *

Cam wanted a "burnt cheese sammich" for dinner and he

wanted to watch TV while he ate. Madison agreed, mostly to avoid a thousand questions about why little boys couldn't eat in the living room; she needed time to think.

She set his plate on the coffee table, in the midst of the entire inventory of fishing lures, and sent him to wash his hands. The doorbell rang. Madison could see a florist's van in the driveway. She opened the door and was handed a vase of long-stemmed red roses.

Cam shrieked and she turned, half expecting to see Dudley, who was skulking around the coffee table, eating Cam's sandwich.

Cam smacked Dudley on the rear. "Bad dog."

"Hey," Madison said, "we don't hit the dog."

"But he took my purple worm and half my sammich."

She stifled a laugh. "Don't worry about it. You wouldn't have eaten all the sandwich anyway, and we'll get you another worm."

Cam's lip quivered. "But it was my glitter worm. And he ate it."

"Maybe he just hid it. It's probably in his bed; you can look after dinner. Now eat."

"Stupid trundle tail," Cam muttered, glaring at Dudley, who eyed the selection of treasures from a safe distance. Cam took a gigantic bite out of his sandwich, then started putting his lures back in the box.

Madison set the roses on the end table and opened the card, which was simply signed, "David." Bless his heart, even after the heavy drama in his office, he was still either unwilling or unable to share emotion, at least in words.

She was reminded of an old letter her father had written her mother from overseas. He was a silent man, generally thought of as emotionless, but Madison knew he was just plain inarticulate. In trying to tell her mother how much he loved her, he'd written, "I feel like a big galoot writing mushy stuff. But if you get the Reader's Digest for November, there's an article that says exactly how I feel."

Madison smiled. David was much like her father in that respect. The roses were beautiful, perfect, fragrant. Damn, now she would have to call and thank him. But she just couldn't. Not until her brain had some down-time.

After she put Cam to bed, she sat down to journal, trying to make herself focus on her emotions, put them down in neat paragraphs that wouldn't get mixed up again because someone did something out of character.

Madison had never really noticed how much David was around until she'd wanted some private time with Park. She and David had had a two-year separation while he finished his fellowship in Memphis, and when he'd moved to Houston, they hadn't resumed a physical relationship.

From the very beginning, their relationship had been odd. Madison had met David when he was a medical student. One day, she'd told him she needed an escort to a concert, and asked him in an offhand way if he would like to go. To her surprise, he said yes. They sort of fell into a pattern, with her initiating their dates, which left her feeling uncomfortable. She tried to repress her feelings for him, but when they finally slept together, she thought it meant he loved her, and she let herself fall for him.

Her passion for David and the longing for a declaration of love, however, made their relationship at work tense, and the status quo went on for years. Park had encouraged her to terminate the relationship, and it had come to a natural end when she moved. For a while.

When David moved to Houston, they had fallen into a similar pattern, except now they were friends without benefits. She had always been the one to initiate sex anyway, and surprisingly, the lack of it didn't seem to bother him much. Or if it did, he hadn't indicated it to her.

Now, threatened by another male in her life, he wanted to fight for her. Was it too late?

She didn't know. Park, whom she'd held in her heart like a hot coal for years, was right next door, maybe even soon to be available. But despite her intense feelings for him, she couldn't imagine having a sexual relationship with him; he was sort of like a soul mate without benefits.

Madison could not understand why she felt that way. She knew exactly why she loved him: He valued her for her intellect and the unusual things that she thought and studied and wrote about. He'd let her be herself in therapy, and understood her complex ideas. He knew everything about her, good and bad, and he *still* liked her. He had validated her for the unusual person she was, viewed her as special instead of odd, thought her worthy of a man's love. She still felt that old rush, like an elevator unexpectedly dropping a few floors, when he entered a room. Sad as she was for the pain a divorce would cause him, she couldn't help but feel a surge of hope that now she might have a chance for a legitimate relationship with him. Claire was abandoning him at the worst possible time, but Madison would take care of him if she had to move him into her house and pay for his medical care herself. And maybe, just maybe, that would make him realize he loved her, had for a long time. She tried to imagine herself kissing him, hearing him whisper, "I love you."

But every time she took Park into her mental arms, he turned into David. David, who had been a solid part of her life for a long time, whose kiss had gone through her like an electric current, reminding her of long nights of passion.

And oh dear God, he was a "man with a slow hand" . . .

* * *

When Park left the house the next morning, Madison and Cam were in the car, ready to go.

"Buckle up," Cam ordered from the back seat. He held the tackle box in his arms, like a newborn baby.

"You taking that to show and tell?" Park asked.

"Show and tell is on Friday, not Thursday," Madison said firmly, as if to end an argument before it started.

"Oops," Park said. "Did I open up a can of worms?"

She smiled. "So to speak. I think the box has become a permanent part of his body. I nearly had to amputate the damn thing to get him in the bathtub last night. And I regret to report that Dudley absconded with your extra-long purple glitter tapeworm."

Park laughed. "Earthworm," he corrected. "I suppose it was the bling that made him pick that one. What did he do with it?"

"He ate it," Cam said. "And I'm really mad at him. I might say Basil Rathbone to him. That'll fix him."

"You won't like the consequences if you do that," Madison said. Park reached back and patted him on the leg. "I've got a better idea. I'll take you to the bait shop, and we'll get you a dozen purple glitter worms."

"I got enough worms. I need a fishing pole."

"Hint, hint," Madison said to Park. "Speaking of eating, did you have breakfast?"

"No."

"Look in that container on the floor. I made some blueberry muffins. Do you think you'd do better with something in your stomach, or not?"

"I don't know. It's probably a toss-up, no pun intended. But they smell good, and I'm hungry."

"That's your coffee on the right. You like it black, as I remember."

"That's very thoughtful of you. Thanks."

She looked beautiful this morning in jeans, a white shirt, and a hot pink jacket, her hair in a pony tail. Park marveled at the change in her appearance. In Memphis, she had been quite obese. She had never worn anything but scrubs, and her face was always slack with depression. This Madison, however, was slender and vibrant. He liked the previous version, but this version was practically irresistible.

"How's the donor search going?" she asked.

"Unfortunately, there's no match in the U.S. database."

"Park, why do you need a donor?" Cam asked. "Are you going to grow a baby, like Mom grew me? Maybe Mom can give you a cell. Mom, if you give him a cell, give him a girl cell. Then we'll have a boy and a girl. Can we get her a fishing pole too?"

Madison groaned and Park laughed. "I need someone to give me some cells, so I won't be sick anymore," he said. "Only girls can grow babies."

"I'll give you some cells," Cam said.

"That's very nice of you. But I need cells from someone whose cells match mine."

"Well, if you're my donor and you gave mom a cell for me, then my cells are the same as yours. Do I have to have a shot?"

"Yes."

"I can do that," he said in a barely audible voice, as if trying to convince himself.

Madison's expression behind her sunglasses was inscrutable. "That's a very brave thing to do, Cam. We are all going to get tested for Park, you, me, and David."

Park was stunned. "All of you?" What did that mean—that she thought Cam might be his son? Or that she really wasn't worried that such information would come to light? "Why would you test a four-year-old?"

She pulled up in front of Cam's Montessori school and looked at Park. "Because he offered," she said, in a "why not" tone. "And he doesn't have to get a shot. We have his umbilical cord blood, which I had frozen when he was born. Itty, bitty, brand-new stem cells."

Brand new stem cells to make brand new bone marrow. Hope surged through Park. He couldn't speak for a minute, fearful that he would burst into tears. "You'd give me his cord blood?" he asked, thickly.

"Of course. I'd give you a kidney, if you needed it. I'd give you a heart."

Park's chest ached as he watched Madi walk Cam into his school, questions floating behind, as usual.

"Mom, what are itty bitty baby stem cells? Is a stem cell what you got from my donor? If my stem cell is like Park's, does that mean he's my dad?"

I guess that question will be answered soon enough, Park mused.

* * *

"I don't like the smell of this place," Park said as they went up the elevator to the clinic at M.D. Anderson.

Housed in an old part of the complex, the clinic smelled like a cancer ward, the odor of death hovering beneath a layer of deodorizer. Park checked in, and they were immediately shown to a standard hospital room. He slipped his shoes off and lay down on the bed. Madison sat in a chair beside him, scooting it back so she could stay out of the nurse's way.

"How did you do after your first treatment?" asked Park's nurse du jour.

"Awful. I was so nauseated, I barely made it home."

"Oh, I'm so sorry. I'll give you some medicine to help with that before we start the drug. And I'll get you a prescription for Emend. You can take that before your next treatment. It's unusual for people to have that much nausea, but everybody's different."

She started an IV and hung two small bags of fluid, one with a steroid, and the other with Zofran, to reduce his nausea. "I'll be back in a little while," she said.

"Madi, thank you," Park said after the nurse left. "I mean, about all of you being tested as donors. And the cord blood—if Cam should match, won't you mind giving it up? He might need it some day."

"You're sick right now. I'm happy to give it to you." It

doesn't matter, it doesn't matter if Park ends up hating you, she said to herself. Just so he lives.

Park was quiet so long, Madison turned her chair around so she could see his face without craning her neck. "Why didn't you want to come into the building?"

He smiled a little. "Still got that intuition, don't you."

"It wasn't rocket science. You wouldn't get out of the car; we were holding up the valet for a block."

"I don't really know. There are so many enormous buildings in this medical center, and they make me feel so small and insignificant. Getting into the building is always the hardest part of this. I'm guess I'm terrified that I'll die in here, like there's some malevolent force that will get me. If I stay outside, it won't happen.

"And then I think, why fight it if it's time for me to die? You rock along through life thinking it won't happen to you, at least until you're old and expect it, and then, all of a sudden, it's here and you're young and you're getting all this toxic treatment, when maybe you should just accept it and spend the rest of your life doing what you want. I mean, what would you do if you thought you had less than a year to live? Rob a bank and travel on the proceeds? Make a list of things you haven't done, and start doing them? Pretend to believe in God because you're scared, pray to go to heaven?"

Park's pre-treatment was finished, and Madison waited until the nurse had started his chemo and left before she answered.

"I've only been in one situation where I was afraid I might die. I had to fly into Washington, D.C. a week after 9/11 for a meeting at the National Institutes of Health. Basc absolutely would not let me skip it. Before I got on the plane, I thought, is there anything I need to do? Any amends to make, any debts to pay, any absolution to seek? The answer was no, I'm okay."

That's not rigorous honesty, said the mother lurking in her brain. You need to get this mess with Park cleaned up. Shut up

Mom, Madison thought. "I owe that to AA," she continued. "If I hadn't sobered up and worked the twelve steps, I wouldn't have had that peace of mind."

"Maybe I should work the steps. I've heard you talk about it often enough."

"Anybody can do it. Basically, you just admit that alcohol – or whatever your poison of choice is – has made a mess of your life, and only a power greater than yourself can fix it."

"You believe in God now? You never used to."

"I don't believe in the God of my childhood, the punishing male authority figure in long, flowing robes, with a white beard. But I believe in a creator, and for the sake of simplicity and being able to communicate with others, I call that creator God."

"What changed your mind? Did you find the book with the answer underlined?"

She laughed. "I underlined it myself, like I told you I would."

"That's awesome. I didn't really think you would find it. What did it say that changed your mind?"

"It gave me proof that it's more likely God exists than not," Madison said. "The author interviewed scientists, medical doctors, psychologists, philosophers, and religious leaders of all types, and asked the same hard questions I would have. Then he put it all together in a believable theory. It was so complicated, I had to make an algorithm. I'll show it to you."

"I wish you would," Park said, his eyes full of pain, "because right now, I'm lost. If I prayed, I don't think my prayers would get past the ceiling."

"That's okay. You and I just don't have the 'God gene.'"

"What's that?" he asked warily, suspecting a joke.

"It's actually a mutation of a gene called VMAT2, discovered by an NIH researcher. The gene controls the flow of mood-altering chemicals to the brain, and allows people to have mystical experiences during intense prayer. So if you can't connect to God like other people can, it's not your fault."

"What if it turns out that there is no God?"

"Doesn't matter. Because when you live as if there is, you are just plain happier in the long run. When I look back on all the wild behavior of my youth, I don't know why I thought it was fun. I can't imagine wanting to drink now, or wanting to feel all drunk and out of control." She hesitated, then said, "I'll take you to an AA meeting when you're ready to put down your beer."

He looked surprised. "Busted again."

"Now I know why you couldn't help me with my alcohol problem," she said.

"I was sober when you were in therapy, but I still didn't have all the answers. Sometimes I think you taught me more than I taught you. I should refund your money."

"That would be great! I could retire on that tidy sum."

Park smiled. "So what's your conclusion about life? What truths are self-evident to you?"

"Well, let's see. I know a ceiling fan can hit a baseball through a double-paned window at about a hundred miles an hour; one purple crayon in a dryer is enough to ruin three pairs of scrubs; the second mouse gets the cheese; women want a man who is strong and sensitive; and men want a nymphomaniac with big boobs, who owns a liquor store and a bass boat."

"Seriously," Park said, smiling.

"I'll tell you another time, but right now I've got a better idea." She fished around in her purse and came up with a notepad and two pens. She tore some paper from the pad, folded it in half, and handed it to him, with a pen. "Let's play Seven Sevens."

"What's that?"

"It's a list that circulates around the internet on the blogs. There are seven categories, with seven items each. Okay, first category: List seven things to do before you die. You have seven minutes to do it. Write."

Madison finished her list and called time.

"Nothing sounds like fun to me," Park said. "Read your list."

"Okay. Get Park well, get a book published, make seven quilts, build a sailboat and sail to Australia, retire, learn ballroom dancing, go hang gliding over the Grand Canyon, hear the man I love say 'I love you.'"

"That's eight."

"So I cheated. Try the next one, it should be easier. Seven things that attract me to my significant other."

This time, neither of them wrote anything. There were two men in her life, but she didn't know which of them was her significant other. She thought about the expression on Park's face when something touched him deeply; the gentle way he treated his patients; how he interacted with Cam. And then she realized that all those things could easily apply to David, as well.

"This is stupid," Madison said. She took the pens and paper and stuffed them back in her purse. "I'm sorry, Park. Elisabeth Kubler-Ross I'm not. Nurses are encouraged to talk to people about death, but we're not taught what to say. Anyway, I don't think you're going to die, but if I say so, that sort of cuts you off. So I guess you'll just have to tell me what you need."

"Just listen when the fear boils over, that's all. And you're doing fine. You should have been a psychotherapist."

Madison laughed. "Hell, I was in therapy for years. I know all the good stuff to say. How does that make you feel?"

"Successful. I taught you some of that good stuff."

The nurse came back in to check Park's IV, and Madison followed her out of the room.

"We have some people who want to get tested as donors for Park," Madison said. "Can you tell me how to do that?'

The nurse gave Madison an information sheet with a number to call to schedule an appointment. "Also," Madison said, "Is there any financial help available for Park?"

"There aren't any fees while he's on the study," the nurse

said. "His study drug and treatment are free. He's responsible for anything outside of that—treatment for complications, and his bone marrow transplant, for instance. However, he can get financial counseling; a payment plan can be made for the hospital bill, at least."

That would help some, Madison thought. She'd move him into her house if she needed to, and if she couldn't handle it financially, she knew who would help without a second thought—David.

* * *

"When do we have to get Cam?" Park asked on the way home.

"By five," she said. "Why?"

"I just wanted to sit outside for a while, and talk. I've missed talking to you."

"Okay. Let's get your prescriptions filled first. How do you feel? Are you hungry? It's almost lunch time."

"A little hungry, maybe. A touch queasy."

At home, she gave him a dose of anti-nausea medicine. All he wanted to eat was potato chips and a soft drink. Madison took a battered quilt from the car, and they walked across the street and sat on the grassy bank of the bayou.

Park ate a few chips, squinting thoughtfully at the green water that flashed in the bright November sunlight.

"Madi, I'm struggling so hard with my feelings about our situation. You once described the therapeutic relationship as schizophrenic, and you were so right. The therapist gets to know all about you, but you can only fill in the blanks about him; and still, an intense connection forms. With luck, the patient gets well, and the therapist becomes a saint. It has to be that way; how much respect would you have, how could you take direction from someone who's a mess, no matter how much education and training he has?"

"I admit that I canonized you," she said. "I saw the exterior of a great life. You had the brains, the soul, the skill, the job, the looks, the house, the car, the marriage. I needed to believe you were all in one piece, so I could believe what you reflected back to me, that I was okay. And I stand by your sainthood."

"But now, our relationship has changed," Park said. "I'm not entirely comfortable with it, but there it is. And there's something I need to talk about. My soul needs you."

"Talk," she said. "I'm okay, Park, really. Five years ago I wouldn't have been."

He took a deep breath, and let it out slowly. "A long time ago, Claire and I had a son," he began hesitantly. "His name was Nathan. Claire got pregnant when we were freshmen in college, and we got married. She quit school. Mother had left me some money, enough for us to get by on until I graduated, if we were frugal.

"For a while, it was heaven. I was an only child; my mother is dead, and I don't know who my father was. I needed people in my life, and I loved having a family. Claire and I wanted lots of children.

"Being a father was the best thing that ever happened to me. The way Nathan looked at me, that ear-to-ear grin when he saw me come home after school, filled me with a love that was different from anything I'd ever known. Sometimes I'd just stand quietly until he saw me, thrilled the moment he recognized me and started kicking his legs and holding out his arms to be picked up.

"I wanted to be the ideal father, to produce a human who passed that ability down the chain, to make the world better. Without a male role model in my life, I had to make myself up. I envied other kids whose fathers took them fishing, coached their Little League teams, led their Boy Scout troops.

"I don't think one parent can do all the things two are meant to do. My mother taught me to respect and cherish women. But there's a built-in drive, I think, to bond with a father, and I missed that."

"I know what you mean," Madison said. "My father is a distant, silent man, and none of us are able to bond with him. I don't even know if he understands how that affects us. He never was the sports dad; he traveled most of the time when we were kids. None of us were in many extra-curricular activities anyway, my mother just didn't have the reserve to do that."

"Mine did. Her whole life was geared around me. I had some heart problems as a child, but she got me on my feet and into every activity imaginable. Still, I remember watching other kids with their dads, wanting to see approval mirrored in my father's eyes, too. I was even envious when my friends got disciplined; to me, it meant 'look how much he cares.'"

"My brothers are all wonderful fathers," Madison said, "almost like they have an instruction manual. They must have made themselves up, like you. I read a statistic recently, that 59% of fathers get more satisfaction from their children than from their jobs. I found that astonishing because I don't see men as creatures that want children. My mother always told us our father didn't want us. My older children's dad abandoned us. I understand the female drive to have children, but male I just don't get, and I always have an instant love for any man who loves his kids."

Park was silent for a long time.

"What happened to Nathan?" Madison asked hesitantly.

"Claire's pregnancy and delivery were easy. Nathan only weighed five pounds, but he was perfect. He had these huge, wistful blue eyes, and a full head of white-blonde hair, so fine," he said, rubbing his fingertips together as if he could still feel it, "that even the smallest breeze or static electricity made it stand up on his crown. His hair always reminded me of a dandelion about to go to seed.

"On Thanksgiving day when he was six months old, Claire had put him down for an early nap. We had friends coming for dinner, and I was supposed to get him up and dressed while she walked to the convenience store for cigarettes. I didn't wake him immediately, because I wanted to see the end of the football game.

"He was on his belly with his knees drawn up under him, his little butt sticking up, like he always slept. I turned him over so I could pick him up, and he just flopped, like a rag doll."

Park dug his hands into the quilt. Every time he thought about that moment, it was as if he were there again—the hot apartment, the limp, blue baby. The smell of the $1.29 boxed sausage and cheese pizza they were having for Thanksgiving dinner, because they couldn't afford turkey and all the trimmings. The shock, the panic.

"He wasn't breathing. I grabbed him and ran outside, screaming for help. We were just kids. Nobody knew what to do," he said, tears blurring his vision. "Somebody tried to do mouth to mouth, and I pushed on his chest like I'd seen on TV, but I felt—I felt the little bones crack, so I stopped.

"The paramedics tried to revive him, but it was just too late. They wrapped him up in a white blanket and I stood there empty-handed as they carried him to the ambulance. The top of his head wasn't completely covered, and I could see the sun shining through his dandelion hair, a vision I will never, ever forget.

"Your children aren't supposed to die before you," he said hoarsely. "It's a feeling of utter desolation that never goes away."

Madison put her arms around him, murmuring, "Oh, love, I'm so sorry. How awful for you."

And then the dam burst, and she held him as he cried. "God, Madi, it's the worst pain you can imagine to lose your child. I was his *father*; it was my job to protect him."

"There was nothing you could have done."

"He was just a baby, a sweet, helpless, beautiful baby. I've never been able to make any sense of it. I never knew life could look so black."

"Did you talk to anyone about your feelings?"

"Not at the time. I couldn't save my son, and I couldn't

help my wife. She was in a psych hospital for six months, and she was never the same. I felt so bad about myself, I didn't want to talk about it. Besides that, men are second-class mourners. They're not supposed to have feelings."

"You were a kid. You were her husband, not her shrink. You needed help as much as she did. What about later, did you get help later?"

"I went through analysis myself as a part of my education, and of course it came up. But there's no calendar on the death of a child; it's with you every day. Especially when you don't know why it happened."

"Was the cause of death SIDS?"

"Yes, sudden infant death syndrome. Claire said it was my fault."

"That's a ridiculous, evil thing to say," Madison said fiercely. "It was *not* your fault. SIDS isn't *anyone's* fault."

"We let him sleep on his stomach! Claire was less than 20 years old when she had him. She smoked. The apartment was hot."

"That's Monday-morning quarterbacking. First of all, we used to be taught to put babies on their stomachs, so they wouldn't aspirate if they vomited. Your son died in—what—1980?—when nobody knew those things contributed to SIDS. They still don't know what causes it. In the end, they'll probably find a dozen different things."

"We should have had a system to monitor his breathing."

"Those monitors are impractical and totally unnecessary for normal babies, and are, in fact, an electrical hazard. And probably weren't even available in the 80s. Look at me! It was not your fault!"

Frowning, she took a napkin, scrubbed the tears from his face, and ordered him to blow his nose. "You're not to torture yourself about this ever again."

Madi had written a letter to him years ago, trying to explain how she felt about him. Because it was such a rare thing for a patient to understand feelings the way she did, he'd read it so many times, he'd memorized it.

"It's important that you understand my feelings for you aren't based on an adolescent, schoolgirl image of the perfect man," she had written, "but on things that are measurable every day of my life. One of my cherished memories is of the day when, in one sentence, you gave me something I had sought for years. You pointed out that I had already given my children the very thing that was withheld from me by my parents. And I thought, 'I did do that, didn't I.' At that moment I fell in love with the man whose intelligence, intuition, and sensitivity gave me the gift of my own children as surely as if he had delivered them, cut the umbilical cord, and placed their battered little selves in my arms."

As eloquent as her words were, he had never quite understood how precious a gift he had given her until now, when she'd returned the favor.

No matter what Claire said, he was not to blame for Nathan's death.

"After we lost Nathan, Claire refused to get pregnant again. She just couldn't risk losing another child."

"You gave up your dream, your need for a family, for Claire."

"Yes."

"You must love her very much."

"I did. But that feeling is hard to sustain if it's not reciprocal. Marriage becomes duty. I did everything I could to make her happy, but once you have a tragedy in your life, it just clings to you, sort of like the smell of onions stays on your hands after you slice them. It was like we died too, and they forgot to bury us. I started studying psychology, to see if I could figure out what to do; even if I couldn't help her, maybe I could help someone else. You always wanted to know why I got into the field. It was for Claire."

"It must make you really angry for her to divorce you, after you gave up so much for her."

"Right now, I'm still in shock."

"Park, I'm sorry if what I did precipitated this. If it will help, I'll talk to Claire and tell her how I got the cufflinks."

"She won't believe it. Anyway, our marriage started falling apart years ago. I was sick before we left Memphis, and never started a practice in Dallas. Claire had never worked, and refused to get a job until all our assets were depleted. I can't blame her. I did well in my career and threw money on her emotional problems when she didn't respond to anything else. I have to say, though, I didn't expect her to abandon me in the middle of treatment. I'm having a hard time justifying that."

"There *is* no justification for that."

"I have to find a job immediately, but I don't know what to do; I had already been looking for work I could do at home during treatment. I'm going to run out of money. She said I can have Cobra coverage on her insurance, but I'd have to pay for it."

"Generous of her," Madison said sarcastically. "She has to pay that, though. She probably thinks she can get away with it because you don't have the money for an attorney."

"Well, she's right. I'm afraid, Madi, and I feel so alone. This is one of the reasons family is so important. And I have none. Not a single living relative."

Madison put her hand on top of his. "You're not alone. You have me and Cam and David and Dud. We're your family now, and we're going to help you. I've got the energy, and David has the resources, and Cam and Dud will love you until you beg them to stop."

Park turned his hand and laced his fingers through hers. "Why would David help me?"

"Because he's a good man. Because he's filthy rich. Because he was raised like that. If he sees someone who needs something, he just takes care of it. He's bought me many a plane ticket to Memphis when I was pining to see my older kids, he paid off my hospital bill when Cam was born, he bought all the baby furniture, on and on. And there are never strings attached. But if you're too proud to accept his help, you can always be a Wal-Mart greeter."

Park smiled. He let go of her hand and lay back on the quilt, and Madison did the same. The day was warm in the middle as so many Houston days were, but black thunderclouds were pushing cool breezes in from the north.

"My mother had a friend like that," Park said. "His name was Mac. We only saw him once in a while; I don't even know where he lived. I don't think he had much money, but when he visited, he'd buy me something like a baseball or a pair of shoes. Once he bought me a bicycle on my birthday. I don't know what his motivation was. I guess he just felt sorry for me because I didn't have a father. What an amazing collection of contradictions we are."

"What do you mean?"

"I mean—I just met David, but I already had a negative preconception about him because you had told me so much about the pain he caused you. Now I'm beginning to understand what you see in him. Do you think David would actually go through with a stem cell transplant for me, on the off chance that he should match?"

"Absolutely."

Park rolled on his side. She regarded him steadily with eyes as blue as the sky. He felt the old connection with her, strong as ever. Wisps of hair had escaped her ponytail, and he tucked a stray lock behind her ear.

"He loves you, you know. It's in his eyes."

"I see love in many people's eyes," she said softly.

Again he felt hope, this time followed by fear as dark as the clouds that now obscured the sun. With his future so uncertain, he had no right, no right at all to give her a reason to expect a future with him. He had mortally wounded her once, and she did not deserve to be wounded by him again.

Furthermore, they had definitely switched roles. With the disclosure of his deepest pain and the comfort and insight she'd provided, she had become his therapist.

Park turned onto his back. God, it was exhausting to think like a shrink all the time. Sometimes he wished he had chosen another profession, so he could just be an ordinary man in love.

A few fat drops of rain fell, then a few more. "I guess we better go in," Madison said, and they walked back to her house, enjoying the smell of the rain.

"What are you going to do for the rest of the afternoon?" Park asked.

"I think I'll write until it's time to get Cam. What about you?"

"I'd like to take a nap in your big red chair."

He was shivering now, and she settled him in the recliner with his pillow and quilt. On her end table, a bouquet of red roses perfumed the air. He could see the card; there was no message. It was just signed, "David."

Despite his earlier guilt, Park's immediate response was blistering jealousy. He drifted into an uneasy sleep, enveloped in the dual scents of her freshly washed quilt, and roses from someone who should not be considered his competitor, since Park himself should not be in a competition for Madi.

* * *

Madison put in a load of laundry and made some macaroni and cheese for dinner, thinking it might be bland enough for Park to eat, and fearing the smell of anything stronger would make him sick. As she worked, she thought about their conversation at the bayou, when he finally told her why he had chosen his profession. It was something she had asked him when she was in therapy; he had deflected the question more than once, and now she knew why. He was the walking wounded, and he knew she could not have borne his pain, had he revealed the loss of his child and the effects on his marriage.

And he was right. Even now, she could not look at him without wanting to cry. She remembered the warm, shapeless weight of her babies as she held them to her chest, love swelling like rising bread in her chest. She could not imagine watching a paramedic carry Cam's or Emma's or Dane's lifeless bodies away, the sun shining through their hair. How did one live after a loss like that?

Lightning arced across the sky, followed by thunder that rattled the windows. The house darkened as thunderclouds advanced, dumping rain as they arrived. Madison had two hours to write before she had to get Cam. She booted her laptop and settled in the other recliner, across from Park. He had fallen into a restless sleep, jerking occasionally and muttering unintelligibly.

She decided to write about the day he had ferreted out her feelings for him. Having him right in the room made her writing much easier—just looking at him made old emotions resurface. The longing to know how he felt about her, even if he could never act on it, was as strong as ever, and she ached with the need. She had tried to write this before, but never could get it exactly right; now, the words came faster than she could type. The scene took place in his office, on a dark, rainy afternoon just like this one, and Madison felt like weeping as she wrote.

"How are you?" Wesley asked quietly, as he always did when she couldn't seem to get started.

"Upright, ninety-eight point six degrees, heart in normal rhythm," she said, as she always did when she felt barely able to cope, knowing he would translate that into "lousy."

"I hate it when you start like that."

Her chest felt tight, and she tried unsuccessfully to take slow, deep breaths. He was going to be as disappointed in her as she was in herself; it seemed that making permanent changes was impossible for her, as if she were running around in an ever-deepening circular groove. And just when they both thought she was doing so well.

Even after six months of psychotherapy, Reagan knew almost nothing about Wesley except sensory things. His teeth were very white; when he wore the blue shirt with the frayed left cuff, his green eyes picked up the color and looked almost turquoise. He seemed to have a lot of shoes for a man, and sometimes he wore odd ties that looked like Picasso in a "red" mood. She knew the exact timber of his voice, which became progressively softer as a subject became progressively painful, and that he had a tenderness that made her lean toward him mentally, even as she pressed herself firmly back in her chair to keep from touching him. His essence stayed in her mind all day, like a fingerprint on the window through which she viewed the world.

"Here's your book," Reagan said, handing him the one he had loaned her a month before. He had underlined and annotated and, to her amusement, corrected the writer's grammar, in orange ink. "You know, Conroy's character Tom in The Prince of Tides *says it's sacrilege to write in a book."*

Wesley frowned. "I saw that movie. I really disliked it."

Reagan mentally kicked herself. Wesley had told her he didn't read fiction, and it never occurred to her that he would know the theme of that book, which was about a psychiatrist who had an affair with her patient's brother. As perceptive as Wesley was, there was no telling where this discussion would lead.

"I haven't seen the movie," Reagan said, "but if it didn't show the agony of the psychiatrist about her relationship with her patient's brother, it didn't do the book justice. I can see how it would be easy for a therapist and a client to become involved."

"Any of the roles of therapist, client, or lover were legitimate separately," Wesley said. "I guess it was just the blurring of roles that was ethically repugnant to me." He regarded Reagan intensely for a moment. "What kind of emotional fallout do you have as a result of your relationship with me?"

She leaned forward and rested her forehead in the palm of her hand, feeling that crawling sensation that meant she was turning either very red or very white, and made a desperate and transparent attempt to field the question. "You mean in regard to the book?"

"I think you know what I mean," he said, looking steadily at her.

Because it seemed self-defeating to lie to him, she was generally truthful; now she would have to tell him how she felt about him. Would he abandon her, like all the others? The demons of loneliness and isolation that he'd held at bay during her agonizing hospitalization and the long months afterward, giving her a blessed respite from pain, came howling from the abyss that was her Self.

Miserably, she lifted her chin and looked unflinchingly at him. "For months, I've sat in this chair and filleted myself. I say I'm sentimental and foolish, and you say I'm altruistic and loving. I say I'm selfish and you say I think about everyone but myself. I say I've been a horrible mother, and you say I've given my children the thing I wanted most and could never have—honesty. I sit here and kick my soul as if it were an unwanted puppy, and you pick it up and stroke it. How can I not love you?"

Reagan crossed her legs and folded her arms tightly across her chest, steeling herself for the stinging rejection and dismissal that were inevitable.

Wesley shifted in his chair and looked away, then said, "I've had a similar feeling. Years ago, I was in therapy for a while, when I was making some major changes in my life. It was a male therapist, a professor who was a role model and mentor, sort of the father I always wanted. The intimacy of the relationship almost guarantees that reaction. And, of course, I made him more than he really was."

Tears overflowed Reagan's eyes, ran unheeded down her cheeks, and merged under her chin. Her feelings for him were multifaceted, mostly relief and joy at finding someone who understood her so easily, but sometimes unexpectedly painful, sending an exquisite shiver through her nervous system, like a paper cut. He had just validated her feelings for him even more, and she wanted to crawl into his arms and cry until she was as dry as a winter cornhusk.

"Sometimes when you're talking to me, I feel like you're holding my heart in your hands. I don't have any illusions about you, Wes. I don't think you're available, I don't think you're

perfect, and I don't think you have all the answers to my philosophic questions, but at least you're honest enough to admit you have the same questions."

It was the beginning of the little lies, lies designed to make him love her. She knew she had a fatal attraction to him, the worst she had ever felt for any man, and it shredded her insides, because she was making a fool of herself. Again.

"God, I miss my mother," Reagan continued. "Ever since we first talked about your belief that people give away the thing they wanted most in life and couldn't have, I've wondered what my mother's special gift to me was. Now I think I know."

"What was it?"

"The one thing she never had—a mother who would let her curl up in her arms and cry."

"That's beautiful," he said, very, very softly.

Reagan grinned, her wicked sense of humor saving her from complete annihilation. "Now I have your heart in my hand, don't I?"

"Yes," he said, his acknowledgment was so faint that she read his lips as much as heard him. "The therapy is doing what it is supposed to do, Reagan. We've obviously connected. But instead of thinking of it as a love relationship, what can you do to get the acceptance and understanding without the pain?"

He could have annihilated her completely, had he chosen his words less carefully, and the fact that he didn't immediately fire her, as she thought a therapist who had a patient in love with him would, only reinforced her desperate love for him. But the message was clear. She could stay, but she could not love him. He thought of her only as a patient, and probably a difficult and boring one at that.

"I don't know what I can do," she said. "This is all I've ever experienced with men. When you love someone who doesn't return the feeling, it makes you feel diminished. I have all these positive feelings pouring out of me like sunshine. It feels wonderful and diminishing simultaneously. I want to say 'I'm sorry I love you.' But I'm not sorry. Why should I apologize because the part of me that has been petrified for so long has been profoundly touched by the best part of you? You tell me to feel my emotions, then you tell me, oh no, don't feel that. Well I can shut that down, all right,

but then the whole system goes down."

Madison looked over at Park, awake now and watching the lightning show, his face creased in a frown. She had felt so humiliated by admitting her love for him. It was such a cliché, the patient who falls for her shrink. But then, confessing love for a man had always humiliated her, because she had never in her life received a reciprocal confession. Still, she had been helpless in her love for him, and despite the pain it caused, had never been able to shut the system down.

Park sat up and gripped the arms of the recliner, swallowing several times. "Madi, is it time for more nausea medicine?"

She gave him another dose and a little soda.

There was one thing left on her list for the day, to make arrangements for Cam's cord blood to be tested. In her workroom, she pulled out the folder for the cord blood banking facility, and dialed the number. She gave the representative her account number twice, and both times was told the account was closed. Fear zinged through Madison's nervous system like the lightning outside.

"How could my account be closed? This has to be a mistake. The fee is automatically deducted from my checking account, annually."

"Yes ma'am, but the account became invalid two years ago. We sent a registered letter to your address on Braeswood, but it was undeliverable. Did you move?"

"Yes," Madison said, feeling lightheaded. Her bank had also changed its debit cards from MasterCard to Visa, which must be why her account had become inaccessible. Evidently, because of the address change, she hadn't received the notification.

"What happens if the storage fee isn't paid?" she asked, dreading the answer.

"I'm sorry, Ma'am, but the blood was discarded. Your contract explained that in detail."

She hung up, heartsick. Not only were the stem cells lost,

but this meant that if Cam matched, he would have to go through the donor procedure. She couldn't bear the idea.

It was time to pick Cam up. Madison grabbed her cell phone and called David on the way out.

* * *

"Yes, I got the roses, they're beautiful, thank you," Park heard Madison say, an odd note of impatience in her voice. "David, I just called about the cord blood, and it's been discarded!"

The door closed behind her. Park watched her back out of the driveway, devastated at what he'd overheard. Maybe Madison was right. Maybe this was the fate he had chosen for himself, and he should just quit fighting it. He hated the idea of Cam, such a little guy, going through the donor procedure. Madison must be pretty sure Cam was his child, or she wouldn't have allowed him to volunteer. Of course, at that time, she'd thought she had cord blood.

The medicine Madison had given him kicked in, and Park dozed until the cheerful commotion of her return woke him. Cam raced to him, cheeks rosy from the cold, and climbed in his lap, Dudley right behind him.

"What, no picture for me today?" Park asked.

"No, we had to write in our journals today."

"What did you write?"

"About my Grandpa. Wait just a minute. I gotta put a picture of him in my journal. I'll be right back." Cam scooted out of his lap. He went to the bookcase, pulled out a bulging old photo album, and lugged it back to the end table. As he lifted it up, loose pictures spilled out across the floor. Park sat up and leaned over to help him pick them up, but stopped with the first picture, looking at it in disbelief.

It was a picture of himself, at age five. He wore a cowboy

outfit, complete with chaps, boots, hat, and six-guns. The outfit was a gift from his mother's friend, Mac.

How dare Madison take something like this! The cufflinks were bad enough. He wondered what else she had taken from his house. The real estate agent must have left her unattended for quite a while, for her to find something like this. It had been in a picture album on the top shelf in his closet.

Madison walked into the room, and he shot her a look of pure venom.

"What's wrong?" she asked, stooping to help Cam pick up the mess.

Park turned the picture so she could see it. "Where did you get this?"

She took the picture from him, frowning. "I didn't get it anywhere. This was my mother's album. There's another picture of that kid. He's probably the child of one of her friends. She kept up quite a correspondence, and she often got Christmas cards with pictures in them. Why?"

"That's me."

"You? Really?" Madison scrutinized the picture more carefully.

"Me. In a cowboy outfit my mother's friend, MacKenzie, bought me."

Madison sat down hard, on the floor. "Oh, how weird. MacKenzie is my father's name." She paged through the album until she found a picture of her dad, and handed it to Park. "Is that him?"

"That's Mac, all right."

"How strange," Madison said. "Our parents must have known each other. I wonder what they had in common."

Their eyes met, and he knew she was thinking the same thing he was. "Do you think it's even remotely possible that he's your father?" she asked, her eyes wide with shock. "That would make us half-siblings."

"I doubt it. He wasn't around very much—he'd just stop in for a couple of hours every once in a while, never overnight. He and my mother didn't seem to have a romantic relationship."

"When is your birthday?"

"October 7, 1962."

"That's my birthday too! We're astrological twins. Curiouser and curiouser. But it would be way too much of a coincidence for us to have the same father and different mothers and be born on the same day. Besides, I can't imagine my dad having an—" She stopped, her eyes on Cam. "Well, I'll just ask Dad about it."

Park opened a bag of M&Ms that was sitting on the table and poured out a handful, picking out the blue ones and dropping them back in the bag.

"Mom and I don't like the blue ones, either," Cam said. "They're bitter."

"That's right," said Park.

"I bet you don't like green bell peppers, either," Madison said.

"Can't stand them," Park said. "I can tell if you even wave a green bell pepper over my food."

"That's because people who are sensitive to the smell can detect it at 0.5 parts per trillion," Madison said.

"How do you know that?"

"My brain collects trivia. It's interesting, isn't it, how smell is so evocative of the past? Like, the smell of coffee and bacon together always reminds me of Sunday morning when I was a kid. It was the only day my mother cooked bacon. She would stay in the kitchen all morning, playing short-order cook as each of us got up."

"Chocolate makes me think of my mom," Park said. "She loved it so much that even brownies weren't chocolate enough for her. She poured a bag of chocolate chips in the mix as well."

"I like the smell of fish," Cam said.

"Don't start," Madison warned.

"I wonder how many smells we can detect," Park said.

"I think I read somewhere that we can detect ten thousand," Madison said. "Did you know babies can detect their mothers by smell? And dogs can literally smell fear."

"I don't smell dinner," Cam said. "I'm hungry."

After dinner, with Cam tucked in for the night, Madison told Park about the loss of the cord blood.

"I know," he said. "I heard you on the phone."

"Park, did you ever attempt to find out who your birth parents were? You might have siblings you don't even know about."

Park sincerely hoped she wasn't one of them. "I didn't even know I was adopted until my mother was dying. She had leukemia, and needed a bone marrow transplant, herself. I had myself tested, although she didn't know it, and that's when I found out I couldn't possibly have been her biological child. I never asked her about it. She was so sick, and I figured she had a good reason for not telling me, beyond the obvious. I investigated some after she died, but every avenue turned into a dead end. She worked in the nursery at the hospital where I was born, and maybe she was able to alter my birth certificate."

"Where were you born?"

"In Memphis."

"Me too. But only because my mother went into labor as we were passing through on our way to Kansas. My dad was being transferred to Wichita. I wonder if we were born in the same hospital. Maybe our parents met when we were born, and kept in touch."

"Maybe."

At ten, Madison went to bed; Park wanted to sleep in the recliner. She gave him another dose of nausea medicine and a sleeping pill, but still, he woke from a nightmare at three a.m. and couldn't go back to sleep.

Madison had forgotten to turn off her laptop. She'd been working on her story, and he read it from the beginning. There were only three chapters. She was as gifted with the written word as the spoken, and he knew anyone who read her story would feel her agony. But she had only been able to guess at his feelings, and he decided to write a chapter for her, about the day they parted.

Surely no therapist had made as many blunders with a patient as he had with Reagan, Wesley thought. He hadn't seen her since he'd told her he was moving. She'd lost weight, and her face was pale and swollen. As soon as she sat down, she started crying. Reagan cried easily, but never had he seen her cry so hard and uncontrollably.

"I can't eat, I can't sleep, I feel like I have a rock inside me a little bit bigger than I am," she said. "I just want to go to sleep and never wake up."

If only he could turn the clock back, surely he could do things better. He would not tell her that she fascinated him, or that he would like to have her for a personal friend. He would get some supervision, he would send her to another therapist, as he should have done. He would not spend extra time with her for his own pleasure; he would make her pay for therapy like everyone else. He would watch his body language.

He would stop love in its tracks.

His original intention had been to validate her, to have things come out differently for her this time, but in the end, he was doing the same thing as all the other men in her life: Abandoning her. And bless her stalwart heart, she ruthlessly examined her own behavior first, and ended up blaming herself.

"I've known this day was coming," she continued. "I remember exact moment I fell in love with you, and I said to myself, 'You're going to regret this'. I know I can't hang onto your coattails for the rest of my life, but honest to God, I think you're going to have to cut my hands off to make me let go. I guess you have, in a way.

"Do you remember the poem I read you by Jorie Graham, the one about the bird she imagined enlarging until it was unrecognizable as a bird? I can imagine it expanding until its

molecules separated so much I could walk around between them. That's how I feel with you, sometimes, like we've both expanded so much we could pass right through each other. I have never felt that way about anyone. Losing you hurts so much, sometimes I think I'll lose my mind."

She looked at him miserably, tears streaming down her face, and said, in the most agonized voice he had ever heard, "And I'm going to feel like this for a long, long time."

He knew exactly what she meant, although he couldn't have put it into words. He thought about how much he looked forward to her sessions, how bleak his work would be without her. She was so much like him, and had validated him as much as he had tried to validate her.

He could have ended their misery a month earlier, before he'd decided to move. She'd split on him, abruptly quitting therapy because she was angry. He had pursued her until she'd come back. Now he wished, for both their sakes, that he'd left it alone.

The problem had started innocently enough. He had mentioned that he'd seen her at a concert, and she'd said, "Well, why didn't you come over and say hello?"

"What's to say?" he'd asked, when he really meant, "My wife would pick up the force field between us like a Geiger counter."

"What indeed. We don't have any small talk, do we? It's all blood and guts, and it's my blood and guts."

"Yes."

"So what happens when you're through shrinking my head? We shake hands and ride off into the sunset in opposite directions, you to your end of the river, I to mine? We pass each other in the grocery store, me blushing because you know where all my soft spots are, like a bruised piece of fruit, while yours remain hidden? I say, 'Hi Wes, how's your—uh—stamp collection?'"

He wondered the same thing—how he could keep this wonderful creature in his life without it appearing inappropriate. "I'll be around for a while," he'd said, an evasive and totally inadequate response.

But she hadn't let him get away with that. "Do you have so many kindred spirits that you can afford to toss one away?"

"You're really angry." Another evasive tactic. He felt like a boxer, dodging her well-aimed punches.

"No, I'm afraid. I feel like I've scheduled the amputation of a perfectly good limb a few months from now, and the anticipation is so painful that I want it over with right now, or I want to cancel the procedure."

"If you could write a script for the future, what would happen?"

"You didn't answer my question. Psychotherapy Rule #1," she said. *"When in need of diversionary tactics, answer a question with a question. I wonder what Alex Trebec would do with that. Maybe he could create a game called Psycho Jeopardy, where instead of answering an answer with a question, you answer a question with a question. For example, the category could be feelings. The question could be, 'What is love?' And the answer would be, 'How do you feel about that?'"*

"Or 'Why do you ask?'" Wesley said, laughing, once again the victim of her blazing intelligence.

"You taught me to ask for what I want instead of expecting others to read my mind," Reagan said. *"Well, I want you to give me a definite idea of how things will be in the future. I want to know I can come have a cup of coffee with you, after we are finished with therapy."*

He suspected what she meant was have a pot of coffee with him, over breakfast. *"I don't think that's a good idea."*

Her face registered shock. He knew she hadn't expected this comment; he had led her to believe they would see each other on some basis after therapy. *"Why not?"* she demanded.

"Because it violates professional ethics."

"Bull. Where's that written?"

It wasn't written, and that was the pinch. The literature was full of opinions on this common problem between shrinks and patients, but there was no hard and fast rule.

"You said you would like to have me as a personal friend," she continued, when he didn't respond. *"What are you afraid of, my feelings for you, or your feelings for me?"*

She had nailed him, and all he could do was deny it. He would have to shift the blame to her. *"Reagan, I just don't think it would work. Be honest, don't you have sexual fantasies about us?"*

She laughed. *"You know, the therapeutic relationship is probably nuttier than the clients are. I mean, you can ask me a question like that, but you would be horrified if I stepped over that line you just drew between us and asked you the same thing."* She glared at him. *"So you want to hear my favorite fantasy?"*

"If you want to tell me," he said calmly, inwardly squirming, knowing it was a mistake to invite a writer to describe such a scene. He wished he hadn't introduced the topic.

"Okay," she said, settling back in her chair and staring at the wall, as if it were a movie screen. *"It's late at night, and we sit in my living room. It is a dimly lit, beautiful room with deep forest green walls. The sliding glass door is open, the cool breeze bringing in the scent of freshly-mown grass and the sound of my wind chimes on the balcony. We face each other on the couch, eyes engaged, maintaining a respectable distance.*

"You are telling me your story, why you have such angst, why you chose your career, who you are behind the I.D. badge. I know I have the same expression on my face as you do when I share my pain. Your voice clots and I can't bear to see you in such agony. I wrap my arms around you and you push away like you always do, then you relax and cling to me.

"We stretch out on the couch, and you gaze down at me with your jeweled eyes. I review your colors, rosy cheeks, white teeth, jade eyes, blonde hair. You touch my face, and I know you are going to kiss me, your mouth pink and moist, nested in your beard."

Wesley's face burned with embarrassment. He crossed his legs and angled away from her, to hide his response to the picture she had just painted. This was a mistake, and he wanted her to stop. "Reagan, please—"

Embarrassed, she had stormed out of his office, and he'd had a message on his machine from her the next morning, canceling her future appointments.

But Wes just couldn't leave it alone, and wasn't happy until he finally got her on the phone and arranged a time for them to meet. Her therapy had gone too well for it to end like that, and he wanted a chance to explain what he meant and what he didn't mean.

"When you made a request for personal information," he

told her, "I had a flash of fear that I had done something wrong—become too emotionally involved or made you too dependent on me, and I retreated behind my professional facade.

"I botched it. I really like you, too. I look forward to talking to you, and I have tremendously enjoyed working with you. And I like the fact that you think I'm a good therapist . . ."

That was the most telling statement of all. He needed his damn ego massaged. Why hadn't he left well enough alone—she had left voluntarily, and would have been better off stopping therapy on her own terms.

She was mostly angry then, but now, her pain and his guilt and their joint feelings of loss were unbearable. It was excruciating to watch. He tented his fingers over his nose and surreptitiously dabbed tears from his eyes with his index fingers.

Still, he just couldn't bring himself to say the words he longed to say, because it would be so unfair to her. And so he said, knowing his words were inadequate, "I'm sorry this is so painful for you."

He saw her for the last time two weeks later. She stood in the middle of his office, scanning the bookshelves as if she'd been waiting to see them empty before she could really believe he was leaving. She wouldn't sit down, and her body language told him she was holding herself together with a dry-rotted rubber band that was ready to snap.

She handed him a small, narrow box. "Here's something to remember me by."

As if he could ever forget her. He opened the box to find a tortoiseshell Waterman fountain pen.

"You shrinks think Rorschach was the inventor of the inkblot test," she said. "Well, you're wrong: it was Lewis Waterman, inventor of the fountain pen."

Wesley couldn't even laugh at her joke. He stood there looking dumbly at the pen, knowing he shouldn't accept an expensive gift from a patient, but it meant so much, he wanted to keep it. His emotions welled up and threatened to spill over.

She finally filled the silence. "If you don't like it, the man at Tobacco Corner said you can exchange it," she said in a small voice.

He looked up, unable to keep the sum of his feelings for her out of his expression and voice. "Oh, I like it."

"It has a spell on it."

"Of course it does," he said, thickly. "I'll write to you often. I will."

She took his hand and choked out, "You be happy, Wes," then turned and walked out of his life, leaving his heart fractured in as many pieces as hers.

Tears ran down Park's face as he finished, but he felt a sense of catharsis and peace, although he didn't know exactly what his motivation was for writing the scene. Did he just want to collaborate on a shrink/client novel, like the one Irvin Yalom and his patient had written? In that case, he should have used clinical language, explaining how idealization and merger with another staved off inner terror, and helped the client create perfection and reduce shame.

But that would be a cowardly thing to do to someone who so bravely faced truth. Even thinking about it, he had to laugh; he'd once tried to discuss her idealization of him. She had already thought it through and was prepared with a stinging rebuttal.

Or he could talk about compartmentalizing, a way of allowing conflicting situations to exist simultaneously without confusion, the "that's different" theory. He was guilty of that. Except for one thing: He believed it really was different.

Perhaps he was being too hard on himself. He'd never told her how much he missed her, and he wanted her to know. She had a genius for describing her inner world that captivated him, the way a good writer can send you off into a reverie with one sentence, thinking, yes, that's exactly the way it is . . . She so ruthlessly turned the microscope on her own behavior that sometimes it was both painful and compelling to be fully present for her, so brilliantly did her words frame her inner darkness, like a doorway to a black tunnel outlined with white lights.

He could hide behind the therapist's couch, but the plain fact of the matter, he admitted once and for all, was that he loved her. And he wanted her to know it.

CHAPTER SEVEN

Madison sat up and groaned when the alarm went off at five Friday morning. She did not want to go to work. Even though she'd gone to bed at her regular time last night, she felt like she hadn't slept at all.

In the living room, Park was still asleep in the recliner. She'd heard him get up several times during the night, and the television was still on, so he must have had a bad night.

She groaned again when she walked into the kitchen. Wrappers from Hershey's Kisses littered the counter, and a nearly empty jar of peanut butter, which she'd just bought last weekend, sat in the middle of the mess. She had absolutely no recollection of eating any of it.

"Dammit," she said, clearing a space to make coffee. She was sleep eating again. That was the ultimate indicator that she was in trouble. She probably needed to see her psychiatrist, Isabella Rose, who had treated her for a few years after she had come to Houston; but in the last couple of years, Madison had gotten along without psychotherapy or medication, and she really didn't want to lose the freedom she'd worked so hard to achieve.

Of course, the initial topic in therapy had been Park, as it would be now; but Dr. Rose had exhibited a cold anger toward him after she'd heard the story, and Madison knew she'd get no sympathy for getting involved with him again. In fact, Dr. Rose might even get Park in trouble.

And Madison certainly couldn't discuss her problems with David or Basc. She would try to call her AA sponsor later, or her sister, Bree.

Park walked into the kitchen, clothes rumpled, bleary-eyed.

"Good morning," Madison said. "Coffee?"

"No thanks." He surveyed the mess on the counters, and started sweeping up candy wrappers and throwing them in the garbage. "Looks like about a 10,000 calorie binge," he said, disgusted.

Madison felt her face burn with shame. "I guess I never told you about my sleep-eating problem." She screwed the lid on the peanut butter jar, and put it in the cabinet. "Makes it hard to keep the weight off."

He looked at her in surprise. "You did this?"

Madison nodded. "I have what's called 'nocturnal sleep-related eating disorder.'"

"I know what it is. I have it, too."

"Really. Well, in that case, I'll let you take the blame."

Park laughed. "No, you take the blame." He looked drawn, and had dark circles under his eyes.

"Bad night?"

"About the same as last time. I'll probably be fine by this afternoon."

"You can sleep it off in the recliner, if you want to."

"Thanks, but I think I'll go on home and get cleaned up. I need to get organized and start looking for a job."

After he left, Madison showered and dressed, then woke Cam.

He was such a precious little boy, sweet natured and generous. Madison smiled, remembering a story the mail carrier had told her—one July day she'd labored up the steep driveway, red-faced and sweat-soaked, and Cam, then three years old, had said to her, "You look so hot. Would you like some ice water?"

The woman was impressed; evidently not too many people cared if mail carriers were inflicted with chronic dehydration and malignant hyperthermia. Madison herself had never thought of offering a glass of water to the one of them.

And the first Halloween she'd taken him trick-or-treating, he'd insisted the proper procedure was to give candy to the person who opened the door, not to receive it himself. When an elderly lady persevered in giving him a treat, he stuck his hand on his hip and said, "Well, excuse me!" and walked off in a huff.

He slept like a tornado, just like Madison did; his head was at the foot of the bed, his quilt and sheet balled at the top. She brushed damp hair away from his forehead and stroked his flushed cheek. Even at four, he still had his rosy little Gerber-baby mouth. She traced the bluish vein on his hand, imagining blood being drawn, IVs started, bone marrow sucked from him, and panicked at the thought.

He opened his eyes and stretched, then sat up and smiled at her. "Good morning, my little Bellibone," he said, putting his arms around her neck and snuggling against her.

"Good morning, my little Poplollie."

He was such an easy child. Getting Emma and Dane up when they were this age had been a lengthy ordeal every morning. Madison could still visualize them sitting Indian-style in their beds, heads bobbing, fully dressed and nearly sound asleep. When they were in grade school, they'd started putting on their school clothes instead of pajamas after their evening baths, to save time in the morning. Madison didn't care; she figured that was why God made permanent press. Besides, it saved on pajamas and laundry.

Cam, on the other hand, would be perfectly content to go to school in his Spiderman pajamas.

Without Park there as a distraction, she got Cam to school and arrived at work with time to spare. After preparing her patient for an embryo transfer, Madison sat at the desk to wait for David, who was doing the cases today.

She booted the desktop computer, then her laptop, so she could view statistics on one computer, and write a report on the other. There must have been some kind of a power problem with the laptop; it opened to Microsoft Word, and there was a recovered document. She hit save, but it was treating the document as a new one, requiring a name. She scanned it, but did not recognize it.

Either she had a new nocturnal disorder—sleep writing—or someone else had created this document. Her heart skipped a beat as she read the first line: "Surely no therapist had made as many blunders with a patient as Wesley had with Reagan . . ."

The author had to be Park. Back when she was in therapy with him, they had toyed with the idea of writing a book this way, she writing from the patient's point of view, he from the therapist's.

She read the scene quickly, her emotions ping-ponging from elation to anger. Park's writing blended seamlessly with hers, almost as if they were the same person. But was his chapter purely fiction, or was he trying to tell her something? Was he admitting that he had, in fact, made exceptions for her because he considered her special? That he had made mistakes? He stopped just short of saying he loved her, but was she supposed to read between the lines?

Damn him, it was the same old story. Maybe he wasn't any better with his own emotions than David was. Once again, she vowed to protect herself from men. All men.

Still, it seemed like both she and Park were unable to forget each other, like the characters in *The Bridges of Madison County*. Maybe she should rename her book *The Bridges of Buffalo Bayou*.

She was re-reading his description of the character's sexual fantasy, heat rising in her face, thinking maybe Park would be better suited to write soft porn, when David walked in. Madison quickly shut the laptop.

His eyes scanned her face and neck. "What's going on?"

"Nothing," she said brightly. She looked at her watch. "You're ten minutes early. As Paris Hilton would say, believing her comment totally original, 'that's hot.'"

"Do I get some Brownie points?"

"No, you just don't get demerits. Hurry up and speak to the patient, then I'll put her on the table while you wash your hands."

They worked together smoothly, like the old days, and the case went well. While Madison recovered the patient, she worked on her report, Park's chapter practically burning through the screen beneath her Excel document. She would read it again later, when she could concentrate on it, and try to figure out what he was saying. If his writing were that cryptic, it probably wouldn't do much good to ask him what he really meant.

In the afternoon, she carried a stack of charts to David's office. "Do you have time to give me some orders?"

He looked at his watch. "Yeah, I have a few minutes before clinic."

Madison sat down, facing him across his desk, and opened the first chart.

"I have a new couple coming from out of town next week," she said. "They want to see if they can get some tests out of the way while they're here for their initial visit. It's a second marriage—she had her tubes tied during her first marriage."

"They can knock out some labs and a semen analysis this time."

Madison wrote the orders, and pushed the chart across the desk for him to sign them.

"Next. You'll love this. I need help shamelessly manipulating Basc."

"I'm in," David said, with zest.

"Hah! I knew I could count on you. I have a 40-year-old female whose husband was killed in Iraq. There's enough sperm frozen to do one IVF cycle only. She's decided to go with donor egg, since her chances are so sharply reduced, secondary to advanced maternal age."

"So what's the problem?"

"I have the perfect donor, but I can't use her, because she's already donated three times and there have been three pregnancies."

"So you need Basc to waive the rule that a donor can't be used after three pregnancies are achieved? I always wondered how she came up with that rule."

"Statistically speaking, in a city the size of Houston, a donor could produce 15 babies before it would be probable for any of them to meet as adults. Since they could potentially donate at other clinics, Basc decided on an ultra-conservative number."

David snorted. "Judging by how much fun an egg aspiration is, I'd want to do it at every clinic in the city, wouldn't you?"

"For sure."

"I bet in reality there are very few siblings that have met, not knowing they were related. I need to figure out a strategy and get a bullet-proof vest. Convincing her to change a rule is no task for the faint-of-heart."

"Grovel if you have to. But start by asking her to be open-minded. That almost always works, because it implies that she's not, and she doesn't like that. And sometimes, depending on her mood, I'll ask for the exact opposite of what I want. Her brain automatically kicks into devil's advocate mode, and she'll take the other side. But that's a gamble. It has backfired on me."

David laughed. "You tricky little fiend. Now I know what to look out for."

"Oh, please. Surely you don't think I would use the same strategies on you," Madison said, grinning.

She opened the last chart. "We need to fire these patients. They've done ten IVF cycles in the last two years, three of them donor egg, the last one donor egg and donor sperm, which is adoption, for all practical purposes. They're still not pregnant. I talked to Basc about this at the last IVF meeting, when you were out of town, and she wants to let them continue. But David, this woman is a wreck. I'm really worried about her emotional state, and I don't know how much more hormone hell she can take."

He took the chart and flipped through the progress notes, then leaned back in his chair and tapped his front teeth with his pen. "Won't they just go somewhere else?"

"You're going to have to convince them that there will never be a pregnancy. And I think she definitely will need psychotherapy. Hey! I know a great shrink who can get her in immediately."

"Ha, ha," David said. "Get serious."

"I am serious," Madison said. "I think it's a great idea. Basc has talked about having a therapist on staff part time. I think I'll ask her if she would interview Park."

"Maybe he should just take it easy until he's through treatment."

"He can't. With the divorce, it's imperative for him to work." As soon as she said it, she wanted to bite her tongue.

David signed the charts and pushed them back across the desk to her, his face stiff. "Park is getting a divorce? I'm surprised. It doesn't seem like something Mr. Wonderful would do."

Madison bristled. "It's not something he would do. His wife is filing."

"Oh. I see."

Madison gathered the charts and headed for the door.

"What time am I picking you up tomorrow?" David asked.

She turned. "Picking me up?"

"You haven't forgotten our date, have you? We're supposed to see a play tomorrow night." When she continued to look blank, he added, "*A Tuna Christmas*? In Galveston? I gave you the tickets for your birthday."

"Oh—is it time for a Christmas play already? It's not even

Thanksgiving yet."

"Well, I don't make the holiday schedule. And you chose the date. How about I pick you up at six and we have dinner first?"

"Okay. I'll see if I can find a babysitter. But it's awfully short notice."

"Park probably doesn't have anything better to do. Why don't you ask him?"

"I'll think about it," she said.

* * *

On Saturday morning, Madison opened the front door to see a UPS truck backing into her driveway. She walked outside and stood on the porch. The driver opened the back of the truck, revealing three boxes, each as big as a refrigerator.

He consulted his paperwork as he walked toward her. "Ms. Templeton?"

"That would be me," said Madison. "But I didn't order any refrigerators."

He smiled. "It's not refrigerators. It seems to be—" he consulted his paperwork again. "A tree house."

"A tree house. Great. Let me guess who ordered this tree house. Would it be one David Thorpe?"

"Yes Ma'am. Sign here please. Where would you like me to put the boxes?"

"Back yard, I guess."

She went inside and called David. "Just curious. Did you happen to notice the dimensions of your tree house before you had it delivered to me?"

"It's there already? Great. Cam and I can build it Thanksgiving weekend."

"Sweet. He'll drive me crazy by then. 'Mom, is there a tree in the tree house box? Because we don't have a tree. But we could grow one. It would take a long time, though. Maybe we could buy one. It will have to be big. I have a dollar, I'll give it to you. If it's not enough, I can earn some money. Maybe I could wash some bayou fish for the guys that fish over there. They don't know the bayou fish are dirty. Mom, how do the bayou fish get dirty . . .'"

"Stop," David begged, laughing so hard that she imagined tears streaming down his cheeks.

"Couple of details. First, there *is* no tree in the back yard, unless you count the spindly little oak that grew from an acorn my resident squirrel planted. Somehow, I don't think it's quite big enough to support the tree *mansion* you ordered."

"Oh, don't worry. The tree is included."

"Thank God for small favors. Second, I don't suppose it occurred to you that I might need to be consulted."

"Nah . . . I figured it would be easier to get forgiveness than to get permission. Gotta go, see ya later . . ."

Exasperated, Madison hung up and opened the papers that came with the tree house. The thing was huge. It sat on a hollowed-out redwood base and had a crooked little house perched on top, siding, shingles, dormer windows and all. A door opened into the tree, and a ladder led up to a trapdoor entrance into the house. She hoped the neighborhood association wouldn't object.

But she had to admit that Cam would love it. She shook her head, half irritated, half touched by David's indulgence of Cam, who had already started nagging her to open the boxes.

By the time Madison done her Saturday chores, it was time to get dressed for the play. Park had agreed to babysit, and arrived promptly at six; David, no surprise, was late.

"Tell me about this play," Park said as they waited.

"It's a comedy about a town called Tuna."

"It's the third smallest town in Texas," Cam said.

"There are only two actors," Madison continued, "and they play all the characters, 29 altogether, plus a dog and an extraterrestrial. Their plays are hilarious. I'll take you to see one, if you're interested."

Park was surreptitiously checking out her outfit. She wore a royal blue coatdress and classic black heels, and had put on a touch of makeup and perfume. Always self-conscious about her appearance, Madison had found herself nervously primping, for which of them, David or Park, she didn't know.

When David finally arrived, 30 minutes late, he gave a low whistle, then kissed her. "Hello, beautiful," he said, dragging out the hello. She could have slapped him. He never behaved like that except when Park was around, and it embarrassed her.

Cam attacked David with a million questions about the tree house, and by the time they extricated themselves, it was almost seven. They left Cam happily ensconced in Park's lap, writing a letter to Santa, stimulated, no doubt, by the Christmas commercials on TV.

"Why are you so late?" Madison asked, as they got in the car.

"I did a 10-K bike ride, and I didn't get back as soon as I thought I would."

"Typical."

"Would it help if the bike ride were for charity?"

"That might mitigate the damages a little. We might as well forget dinner. Let's just grab some fast food on the way."

David pulled into a Sonic and ordered a burger and fries for himself, and a salad for Madison. While they waited, he turned in his seat so he could look straight at her.

"I'm sorry I've upset you," he said. "I really wanted some quiet time to talk before the play."

"You remind me of Emma. Always late. I guess I'm sort of sensitized to that, because it was always such a battle to get her anywhere on time. She used to do it deliberately, just to make me mad."

David took her hand and squeezed it. "I didn't do it to make you mad. I just don't have any sense of time. I'll do better."

"Sure you will."

"Hey, I made it to the embryo transfer ten minutes early."

"Do that every day for a year, and you'll establish a little credibility."

"I'm afraid I won't be able to do that."

"Okay, do it for a month."

"Madison, I have something to tell you," he said, his voice serious.

Her expression turned to alarm. "What's wrong, are you sick?"

"No, I'm fine. I just—I don't know if you care—but I'm moving back to Utah."

"You can't do that! You've barely been in Houston a year. What will Basc do without you? And Cam?"

"You didn't mention yourself. Won't you miss me?"

"Of course I will, don't be ridiculous. You're my best friend."

She jerked her hand out of his. "When did you make this decision? Why are you doing this?"

"I'm not happy here, Madison. You know that. Basc treats me like I'm still an intern, instead of her partner. I have no autonomy at all. And I don't see that changing."

"Why can't you just follow the rules? When you're the director of an IVF program, you can be the boss. You need to grow up. What are you going to do in Utah?"

"I'm going to be a country doctor, like I planned to do when I started medical school. I'll have a base office, and fly my Cessna to outlying clinics."

"But you're a Reproductive Endocrinologist. You can't use those skills in the middle of nowhere!"

"Don't forget, I also did a Family Practice fellowship."

"And you hated it. You'll have to do Pediatrics again, and you hate Peds."

"Kids are growing on me."

"David, please don't leave me. Please."

"I don't want to leave you. I want you to come with me."

"Come with you? In what capacity?"

David opened the glove compartment and took out a turquoise box tied with a white ribbon. She could see the words "Tiffany and Co." on the top.

Oh, dear God, she thought. Don't let him propose in the middle of all this confusion.

He untied the ribbon, lifted the lid, and took out a blue velvet ring box. Inside was a heart-shaped diamond solitaire that must have weighed at least two carets. He slid it on her finger.

"Madison, will you marry me? You don't have to make a decision right this minute. Just wear the ring, and think about it. We're good together. We belong together."

It was a moment she had once longed for, dreamed of, tried to make happen for years. Eventually she had abandoned hope of marrying him. Why was he proposing now? David had been uncharacteristically possessive lately, and she distrusted his timing. If he were proposing simply to eliminate Park from her life, the marriage would never work.

"It's beautiful," she said. The large diamond might have looked gaudy on a smaller hand, but it was perfectly proportioned for hers. "When did you get it?"

"Right before I left for Utah."

That would have been before Park arrived in Houston. She shook her head. "I don't understand you, David. For years I dreamed of this moment, but I finally got tired of chasing you. I gave up on you, and it seemed like you didn't even notice. Nothing changed, except that we drifted into a brother-sister type relationship that seemed just fine with you."

"No, it wasn't. I'm just hopeless at the boy/girl stuff. Don't forget, I grew up in all-male boarding schools, and I had no model for how to romance a woman. The only close contact I ever had with a female my age was the housekeeper's daughter, and I only saw her on holidays. You made it easy for me, always taking the initiative, and when you stopped, I didn't know exactly what to do. I respected your wishes, but Madison, I had to be near you."

The statement rang true. As far as she knew, he had never dated anyone else. In fact, people speculated that he was gay, although he had not one effeminate bone in his body.

"And then you had Cam, and I respected your maternal instincts."

"I had no idea you were still romantically interested," she said. "I thought we were just friends, and that you liked little kids."

"I thought Cam was my child, and that you would tell me when you were ready. We've done a lot of growing together, so that seemed reasonable. When I first met you, I was an immature, spoiled rich kid, not ready to assume the responsibilities of a permanent relationship, which in your case was complicated by the two children you already had. And I got mixed signals, with you constantly in and out of relationships with other guys."

"I wouldn't have been, if I'd thought I stood a chance with you."

"But haven't we been making progress? You were less distant right before I left for Utah. You'd been out of psychotherapy and off antidepressants, and it seemed like you were waking up."

It was true; for a while, she had been coping without her psychological crutches. But that was a fragile, hard-won state.

"I just don't want to lose myself again," Madison said. "I've worked so hard to make myself into a real person, who doesn't require a man for validation."

"Is it me who will make you lose yourself, or just anybody?"

"It's anybody. I mean, what would I do in Utah? I'd get all dependent on you again."

"You can do whatever you want. Be a full-time wife and mother. Or be my nurse. You want a Master's in creative writing, so go to school. For once in your life, let someone take care of you instead of you taking care of everyone else."

She groped blindly for his hand. Maybe he did understand and love her more than she thought. "I don't know if I can live without a quilt shop fifteen minutes away in any direction that I point my car."

"That's what the internet is for, sweets. Or I can fly you wherever you want to go. Hell, I'll buy you a quilt shop. I want to build a home near the family lodge and vineyard. We can design it together. It's beautiful there Madison. You can see it on the website, or we can visit. Mother is dying to meet you."

"What about Cam?"

"He'll be fine. I grew up there, and I turned out all right, didn't I?" She shot him a doubtful look, and he laughed. "We'll home school Cam, and send him to the very best college and medical school."

"But what will he do for fun? The place is so isolated."

"He can enjoy the great outdoors. He can have horses. He can fish!"

Now Madison laughed. "If he says the "F" word to me one more time, I'll scream. Where'd he get the fish obsession, anyway?"

"Well . . . he might have heard me talking about fishing the Colorado River . . ."

"That river is too dangerous. I don't like your daredevil stuff and I don't want you teaching my son dangerous sports."

"Okay. Then we can hike the Grand Canyon. I'll take both you to Pine Mountain to see the ladybug migration. They cover every surface for miles."

"Are you crazy? You know I don't go outside. I only go from one air-conditioned place to another. Besides, I hate ladybugs."

"You do? Why?"

"They bite."

"That's ridiculous. Who ever heard of a sweet little ladybug biting someone?"

"Well, one bit me, and I don't like them."

"Okay, no ladybugs for you."

The food came, and they ate silently for a while. David did, anyway; Madison just pushed her salad around with her fork. "David, what if Cam turns out to be Park's son?"

"He won't."

"We have to think about that possibility."

"Okay, let's say he's Park's. So what about Park. You once told me you loved him."

"Yes."

"And you once told me you loved me."

"Yes." She didn't like to remember either of those humiliating, one-sided confessions.

"So which is it, Madison?"

She looked into the distance, groping for an answer. "I don't know, David," she said, miserably. "He fills up my soul. You fill up my life."

"I am going to fill up your heart," he said softly, kissing the hand that wore the heart-shaped symbol of his love, and once again a million neurons fired, all the way to Madison's toes.

* * *

A Tuna Christmas was entertaining, but not entertaining enough to keep Madison from obsessing about the new turn of events. All she wanted was to get home and have some quiet time to think.

David walked her to the door. She turned and looked up at him, searching his face for confirmation that he was serious about his marriage proposal, for he'd said all the right things except one: I love you.

Then he kissed her. She put her arms around him, her body conforming to his familiar shape, and allowed herself the pleasure of holding him again. A master at seducing her with only his mouth, his passion nearly convinced her of his sincerity; but she still wanted to hear the words.

"Let me come in," he whispered.

"No, you know Park is here."

He took her hands, held them behind her back, pulled her against him, and kissed her again.

"Make him go home," he breathed in her ear, then kissed her again.

"Stop," she said unconvincingly. He nuzzled his way down her neck to that exact place he knew turned her to hot lava, and her knees buckled. "Cam—"

"Is probably asleep, or will be soon."

He took her keys and opened the door, following her inside. Park was sound asleep in the recliner, with Cam wedged on one side, Dudley on the other. The living room was littered with toys, junk food wrappers, juice boxes, soft drink cans.

David picked Cam up, saying, "Come on, Spike. Bedtime."

Cam put his arms around David's neck, the usual volley of questions trailing behind as David carried him to his bed. "David, did you like Tuna fish Christmas? Was it an ocean tuna, or a bayou tuna . . ."

Park stood and said awkwardly, "Well, I guess I'll go."

Madison walked him to the door, feeling like she was forcing him to leave, like he could feel the sexual tension in the air. She followed him onto the front porch.

"Thank you for babysitting," she said. "I really needed the break."

"Anytime," Park responded, looking desolate. "I'll talk to you tomorrow."

Madison locked up and went to check on Cam. David came out of his room, and shut the door. He put his arms around her, fused his mouth to hers, and started walking her backward to her bedroom.

Oh God, she was so confused. She loved both of them emotionally, but she had a deep spiritual connection with Park that was missing with David, and a physical connection with David that she had experienced with no other man in her life, and could not imagine with Park. In fact, she could not really imagine having sex with him at all, because she would rather talk to him.

And deep, deep down, her trust had been damaged by both of them, by David's lack of commitment, by Park's abandonment. She didn't know if that could be repaired.

But right this minute, her body could not possibly have cared less about all that. It was screaming David, David, David . . .

CHAPTER EIGHT

On Thanksgiving morning, Park woke with a disquieting sense of anticipation, mixed with guilt. He was looking forward to spending the day at Madi's; but Thanksgiving was the anniversary of Nathan's death, and enjoying the day felt like a betrayal of both his wife and his son. He closed his eyes, trying to suppress rapid-fire images of that long-ago day—lifeless baby, dandelion hair floating in the sunshine; empty crib; grave in Memphis, headstone no bigger than a Golden Book: Nathan, Beloved Son.

Park was also worried about Claire being alone today. He decided to call her later, even though he expected an icy reception, just to let her know he was with her in spirit. More than that, he could not do. He fervently hoped she would be with loving friends, or her parents.

Madi was right; trying to take care of Claire had prevented him from working on his own closure over the brutal loss of the baby. As a therapist, he knew that, of course, but the knowledge didn't translate on a personal level.

Intellectually, he knew that after more than twenty years he should be able to compartmentalize the pain, like a tiny white coffin in a corner of his mind; emotionally, he knew it was a process he hadn't even started. It was pushed away on a weekly basis, like planning a diet—enjoy just one more weekend, and get serious on Monday. And once again, for one last Thanksgiving, he needed to put off working on the issue; there was just too much chaos in his life right now, too much pain. So with apologies to Nathan, Park closed the mental door of the room where his baby son lay entombed.

Madi was cooking a traditional Thanksgiving dinner, and Park's spirits were buoyed by the feeling of being part of a family at holiday time. His assignment for the day was breakfast, and he made a run to Starbucks and the neighborhood bakery, arriving at Madi's at eight with kolaches and coffee. A shiny red BMW motorcycle was parked on her front porch.

Cam opened the door, looking like Dennis the Menace in blue jean overalls and a red and white striped knit shirt. He jumped around like a hungry flea that was anxious for a vacationing dog to return home.

"David brought donuts," he said. "I ate two. Mom says I'm wired, no more sugar for me today. But she'll give me some pie. I'm making a sign for the tree house. You can help me."

Miffed that David had upstaged him with donuts, Park followed Cam as he buzzed off to the kitchen, where dinner preparations were already in full swing. Madi and David were making pies.

Park set the tray of coffee on the counter, and David gave it the hairy eyeball.

"Don't start," Madi said to him.

"What's wrong?" Park asked. "Someone allergic to coffee?"

"David's a fan of Mom and Pop coffee shops. The greedy, multi-national Starbucks Corporation, evil icon of capitalism, is pushing them out."

"Plus, their coffee sucks," David said. "Did you bring Madi a mocha frap? That's what she likes."

Madison took a cup of plain old coffee from Park. "A frap is the last thing I need today, with all the calories we're going to consume."

Cam sat at the kitchen desk, laboriously lettering a sign: "Keep out! Boys only. Xcep Mom." Park handed him a hot chocolate.

"Oh, that's a good idea," David said. "Give him another jolt of sugar."

Madi elbowed him in the ribs. "Stop it, right now," she said under her breath, "or I'll send you home. Besides that, you're the one who gave him the first jolt."

David rinsed a handful of green tomatoes and Granny Smith apples, and set them on a cutting board. Madi handed him a towel. He dried his hands, picked up an apple, and held out his hand. She slapped a paring knife in it, then put a bowl on the counter, next to the cutting board.

Park watched Madi and David work together. David focused on his task, and Madi watched him, ready with the next thing he needed. He never looked up or said a word, as if everything had been choreographed in advance. Park supposed that was the way doctors and nurses worked in the Operating Room.

David sliced the tomatoes and added them to the apples.

"Mom," Cam said, disgusted, "David just put tomatoes in the apple pie."

David looked up, surprised. "That is what you told me to do, isn't it, Madi?"

"That's what I told you to do."

"I'm not eatin' any of it," said Cam.

David looked at the tomato/apple combination, clearly unable to make it compute.

Madi laughed. "It's my 'Thanksgiving Surprise Pie.' When Emma and Dane were little, I cooked dinner for the whole family. The last of the tomatoes from the garden were on the windowsill, taking forever to ripen. I threw them in with the apples and some brown sugar, and made kind of a sweet and sour pie. The first one disappeared in a hurry, but when Emma discovered the tomatoes in the second one, that was the end of the pie eating."

Park smiled. That was so Madi.

She handed David a cup of brown sugar and cinnamon. He dumped it in the bowl, then held out his hand; she slapped a wire whisk into it. He stuck it in the bowl, then took it back out and looked at it, then at her. "What's that for?"

"Well, you surgeons always say gimme what I need, not what I ask for. You figure out what to do with it." She turned her attention to Cam. "Did you finish sorting the pecans?"

"No, I gotta finish my sign."

"If you want Thanksgiving dinner, you 'gotta' help."

"I'll help David build the tree house."

When she turned around, David was still puzzling over the whisk. Laughing, she snatched it from his hand and threw it in the sink. "I'm kidding, dummy. Why don't you and Cam go outside and play. Park can help me."

"Yippee!" said Cam, grabbing his sign and running to the back door.

"Suits me," David said. He rinsed and dried his hands, then opened the small drawer where Madi kept her tools. After fishing around for a minute, he said, "Don't you have a hex screwdriver?"

"I don't know," she said, "maybe. What's it look like?"

"Jeez," David said. "This is pathetic."

"Look, I'm just a girl with a nail file. I call a man with a toolbox when I need something done."

"Me too," Park said.

"That figures," David said. "Okay, come on Spike, I'll teach you to improvise."

"Just pretend you're at the county hospital," Madi said, "where the motto is, 'If it don't fit, force it.'"

Dudley followed Cam and David outside. Madi left the door open, so she could keep an eye on them. "Maybe I can get some work done, now," she said.

"What do you want me to do?" Park asked.

"Go through those pecans and pick out the bad ones and any pieces of shell." She rolled out a pie crust, deftly turned it into a pan, and added the tomato/apple filling. "I'm dying to know how your interview with Dr. Bascomb went."

"I'm not sure. She was kind of distant at first, except where you're concerned, when she's like a female gorilla with a newborn. I gather she doesn't approve of me."

Madi put the top crust on the pie and pinched the edges together. He waited for her to speak. Finally, she became uncomfortable enough to say something.

"Dammit, Park, don't start with the shrink technique. Of course she distrusts you; she was there for me through the whole ordeal of you leaving. She absolutely insisted that I move to Houston, and not just because she wanted me to work for her. She thought a geographical change would help me, because everywhere I went in Memphis, there was a constant reminder of you. You worked where I worked, lived near me, we even shopped in the same places. So cut her some slack. In time, she'll love you. Did you two just snipe at each other, or were you able to talk about the patients and the job?"

"Once we got into that, we did fine. It turns out that I have rather a good reputation as a shrink. She, on the other hand, doesn't seem to have much compassion for the patients."

"It's not that. She depends on the nurses to take care of the warm fuzzy stuff. She says she loses objectivity if she gets emotionally involved, and that can be dangerous when making medical decisions."

"At any rate, she's a brilliant woman. I can understand why you like her so much. But she sure has some unconventional ideas."

Madi put the pie in the oven and started the filling for the next one. "Do you think you'll get the job?"

"She said she'd let me know by the end of the week. I'd start on an as-needed basis at first, so I don't know how much income it will generate. But it's a start."

"I guarantee you're needed plenty." Madi took the pecans from him, dumped them in a pie crust, and poured the filling over the pecans. "Honestly, I think every IVF couple needs counseling, or at least an evaluation. They're usually pretty beat up by the time they get to us, and our treatment is the most stressful of all."

"Tell that to Dr. Bascomb," Park said.

"I did. That's how the position was generated."

Madi put the pecan pie in the oven, washed bowls and utensils, and set up to make dressing.

He loved everything about this woman, but most of all, he loved the way she worried about everyone's welfare, even though it took its toll on her. Finding balance was something they'd worked on in therapy, but obviously not too successfully. He wondered how she would handle Cam donating bone marrow, should he be a match.

"How did Cam do when he had his blood drawn?"

"He did okay. David and I went first, so he could see it was no big deal. Still, when they came at him with the needle, you could see the whites of his eyes all the way around, and at the last second, he looked at me like, 'Help me, Mom.' But he didn't move a muscle."

"He's a brave little kid," Park said. "But what would one expect? He's yours."

"Thank you."

"I'm very grateful to all three of you for being tested."

Madi flashed him a look that melted his heart. "I'm happy to be able to help you, for a change," she said quietly.

"Did the coordinator talk about the donor process?"

"Yes—she explained that it wouldn't be a conventional bone marrow transplant; that blood would be taken from the arm of the donor, and after the stem cells were separated out, it would be returned."

"When did they say the results should be back?"

"We should know something by tomorrow or Monday."

As much as Park wanted Cam to be his son, he almost hoped he wouldn't be, so the child wouldn't have to go through the stem cell donation.

"Okay," Madi said. "Your turn to help."

Park went to the counter, and she set a knife and two onions on the cutting board, then took an old-fashioned apron off a hook.

"Oh, no," he said, holding up his hands. "I don't do onions."

"Oh, yes you do." She slid the apron over his arms and tied it in the back.

"But they make me cry."

"They make everybody cry. Crying is good for you. You should know that. Get busy."

"Yes, Chef," he said. He cut the ends off the first onion, peeled it, and started slicing it.

Madi took the turkey from the refrigerator, washed it, and left it draining in the sink, then started butter melting in a skillet. She checked Park's onions, and, evidently dissatisfied with them, took a cleaver from her knife rack and handed it to him. His heart sank when he noticed a diamond solitaire ring on a long chain around her neck, flashing in the sunlight as she leaned forward.

"Chop those onions, Mister," she said.

"Yes, Chef." With the cleaver, he pointed to the ring. "Is that an engagement ring?"

"Yes."

"Why are you wearing it on a chain?"

She dropped it down inside her sweater. "Because I haven't decided if I want to accept it."

"David's?"

"Yes."

"You don't seem happy."

She raised those devastating blue eyes, full of pain and confusion, and held his gaze. "I'm not sure how I feel."

Park knew that if he were half the therapist she thought he was, he would encourage her to marry David. They seemed so right for each other. And Madi had grown so, learned to acknowledge her accomplishments and be her own person instead of validating herself through attachment to any old male who strolled through her life. She'd conquered her addictions, even her food addiction, the hardest of all for her to relinquish, the portable, acceptable quick fix. If she married now, it would not be out of neurotic neediness.

He broke her gaze and started chopping the onions. His eyes started burning, and tears streamed down his face, only half of them from the onions. Madi took a clean dishcloth from a drawer, soaked it in cold water, and dabbed at his eyes. He looked at her sweet mouth, then engaged her eyes again. Her long lashes and deep-set eyes always made him think of cornflowers.

"Park," she said, "the scene that you wrote for the novel. How much of that was based on truth?"

"Most of it," he said, loathing himself for his inability to take the high ground.

"The therapist said he would stop love in its tracks. Please, for once, just give me a straightforward answer. Were you saying you loved me?"

Park opened his mouth to say yes when the back storm door opened; the word froze in his mouth. Still wiping tears from his eyes, Madi turned to see what had surprised him.

Cam stood in the doorway. "Mom, why didn't you answer the door? Claire is here."

Claire stood behind him, a plastic Kroger bag in one hand. Park was shocked to see her, but even more shocked at her appearance. Her white-blonde hair was skinned back from a face bleached of color. She had lost weight, so much weight that her face looked like nothing more than bones with skin painted on. Her black jumpsuit clung to a Tinker Toy body—big joints hooked together by skinny sticks.

Claire dropped the bag on the floor. "I came to give you one last chance, and here you are with *her*. Cooking *Thanksgiving dinner*, no less." She switched her blazing eyes to Madi. "We don't *do* Thanksgiving. That is the day we memorialize our baby son."

She ran back outside, Park following at her heels through the boxes, lumber, and tools Cam and David had spread out in the back yard. Park jerked off the ridiculous apron as they reached the front yard. "Claire, please stop. I want to talk, but I'm not going to run after you."

She turned on him so quickly that he nearly ran into her. "How could you, Park! How could you forget Nathan?"

"I will never forget Nathan, and don't you dare accuse me of that. The image of the paramedics carrying him away is burned into my very *retinas*. But I need to move on. Surely you don't think Nathan wants his parents to live their entire lives in misery."

"Yes," she hissed, "I do."

"When are you going to get some help? This whole thing is pathological. And you've stopped eating again. You couldn't weigh more than 80 pounds. You need to be in a hospital, right now. *You are going to die* if you don't get some treatment. Do you hear me?"

"You don't have to concern yourself with that anymore."

She got in the car, rolled the window down, and shoved an envelope at him. "Here's an early Christmas present."

Park watched her drive away, torn between fear, compassion, and dislike for his wife.

The mood of the day was fractured now. He stopped at his house and guzzled a beer, then opened a second bottle. Nine o'clock in the morning, and he was drinking, although that wasn't unusual on Thanksgiving. His gut was burning, and he grabbed his ulcer medication on the way back to Madi's.

David followed him into the kitchen. Madi was sautéing onions and celery. Park sat down heavily at the desk.

"You okay?" Madi asked.

"Not really. She's upset because I'm not observing Thanksgiving properly. We always have the same meal we cooked the day Nathan died. I can tell you, to the last item, what's in that

Kroger bag. A pizza mix, an onion, chopped black olives, mozzarella cheese, and a roll of hot sausage."

Madi picked up the bag and looked in it. "Exactly."

"I just thought, if she's going to leave me, I can finally take off my hair shirt. My God, isn't twenty-four years of mourning enough?"

"Way more than enough," Madi said.

Park opened the envelope Claire had given him, his face crumpling when he took out divorce papers. He clutched his stomach and bent over for a minute, then straightened and opened his ulcer medicine, tossing back a handful of pills and downing them with beer.

David frowned and looked at Madi.

"He has a peptic ulcer," she said.

"You're taking ulcer medication by the handful? Damn, what is that?" David picked up the bottle and read the label. "Who in the hell gave you this shit?"

"I get it off the internet," Park said. "Why?"

"How long have you been taking this?"

"For years. Why?"

"Why do you get it off the internet?"

"It's cheap, cheaper even than the insurance price. It comes from Mexico. The doctor there even writes the prescription. No hassle. I never have to leave the house."

"Does your doc at M. D. Anderson know you take it?"

"No, I didn't think to tell her; isn't the stuff kind of like Tums?"

"Oh, my God, you idiot," David groaned, giving himself a dope-slap on the forehead.

"Why are you yelling at him?" Madi asked.

"Because we don't prescribe this anymore. And one of the reasons is that it causes aplastic anemia!"

Now Madi's mouth fell open. "He's had years of treatment for something that's a drug reaction? Maybe if he quits taking it, he won't need any more treatment!"

"He'll have to talk to his doctor about that, but I think it's quite possible. Damn those internet drug sales!" David poured the pills down the garbage disposal, chunked the empty bottle in the trash. "They can give him something else for his ulcer."

"You mean I might be able to stop the chemo?" Park asked, hope rising in his chest like a hot air balloon.

"Maybe," Madi said. "And maybe your bone marrow will regenerate without a transplant!"

Outside, Cam let out a howl of rage, and Madi ran out the back door to see what was wrong.

"You may have saved my life," Park said to David. "I'm deeply indebted to you."

"Pay me back by releasing your hold on Madison," David replied. "I've asked her to marry me."

"So she said. But I don't have any hold on her."

"The hell you don't. I've been invisible to her since she met you."

Good, Park wanted to say. "When Madi started therapy, she told me she distanced herself from men because they always abandoned her. I respected that, and I truly thought that I could provide a different experience for her, where she would be understood and validated, and it would make her stronger."

"That's bullshit," David said.

"No it's not."

"Sure it is. You were massaging your ego with her admiration for you, and you damn well knew she was in love with you."

"I know she thought she was in love with me. In a really good therapy, for the patient and therapist to feel a kind of love for each other is more the rule than the exception, but I've never given her a reason to believe we would have a relationship beyond that." It wasn't the truth, and he hoped it didn't show on his face.

"You condescending jackass," David snarled, "you've had

her head tied in knots for years, and you know it. You didn't have the balls to leave your wife for Madison, but now that your wife has left you, things are different."

"Madi originally came to me because *you* had her head tied in knots and refused to make a commitment, so don't point the finger at me. If you're really in the running, why hasn't she accepted your proposal?"

"I think she's waiting to see if Cam is your kid or mine."

"My kid? How could he be my kid?"

"Oh please don't pretend you weren't sleeping with her. Don't you have any scruples about screwing your patients? It seems a little predatory to me. I think you could lose your license."

Park sucked in his breath, assaulted by emotions. He was overjoyed to know his suspicions that Cam might be his child were correct, surprised that Cam might also be David's, and furious that Madi would sully his professional reputation by claiming she had slept with him. No wonder Caroline Bascomb had been so hostile. "I do not screw my patients," he said, through clenched teeth.

"Oh. So what was it, immaculate conception?"

"That may be a fairly accurate description, if my suspicions are correct. There is one, and only one way that Cam could be my child. And that is if Madi used my sperm for insemination."

"I don't understand. How would Madi get your sperm?"

"It was supposed to be banked at her clinic before I had my first round of chemo. But the clinic called and said it was discarded because it had been contaminated."

"Are you implying that she stole it and had someone tell you it had been thrown away, then used it for an insemination? I can't believe she would do that."

"I'm not implying anything," Park said. "I don't know what happened. I don't know if anything happened. But I'll tell you one thing, if Cam is my child, that is the *only* way it happened."

"I suggest we ask her. Here she comes."

* * *

Even though the sun was shining, it was raining lightly when Madison ran outside to see why Cam was screaming. He stood by the tree house with his hands held over the sign he'd nailed to the door, trying to keep the rain off of it.

"Come here," she called.

"No," he wailed, "my sign will get wet."

"Come on, we'll make a better one that rain can't hurt."

He stomped across the yard. In the kitchen, the air was charged. David and Park looked at each other like two bulls squaring off. On the stove, the butter she was melting for the dressing was burning.

Wondering what in the world had happened in the minute she was outside, she took the pan off the stove and turned off the burner, then dried Cam's face, hair and arms. "You're tired. I want you to go in the living room and rest. I'll bring you a sandwich."

"I'm not tired," Cam protested. "And I'm not hungry. I just need a new sign."

"Don't argue. Go on, you can sit in my red chair. Scoot."

"Fine," he said sulkily. "Come on, trundle-tail." Dudley obediently followed him out of the room.

Madison took the turkey out of the sink and plopped it in the pan she had prepared, then put the onion pan in the sink and ran hot water in it, sending up a sizzling cloud of steam.

"David," she said irritably, "why didn't you take the pan off the heat? Can't you smell something burning?"

"I guess I was preoccupied with a conversation about paternity."

Madison's heart lurched. She took bologna, bread, and mayonnaise from the refrigerator and busied herself making Cam's sandwich. Her hand shook as she cut the sandwich in quarters.

"It seems that some of Park's sperm may have been misappropriated from the Memphis clinic," David continued. "Do you know anything about that?"

Damn it, Park must have figured it out and told David. Now she would have to explain it to both of them. The thought made her physically ill. "No," she said.

She delivered Cam's sandwich, came back, took the pies out of the oven, put the turkey in. Forget the dressing, she needed out of this room.

"We need to talk about this," David said.

"There's nothing to talk about."

David set his jaw, and red crept up his neck. "Oh, yes there is. Park, you got any more beer?"

"No."

"Fine. I'll go get some. Then the three of us are going to sit down and have a long, detailed discussion about our problem."

"There's nothing to discuss," Madison said.

David disappeared around the corner.

"Take my car," she yelled. "You can't carry beer on the bike."

"Do it all the time," he yelled back.

"Well, put your brain bucket on!"

Swearing under her breath, Madison washed the onion pan and wiped the counters. Outside, David revved the motorcycle, and she heard him peel out. She took out dishes and silverware to set the table for dinner, and found napkins and the Thanksgiving tablecloth. She was running out of things to do. Park just sat there, staring at her.

Finally, he said, "Did you tell David I slept with you?"

There was a hard note in Park's voice that she'd never heard. Madison willed time to stop. She could not face this moment. In the distance, she heard a siren, someone having a worse day than she was. If that were possible.

"Well, did you?" Park asked.

She didn't want to reveal her secret unless she absolutely had to, although her conscience urged her to confess. If only she had the results of the blood tests, she would know who Cam's father was; she would know what to do. "I never told anyone I slept with you," she said. That was technically true. She hadn't told David she'd slept with Park, although she'd let him assume it. "David is jealous of you, and he has his own ideas about us."

"Okay. Then why does he think Cam might be my child? There's only one other way. You know it, and I know it."

She couldn't meet his gaze. In slow circles, she continued to wipe the already spotless counter. Silence spun out. The siren came closer.

"Excuse me just a minute," Madison said, "it sounds like that siren is in the neighborhood." She escaped to the living room. *Think*, she urged herself. *Think fast.* Pretending to be concerned about a disaster outside wouldn't deflect Park's questions for long.

As she expected, David's motorcycle helmet was still on the coffee table, where he'd left it earlier. Stubborn ass; didn't he know most accidents happened within a mile of home? Besides that, he was a doctor. He'd treated enough victims of motorcycle accidents to know that medical personnel called them "donorcycles."

She looked out the front window, where the street sloped down to intersect with MacGregor. A black SUV was stopped in the intersection. Madison's heart skipped a beat, lurched into the arrhythmia. David's motorcycle was on its side under the SUV, and he was sprawled in the street beside it.

She starting running on jelly legs, wanting to get there quickly and not at all. It seemed like she was running in slow motion. She could see blood running down the side of David's head, pooling on the street. *God, please don't let him be dead. Please, please, please.*

A man with a cell phone in his hand stood beside David, looking dazed. "He tried to stop, but the streets are slick, and he slid right under me. I think I dragged him a little."

Madison knelt beside David and called his name. He didn't respond. A huge gash across the left side of his forehead spurted blood. She pressed her palm against the gash to stop the bleeding, but otherwise, her mind was blank, her medical education inaccessible. She didn't know what to do next.

The sirens were deafening now. A firefighter appeared and knelt at David's head.

"My name is Randy. I'm a paramedic," he said.

"Hi Randy," she said, responding like she was in an AA meeting.

He checked for a pulse, watched David's chest rise and fall, placed his hands on either side of David's head, holding it gently in alignment.

"You keep that pressure on his forehead, Ma'am, just like you're doing, but we don't want his head to move one inch."

More firefighters surrounded them, carrying bags of equipment. Randy started barking orders, his intensity frightening her even more. "I want 100% oxygen, and get an IV in him."

Everything seemed to be happening at once. David's vital signs were checked, and a cervical collar was put on his neck. Somebody took Madison's hand off his forehead, and applied a pressure dressing to the wound. "Okay, Ma'am, you can step aside, now."

Madison moved to the curb, David's sticky blood drying on her hand, copper smell nauseating her. In the early part of her career, she had worked in the Operating Room of a trauma center, and had known exactly how to care for someone with injuries like David's; but she was not trained as a first responder, and was now relegated to the role of helpless onlooker.

Not until David was on a spine board with foam wedges on either side of his head secured with tape and a cervical collar on his neck did the firefighter release his head. An ambulance finally arrived, and a paramedic strode toward them, firing questions.

"Is he breathing? Does he have a pulse?"

"Yes," Randy replied.

"Is he conscious? Was he wearing a helmet?"

"No helmet. Responsive to painful stimuli only. Blood pressure is low. A little road rash, but no fractures. You're good to load and go."

Now the police were asking Madison questions, but she couldn't answer; she was focused on David's swelling face, the blood trickling from his nose. A circle of onlookers stood around them. Flashing lights on the fire truck, ambulance, and police car gave the scene a surreal feeling. She heard a child crying, and turned to look back at her house. Park stood on the front porch, holding Cam on his hip, trying to calm him.

They loaded David into the ambulance and strapped Madison in the front seat. "Where are you taking him?" she asked.

"Ben Taub."

"No, take him to Methodist."

"Sorry, Ma'am. We have to follow protocol. He goes to the trauma center."

It's better, she said to herself. The trauma center is better. She could move him to a private hospital later. They left with lights and siren, and she craned her neck to see what was going on in the back of the ambulance.

She couldn't see the EKG monitor, but she could hear it beeping. She mentally calculated his heart rate. Too fast. The paramedic checked David's blood pressure again, then flipped the IV wide open. He was giving David a fluid bolus, which meant his blood pressure was too low. David lay flaccid on the stretcher, blood soaking through the bandage on his forehead.

Madison frantically searched her memory for her neuro education, but it escaped her. All she could think of was closed head injury, bleeding in the brain. Blood pressure low, heart rate high. Shock.

Death.

The paramedic picked up a radio mike. "Ben Taub, this is Houston Fire, Unit 32."

Madison heard some static, then, "Go ahead, Unit 32."

"Ben Taub, we're in route to your facility with a 42-year-old white male, motorcycle versus SUV accident. Victim was the driver of the motorcycle, found unconscious on scene, no helmet. Still unconscious but responsive to pain, vital signs . . ."

All of this started with a single, dishonest act. Madison saw herself in Memphis, sliding Park's sperm into her pocket, walking out of the clinic. Years later, David lay in an ambulance, possibly dying, all because of her stupidity. Her mind jumped to the Operating Room, visualizing him on the table, bags of blood and IVs with orange stickers keeping his blood pressure up, clumps of thick, wavy hair falling to the floor, drill in a neurosurgeon's hand to open up his skull, swelling in his brain reducing him to a vegetable.

Her stomach cramped and her chest heaved as she tried to hold back tears. A tiny whimper escaped her.

"It's okay, let it out," said the driver, manipulating the ambulance onto the freeway, weaving in and out of cars. That did it; the floodgates of her grief opened and it all came out.

By the time they arrived at Ben Taub and backed into the ambulance bay, she was under control again, although she was shaking all over. On wobbly legs, she followed the stretcher into the Emergency Room.

The hospital was freezing and smelled like an elementary school bathroom, Pine Sol covering up urine. Emergency room personnel converged on David, while the paramedic gave report. Madison was sent to register him while a CAT scan was being done. She went to the bathroom first. She looked like hell, face ashen, long hair tangled, David's blood caked on her hands and smeared across her clothing.

David's blood. She watched it run down the drain as she scrubbed it away. "Please don't let him die," she whispered to the amorphous God in whom she tried to believe. "Don't let him die because of me."

If only God would let him live, she would make it all right.

Somehow.

* * *

David's CAT scan was negative, but he had a concussion, and he was admitted for observation. Madison stayed at his side, assessing his neuro status hourly, which she knew the county hospital staff probably wouldn't do adequately, if at all. He looked like Godzilla. The left side of his face was black and blue, his eye was swollen shut, and he had a huge knot on his head. The skin on his right arm and leg looked like it had been sanded. The wound on his forehead had been repaired by a plastic surgeon. But it seemed he had escaped serious injury.

Madison bowed her head and said a prayer of thanks. Thanks that he was okay, and oddly, thanks for the accident. For it had taken seeing him in the middle of the street, bleeding and unconscious, to make her realize that it was David she loved, always had loved, and every other relationship in between was only an attempt to find a substitute for him.

She remembered a conversation with her psychiatrist, Dr. Rose, who had tried to explain the difference between true love and transference to a therapist.

"A good therapist provides unconditional acceptance, like a parent. Don't you remember the feeling of being daddy's little girl?"

Madison had looked at her blankly. Her father, a traveling salesman who was home for maybe one weekend every couple of weeks all her life, was a kind but distant man who mowed the lawn, had his car serviced, watched the football game, spanked her oldest brother for his ongoing list of crimes, and left town again. He never refused a request from his children, but neither did he show any interest in them, whatsoever.

Daddy's little girl? She had no conception of such a feeling. Mommy's little albatross was the feeling the children in her family grew up with, because most of the burden of raising a large family had fallen on her.

194

Like the father she wished she had, Park had provided that special feeling of being understood, of unconditional love. But Park went home when the fifty-minute hour was over, and had moved out of town at the worst possible point in Madison's therapy.

David, on the other hand, had been with her from the time she had met him, patiently helping her through crises, returning to her side without bitterness after she had pushed him away.

He was the one who was her Lamaze coach, who cut the cord when Cam was born, who brought antibiotics and Pedialyte in the middle of the night when Cam was sick. He'd worked tirelessly at her side after her house flooded, helped carry her soaked belongings to the curb, paid for repairs she couldn't afford, held her when she cried bitterly over the loss of uninsured belongings, replaced her furniture. Unlike most people, he got her subtle jokes. He was a competent and compassionate physician, and she loved working with him because he valued her opinion about the patients. When she'd been an Operating Room nurse in Memphis, he'd demanded her for his circulating nurse, ever appreciative of her attention to detail and her obsessive care of patients under general anesthesia, who couldn't speak for themselves.

Madison took the ring off her necklace and slid it onto her finger. It was a beautiful ring, exactly what she would have chosen. David always knew exactly what she wanted, when it came to material things. Maybe she would just have to accept the fact that he wasn't good at expressing his emotions in words, and had to show his love with gifts.

Over the years, they had settled into a comfortable and stable life, like a marriage that had survived the storm of romantic love, and she couldn't imagine life without him.

When she looked up, he was awake, giving her a crooked grin. He looked at her hand with his good eye. "Is that a yes?" he asked, through a fat lip.

She wondered if he realized he still hadn't said the words

she longed to hear. From David, just one "I love you" would be enough to last a lifetime. But that might never happen. "It's a yes, Dr. Frankenstein."

"Do I look that bad?"

"You look that bad."

"I want to see." He tried to sit up, but the pain stopped him. "Damn, I feel like I've been hit by a truck."

Madison laughed.

"That's funny?" he asked, sounding genuinely confused.

"You *were* hit by a truck, you dummy."

"Oh. Judging by the reverb in my head, I'd say I got a pretty good head bonk. Do you think there's any permanent brain damage? Will I still be able to play the piano?"

She smiled, and fed into the old joke. "Sorry, you won't be able to play the piano, Sir. But on the other hand, you couldn't play the piano before your head bonk. And as for permanent brain damage, you would have to have a brain first."

David slid his hand into hers. "Do you know that I love you, Madison Templeton?" he asked quietly, and she wished she could live the rest of her life in the silken waterfall of endorphins that his words produced.

"I love you, too, David."

"Get the hospital chaplain. I want to get married before you change your mind."

"First, we have to talk about your apparent death wish."

"What death wish?"

"Don't you remember what happened today?"

"Not really," he said. "I remember working on the tree house, but nothing after that. I guess I dropped the bike?"

"You were going to the 'Stop-and-Rob' for beer. It had rained for a few minutes, and the streets were slick. Of course, your helmet was protecting the living room table, instead of your thick skull. You skidded at the end of the street, and wound up under an SUV. You're damn lucky to be alive. The neurosurgeon said you might have some short-term memory loss. Do you remember who the current president is?"

"Saddam Hussein?" David said, attempting to laugh when she took him seriously.

"Not funny, David. Just for that, I won't help you to the bathroom. You can use a nice, cold bedpan."

"Okay, okay, uncle."

"Promise me, no more motorcycles."

"I'll get rid of the bike tomorrow."

"Well, you may have to surgically remove it from the bottom of the SUV first. You also need to get rid of the hang glider."

"Now, I don't know about that. You may want to take one trip over the Grand Canyon before we get rid of it. It's like being a bird."

"No fair," she said. He knew about her frequent dreams of flying over the countryside, and that if she had to be reincarnated as an animal, it would be as an eagle. "Speaking of the Grand Canyon—do we have to move to Utah?"

"Madison, you'd love it there. Why don't you want to move?"

"It's just so far from Emma and Dane." And Park, she thought, who still occupied a large portion of her heart.

"I have a plane, remember? I'll take you home anytime you want to go."

"I'm not sure I want to go flying with you, Humpty-Dumpty."

"We'll wear helmets."

"Now why didn't I think of that? Helmets will make it perfectly safe. When were you planning to move? I just can't go off and leave Park, until something is settled about his treatment. He needs help. And I'll have to train another IVF nurse."

David's smile gradually faded. His fingers searched out the ring on her hand, as if to reassure himself that her commitment hadn't disappeared when she voiced her concern about Park.

"Don't worry, love," Madison said. "I've got it figured out now, and I'm not going to change my mind. Go back to sleep, and we'll talk when you're feeling better."

He drifted back into sleep, his hand clenching hers like a toddler whose mother was leading him from a blazing house.

Madison called Park to fill him in and check on Cam, then went to the cafeteria to get a cup of coffee. When she came back, Basc was coming out of David's room.

"He looks like hell," she said, smiling. "Serves him right. How are you?"

Madison swallowed hard. "Basc, I never felt so helpless. I thought he was dead, I forgot everything I ever knew about medicine, all I could think to do was put pressure on his head, where it was bleeding."

Basc put an arm around Madison and walked her to the lounge, listening to the story that came out all on one string.

"I didn't even think to see if he had a pulse or if he was breathing," Madison said. "How dumb is that? I'm a nurse; I can think on my feet; what was wrong with me?"

"It's called shock," Basc said, soothingly. "That's why we don't treat our own families and friends. We can't think clearly."

"David has to stop acting like Evel Knievel."

"He still has some growing up to do. And I'm not sure being around me is helping him."

"Well, he still feels like he's just an intern, without a say in anything."

"I've heard he had a job offer at the University of Utah in Salt Lake."

"Really?"

Basc eyed her. "He didn't tell you?"

"No." It was true; he wanted to move to Utah, but he hadn't mentioned a job in Salt Lake. "How did you find out?"

"I know the Dean at the university. Madison, if you know

what his plans are, as a friend, you need to tell me. The current Fellow finishes in June, and we'd like to offer him David's job. But he has other offers, so it's imperative to find out now."

"I think you should ask David," Madison said. "I don't know the answer, but even if I did, I wouldn't feel obligated to betray a confidence for your convenience."

Basc seemed affronted by Madison's blunt refusal to provide the requested information. "There are times when it's appropriate to share confidential information."

"Maybe, but his isn't one of them, in my opinion."

"Am I going to have to torture it out of you?"

"What are you, the Mafia?" Madison asked, laughing to break the tension.

"What are you, the moral majority?"

Madison saw an opportunity to find out what Basc would do about the sperm heist. "Sometimes, I can't fight my way out of a wet paper bag in terms of morality. For instance, I'm working on a new novel, but I'm stuck with a dilemma. Here's the plot: An IVF nurse is asked to throw away sperm contaminated with soap residue. She discovers it's the sperm of her shrink, with whom she is insanely in love. She has a baby, but the paternity is uncertain. The IVF director finds out. What should she do?"

"Well, first, she needs make sure the nurse and the baby haven't contracted anything, like AIDS or hepatitis C, et cetera."

Sweat popped out on Madison's brow. She hadn't even thought about that.

"Then," Basc continued, "the director has no choice but to fire her, and report her to Human and Legal Resources."

"Don't you think that's a little harsh? After all, the sperm was headed for the garbage."

"She took his DNA!"

"Well, the police take DNA out of the garbage all the time."

"They don't make babies with it."

"Okay, suppose the baby is not the result of the insemination."

"That just means parental rights won't be an issue. The nurse's behavior was unethical and immoral, and she should be reported to the State Board of Nursing."

Basc's reaction was worse than she anticipated. "What if the shrink's behavior was unethical, which caused the nurse's judgment to be impaired?"

"The shrink! What did he do?"

She should have known that playing the human weakness card wouldn't work with Basc, who seemed to have lived a life without mistakes. Madison wondered if any of the major traumas of life—the death of a parent, the empty nest, the loss of a great love—would soften her up. She needed another tactic; she'd try Psycho Jeopardy. Answer a question with a question. "What if the nurse were someone the director loved?"

"No one I love would do that."

Wrong, wrong, wrong, Madison thought. "That's cheating. Try to be open minded. Imagine that you have a daughter, Caroline Jr., and she's the culprit."

"Then Caroline Jr. would probably go to jail. I've got a better idea for your plot. What if there had been some kind of mistake," Basc said. "What if the sperm had been mislabeled? It sounds like there were some unusual things going on in the andrology lab that day. Put a new employee in there or something."

"That won't work. It will change the whole premise of the story."

They walked slowly back to David's room. He was sleeping. Someone had put an ice pack on his head.

"He needs someone to watch him tomorrow," Basc said. "I'll pick him up in the morning. He can spend the weekend at my house."

"That's okay. He's going home with me. I'm off until

Monday."

"Okay. I'll check on him tomorrow. Call me if you need anything."

"You could drop off a set of scrubs. They cut his clothes off in the ER."

"You got it."

Throughout the night, Madison obsessed about her problem. She'd told herself that Cam's conception was nobody's business but hers. She had never expected to see Park again; hadn't she lost people all her life?

But Park had turned up again, and now she saw the ripple effect of her actions: Cam pining for a father; Park's marriage and reputation adversely affected; David's distrust; the possible loss of her job and nursing license; possible criminal charges; her child a source of a cure for an adult's disease, loss of Basc's respect, her own confusion and guilt. The problems just kept multiplying, and she needed to put an end to it. She couldn't go on living this lie. Spending the rest of her life looking over her shoulder was a direct path back to the bottle.

And that was simply not an option.

CHAPTER NINE

After the ambulance left, Park took Cam back in the house. The little boy stood at the front window, hiccupping and sniffling, watching as the accident scene was cleared. Efforts to distract him were rebuffed, and Park decided to leave him alone until he voluntarily left the window.

Park felt restless, at a loss for what he should be doing. The aroma of turkey was filling the house. He didn't know if it took one hour or ten to cook a turkey, or if there was anything he needed to do to it; but he had a vague idea that it need basting, or something.

In the kitchen, he peeked in the oven. The bird was in some kind of a bag, so apparently it didn't need basting. It had a red thingie stuck in its chest. Park fished through the garbage until he found the soggy turkey wrappings, and read the instructions. Apparently the red thing would pop up when the turkey was done.

He let Dudley in and gave him some water; the dog seemed to be upset too, panting and pacing nervously. Not a dog person, he patted the little guy, not really knowing how to comfort him.

Park was not much of a hand in regular life, he realized. He and Claire had been suspended in a bubble of unreality, floating above life in an attempt to avoid the sinkhole of pain that threatened to engulf them. They attended the opera and ballet instead of cuddling up on the couch to watch a movie; went to expensive restaurants instead of cooking dinner together; hired a gardener instead of working in the yard. And Park was always working, working so his brain could never settle down to the baseline of his failed marriage, working to make more and more money for Claire to squander.

Cam was still at the window when Park returned to the living room, and he decided just to sit quietly beside the child until the drama outside released him. Writing often helped Park figure things out when his emotions were tangled, and he booted Madi's laptop and started free-associating, pain flying from his fingertips.

His thoughts turned to the other Thanksgiving day filled with the flashing lights of emergency vehicles, a day that had changed his life irrevocably. Now Madi was having a Thanksgiving day from hell. He wished he could be there for her, to help her wait for the outcome, catch her when her knees buckled from fear, let her know she wasn't alone.

He didn't know the extent of David's injuries, but the accident alone made Park's fear of death flare; life could be over far sooner than one expected. Park had things to do before he died: Write a book, teach aspiring psychologists what he knew, tell Madison he loved her.

The accident might provoke a similar feeling in her, and he didn't know which way it would push her. Although she knew he and Claire were having problems, she didn't really know what was going on in Park's head. She might accept David's proposal; there was no time to waste. It had taken a while, but Park was now certain that his feelings for her were genuine, and not countertransference. Madi had paid him to listen to her and say all the right things; she had fallen for him, even though she really didn't know him. But he hadn't paid her. And although he was keenly aware that a therapist's perception of a patient was largely dependent on how honest and self-disclosing the patient was, he still believed he knew Madi well, and that she was the same person, inside or outside of his office. They were fundamentally alike, and belonged together. Ethics be damned, he wanted her in his life permanently.

After an hour, the last emergency vehicle roared away, taking David's twisted red motorcycle. So much for that little Beamer, which had probably cost more than his own car, Park thought, Shakespeare's "green ey'd monster" overtaking his better self.

Cam crawled up in his lap, and he kissed the little boy on the top of his head. Cam smiled up at him, sweetly. "That's what Mom does when I feel bad; she kisses my head on the top." He snuggled deeper into Park's lap. "Are you writing down how you feel? Mom does that all the time. I can't read it, though. She writes in cursive when she feels bad."

"That's called journaling, when you write about your feelings."

"Yeah, I know that. I got a journal, remember? I write on my computer, but Mom writes on black paper with special pens. Her tablets are in the basket under the table. Do you want to see?"

Do I ever, Park thought. He never could resist peeking into other people's heads, Madison's especially, but he said, "Well, maybe I should ask your Mom first." It sounded saintly, but it was a lie; as soon as Cam was asleep, Park knew he would go for her journals. Maybe she had written something about her current state of mind.

Park had never experienced love as passionate as he felt for Madi; he could not believe some of the things he was thinking, doing, saying. He should document his own behavior. It certainly was out of character. If he and Madi ever got around to writing their shrink/client book together, those emotions would need to be explained. Because even if there were no rules written in stone, he would feel obligated to justify his behavior.

Or rationalize it, he amended, with a bit more honesty.

He opened a new document and moved the laptop over so Cam could reach the keys. "Let's see if you can write down some feelings."

"What should I write?"

"How about a story about your day? First give it a title, like 'Thanksgiving Day.'"

"Okay." With two fingers, Cam laboriously typed, "how klar messed up thanksgiving."

"Do you mean Claire?"

"Yeah, 'course. That's what I wrote."

Equal parts of amusement and pain balled up in Park's chest. Cam was right; things had been going fairly well until Claire showed up. "You spelled 'Thanksgiving' perfectly. That is so good."

"Yeah, my teacher wrote it on the board when we were learning about the pilgrims." He pushed the computer back toward Park. "You write. It's too hard for me. I'm just a kid."

"Okay," Park said. "What do you want to put in your story?"

"I don't know."

"Well, how did your day start?"

"Good."

Park typed, "It was a good day."

"And then me and David built the tree house, and it rained on my sign, then Claire came over and everybody got mad."

Park added that to the story. "What happened next?"

"David fell off his bike and caught on fire." Cam looked up at Park, his eyes filling with tears. "Did the fire truck put him out?"

"David wasn't on fire, Cam."

"Well, did he get a head bonk? He didn't wear his brain bucket. That's a rule."

Park nearly burst out laughing at Cam's use of his mother's terminology. "David is going to be just fine," he said, even though he didn't know if it were true.

Cam turned and put his arms around Park's neck, laying his head on Park's shoulder. "I hope you always live next door," he said.

Park rubbed Cam's back, the warm weight of the child on his chest filling a place that had been empty too long. "Me, too. I bet you're tired. Why don't you lie down for a little while?"

He moved Cam to the daybed, surprised not to get an argument. The child fell asleep immediately, and Park dived for Madi's journals.

There were multiple spiral-bound books of black paper, with pages and pages of writing in opaque pastel pens, documenting Madi's struggle with alcohol. The three-month pink cloud, a promise of a better life, falling through the mist into depression again. Pushing through the pain, doing the hard work. Page after page begging God to remove her desire to drink.

Sessions with her Houston psychiatrist, Dr. Rose. Park's own lack of understanding of the three-pronged attack of alcoholism—emotional, spiritual, physical. His inability to help her, his needs contributing to her confusion. Dr. Rose's disapproval of him, her upper lip curled in distaste. Madi's defense.

Dr. Rose: He should have found you another therapist before he left.

Madi: He tried. I refused. I honestly believe he just looked up and found his emotional boat way out in the navy blue water with me, with no idea how he got there, and no idea how to get back.

Dr. Rose: And then he gets scared, asks himself if he is "too interested in this woman," a telling question. Deserts you, leaving you with the same loves me, loves me not confusion that was the reason you were seeing him to begin with.

Madi: In all fairness, there simply wouldn't have been an easy way for us to disengage.

Dr. Rose: It was the holding you needed, not an emotional

affair. Therapy is about the holding.

Madi: That's exactly what he did. He held me. With his eyes, with his sweet, soothing voice, with his words. He held my soul in his arms like an armful of flowers. No wonder I wanted to spend every second with him. No wonder sex with him was unthinkable; no wonder I would rather talk to him, rather sit in his lap with my head on his shoulder, thumb in my mouth, than sleep with him.

Park's eyes skidded back to the beginning of that last innocent-looking sentence, his plans to pursue Madi grinding to a halt.

He'd had it right all along—these were the feelings of a child for a parent. This was transference. It wasn't her fault that he'd been misled; he could not imagine a more honest, disclosing, hard working patient, a delight to him, both personally and professionally. No, the fault was his.

Having just admitted to himself that he truly loved her, this was an unbearable blow. Sitting in her house, reading her intimate thoughts, loving her child, out in the navy blue water with her again, Park thought bitterly about why shrinks needed to be vigilant about maintaining professional boundaries. As Cam had said, with the simple wisdom of a four-year-old, "That's a rule."

And if Park had followed the rule, he could have saved both Madi and himself a lot of pain. But the truth was, if he had it all to do over again, he would probably do the same thing; he was helpless in his love for her. For the first time, he felt the full impact of the pain she must have felt when he'd left her.

There was one beer left in the fridge, and Park went for it, dulling his pain the same way she used to. Now he wanted out of her house, away from her, so he could hide and lick his wounds. No wonder she had moved to Houston. In Memphis, like she said, she would have been reminded of him everywhere she went; they worked in the same place, lived in the same area, even ran into each other doing recreational things. Now karma repaid him in like fashion.

At three, Park checked the turkey. Its red navel had popped out, and he took it out of the oven. Following the directions on the box, he managed to make a reasonable facsimile of dressing, so dinner would be ready when Madi came home.

He tried to call Claire; no answer. He tried to call her parents; no answer. Another big problem eating at his soul; another woman in serious trouble because of him.

Madison finally called at five. "Hey Park, sorry I ran off and left you with Cam. I was just insane, seeing David lying there in the street, unconscious, with blood gushing out of his head."

"Of course you had to go with him. How is he?"

"Banged up, but okay. If you don't mind watching Cam, I'm going to stay at the hospital tonight. David needs his neuro status checked every hour, to make sure his brain isn't swelling."

Park's heart sank. Now he would be stuck in her house all night.

"Sure," he said, hollowly. "Cam and I will be fine. Dinner is ready—the turkey is done, and I made the dressing, although it doesn't have onions in it."

"What, no onions? Shame. Well, Cam will eat the dressing that way, but don't try to feed him turkey. It gags him. Just nuke a frozen dinner for him."

"Okay. How will we coordinate things in the morning? I have to be at Anderson at eight."

"Do you mind dropping Cam off at school? I doubt if David will be discharged that early. We'll just take a cab home."

"That's fine. And Madi, at some point tomorrow, I want to finish the discussion we were having when David got hurt." He needed some closure on that conversation; no matter what had happened, he could not let her tarnish his professional reputation by letting people think he slept with his patients. And he had to find out if there were a possibility that Cam was his son.

"Okay," she said, her voice small. "We'll talk tomorrow."

Park stared moodily out the window, across the street at the grassy banks of the bayou, where his love for Madison had exploded. Now he had to gather it up and put it away again. But it would be like picking ten pounds of confetti out of a field of Bermuda grass.

* * *

On Friday morning, the bruises on David's face, arms, and legs had deepened to variegated hues of navy and purple. He was stiff and sore, and, no surprise, had a pounding headache. Brows drawn into a frown, he'd slept restlessly, jumping awake at intervals, hand scrabbling for Madison in the dark.

"I'm right here," she'd said a dozen times, and he would drift back into his twilight sleep. At one point he'd mumbled, "I'm gonna be hurt really bad," and, "She's gonna be so pissed."

Madison presumed that meant her; normally, she did get mad at his carelessness. But happy as she was that he'd agreed to give up some of his dangerous hobbies, it hurt her to see this David, finally suffering the consequences of his devil-may-care behavior. It was as if he'd lost a part of himself that she loved, the exuberant, invincible little boy, exasperating as he might be.

Before breakfast, she washed his face and hands, gently scrubbing away blood and muddy gravel and brown antiseptic. She helped him into the scrubs Basc had brought from the office. He followed her instructions as if they were something he wouldn't have thought of, left to his own devices.

After another brain scan, he was discharged, and they took a cab to her house. With his battered face and the bandage wrapped all the way around his head to keep the dressing on his forehead in place, David looked like a wounded veteran, returning from war. Madison steadied him as he limped into the house.

"If this keeps up," he said, "you're going to have to name your house 'The Madison Templeton Memorial Hospital.'"

"Yeah, well, housekeeping in this hospital leaves something to be desired," she replied, kicking toys scattered across the living room floor out of the way. Her tables were covered with dirty dishes, juice boxes, and books. Dudley had a silver candy wrapper, a shriveled-up pickle, and a turkey bone in his bed.

"Aw, give 'em a break. Guys can't help being messy."

"Yes, I've noticed that their retinas are not completely developed. They can't see dirty clothes or dishes or junk on every flat surface," she said, putting the turkey bone on the dining room table, so it wouldn't lacerate Dudley's small intestine.

David laughed. "Madison Templeton, squasher of all fun. I need to loosen you up."

"Not."

She settled him in her bedroom, where it would be dark and quiet, and ordered him to sleep for a while. Then she started setting her house to rights, kitchen first, irritated with herself for being irritated. After all, she'd left Cam with Park, who knew nothing about taking care of a small child, and obviously, even less about running a house; now she wanted to critique the job.

The most important thing, she scolded herself, was that Cam had been taken care of properly. Park had finished cooking the turkey and even managed to make the boxed dressing, but he'd left the kitchen in a mess. Toys left out were one thing, but dirty dishes drew "hoarches," as she had dubbed her occasional visitors, the disgusting four-inch long Texas palmetto bugs that she said were a cross between a horse and a roach.

She straightened up the living room and Cam's room, then took a shower, washed her hair, and, with a sigh, sank into her recliner for a nap.

At noon, Park called from the transplant coordinator's office at M. D. Anderson. He sounded funny, and Madison assumed that neither she, Cam, nor David had been a match. "What's wrong?"

"Nothing," he said, but his voice had a note of discomfort that contradicted his words. "I just wanted to tell you that the test results are back, and we have a match."

"Really? That's great!" Madison's spirits simultaneously soared and plunged. Cam was the only one who could reasonably be expected to match, which meant he was Park's son and could donate stem cells that would save Park's life, if he needed a transplant. And it meant that Park had to know she'd stolen the sperm. Heart pounding, she said, "Cam matched?"

"Not Cam. You."

"Me?"

"Yes, you're a nearly a perfect match."

Madison's spirits sank. "Oh, great, they've mixed up my specimen with Cam's." She'd assumed M.D. Anderson would be flawless in handling potential donor specimens, but apparently, they were just as subject to laboratory error as any other hospital. Now she and Cam would have to have blood drawn again.

There was silence on the line, and Madison realized she'd prematurely given herself away by implying that only Cam could match Park. There would be no further waffling—she would have to tell him the whole story—today.

"They didn't mix up the specimens," Park said. "Cam has antigens from his parents—you and David, although he is a two-antigen match for me."

So David was Cam's father, and she had revealed her ugly little secret unnecessarily. "How many antigens did I match?"

"Six."

"Six! But—doesn't that only happen in siblings, who have antigens from each of their parents?"

"Yes. They're saying I'm your brother."

Madison took the phone away from her ear and looked at it as if it had turned into a hoarch. David shuffled into the room and lay down on the daybed.

"Well, that's crazy. I'm not related to you," Madison said, but data points were rushing into her mind, all the things that she'd thought were some sort of metaphysical magic but perhaps were neither serendipitous nor coincidental: That she and Park had lived so close to each other, liked the same things, shared a birthday, went to the same high school. That her father knew Park's mother, that Park's picture was in the family photo album.

"I told them that, but they say the odds of an unrelated donor matching that closely are incalculable."

"My God," Madison said, her mind reeling with the implications.

"Madi, can you call your father and ask him about this?"

"Yes, of course."

"Okay. I'll be home in an hour."

She hung up, staring at David in shock.

"What was that all about?" he asked.

"That was Park. I'm a donor match."

"You! Man, that's odd. How many antigens?"

"Six."

"But a match that close only happens in siblings."

"Right. That's exactly what they're saying."

David laughed. "Yatzee! This gets worse and worse. You screwed your brother. Who was your shrink."

"David, I know you have a concussion, but do you really have to be so inappropriate?"

"Well, did you sleep with him or not?"

"Not," she said emphatically. "I did not."

"Then why did you think Park might be Cam's father? Did you use his sperm for an insemination?"

"Yes," she whispered, her heart twisting with pain. "How did you know?"

"Park suspected it."

"I was supposed to discard the specimen, but I took it, instead." Madison walked across the room and perched on the edge of the coffee table. "David, I was so devastated when Park left, I became completely obsessed with him. I did a lot of things I regret."

"And did the insemination work?"

"No. Cam is your son."

David just smiled, as if he knew it all along. "Then everything is okay."

"No, it's not. I have to get this straightened out. I have to explain it to Park, and I have to tell Basc."

"Why do you have to tell her? That's suicide."

"Because my actions are reflecting on Park professionally. And I can't live with that."

"You know how inflexible Basc is. She'll probably fire you, and maybe even prosecute. Did you ever let her think you'd had an affair with him?"

"No. She just thought he used me to bolster his ego."

"Then I don't see what telling her would accomplish. It just sounds like self-flagellation, at Cam's expense. Stop being a martyr and think a little bit."

"I'm not trying to be a martyr! I'm just trying to keep my life on the straight and narrow. At the time, it seemed like it would be my secret. I never dreamed of the complications it would cause. And I certainly never thought you, Cam, and I would be a family."

"A family," he said, tasting the words like they were a bite of chocolate chip cookie, straight from the oven. "When shall we tell Cam?"

"I don't know. Right now, I need to call my father and ask him some hard questions."

"Okay. I'll give you some privacy." David kissed her, then shuffled back to her bedroom and closed the door.

Madison did not want to call her father. She had a bad feeling about this, like she was about to force her father into revealing a secret he intended to take to his grave. He answered on the fourth ring, sounding out of breath.

"Hi Dad," she said. "Are you okay? Why are you breathing so hard?"

"I was out in the garage."

"Dad," she said hesitantly, "something really strange just

happened. I was tested to be a bone marrow donor for a friend, and the test came back showing that he's my brother."

"What's wrong with him? Is it serious?"

Not "that's crazy," or "boy, they better do that test over," but "what's wrong with him?" There was fear in his voice, urgency. She knew it was true, then.

"He has a condition called aplastic anemia, but we think he's going to be fine. Dad, did you have a kid with another woman?"

There was a long silence and she could picture him in his standard yard work attire, a threadbare khaki jumpsuit and beat-up black wingtips, both covered with the graffiti of myriad projects, paint and grease and grass stains. Mopping his brow with the white cotton handkerchief he always had in his pocket.

Finally he said, sounding weary and defeated, "I knew this would happen sooner or later. Yes, you have another brother. His name is Park. But I didn't have an affair. We allowed him to be adopted."

There was so much pain in her father's voice, she knew the decision about Park had not been taken lightly. Her father seemed more of a stranger than ever, but more understandable, a man with a pocket of pain deep inside, like a sterile abscess.

"We always wanted to tell you kids," he continued, "but we talked to two psychiatrists who said to leave it alone, that Park would find us if he wanted to."

Madison tried to imagine what it would be like to find out as an adult that you were adopted. Maybe like growing up Catholic and suddenly finding out you were really Jewish, trying to assimilate different rituals and language and customs that seemed completely bizarre, even if they were, in reality, no more bizarre than those you knew.

How could you function in a family you didn't know? What if you didn't know your Dad got palpitations when he drank coffee, your youngest brother was allergic to sesame seeds, your sister was born without a thyroid and was dependent on medication to stay alive? What would bond you to your brothers if you didn't know their secrets: That one could fake your mother's signature on an excuse if you wanted to skip school, one knew where your sister hid her diary, and all the places your mother hid cash? How could you not know all the names of the family dogs, Pugsley and Charlie Brown and Cujo? That Dad liked to make popcorn with bacon grease, garlic salt, and pepper? That your mother couldn't pass up a cinnamon roll, and was a tyrant with the broken heart of a little girl who felt unloved by her own parents?

"I don't understand," she said. "How did one kid get adopted? What difference would one more kid have made in a family as big as ours?"

"It wasn't like we just decided to give one of our children away. We certainly didn't want to do that, and your mother grieved over him until the day she died. What happened was, in 1962, I was driving the family to Kansas, where the company had transferred me. Your mother went into premature labor. We had to stop in Memphis for her to deliver the babies."

Madison felt the blood rush from her head. Did he say "babies," not "baby?"

"You weighed five pounds, but your brother Park only weighed three. He had a heart problem and all kinds of complications, and he wasn't expected to live."

He *did* say babies. Pleural. Park was not only her brother—he was her *twin* brother. Duh, she thought. His birthday is the same as mine, of course he's my twin.

"They transferred him to the children's hospital. You and your mother were discharged two days later. We were very poor, and I ran out of money quickly. With a new baby and two other children to care for, no place to live and no job in Memphis, we had to go on to Kansas.

"A nurse named Barbara Palmer became very attached to Park, and promised to watch over him until he was well and we could come back for him, but he had one complication after another, and required several surgeries. Barbara took him home during the brief periods when he could be discharged. Even then, he required round-the-clock nursing care.

"He was four years old before he was reasonably stabilized, but he still had a lot of problems. By then, Barbara was the only mother he knew, and she wanted to adopt him. We allowed it for his sake, although it tore us up. Barbara sent us letters and pictures of Park, which we kept in a special box for him, along with letters your mother and I wrote to him over the years. We made a sort of time capsule for him."

"And you visited him," Madison said softly.

"Yes, when business took me through Memphis, I visited, and eventually, I was able to move the family to Memphis. We bought that house a couple of blocks from Barbara and Park, so we could occasionally get a glimpse of him. I guess I was hoping the truth would come out. I visited him from time to time, and we sent Barbara what we could for support.

"We posted information everywhere that would help him find us, if he wanted, but he never did. It broke your mother's heart. Madison, I need to talk to him. I don't want him to form an opinion about what happened, then have to adjust it when he talks to me. I want to be the one who tells him I'm his father."

"I think he's already figured it out, Dad. But don't worry, he's a kind man, and I think he'll understand. I'll have him call you."

She hung up, so stunned at the news that she couldn't even react to it, only one thought in her head: How close she'd come to having a physical relationship with one of her brothers, and having his baby. Now Basc's strict rule about limiting egg donation to lower the chances of siblings meeting and becoming involved didn't seem so stupid.

* * *

Park got home an hour after he talked to Madi, and went

straight to her house.

There was an awkwardness between them, an inability to dive right in to the issue at hand. Madison made iced tea and small talk.

"How did chemo go today?" she asked. "Have you taken any nausea medicine?"

"I don't need chemo anymore."

"Was that your idea, or your doctor's?"

"We talked over the pros and cons. She was shocked when I told her how much of the ulcer medication I'd been taking over the years, and she thinks the anemia will resolve spontaneously. I'm going to take some stuff to build up my blood count. If it doesn't work, I can always resume treatment. And guess what else? The chairman of the Psychiatry Department at Baylor called me. There's a position open in that department, and Caroline Bascomb recommended me. I'll interview on Monday."

Madison smiled. "That's wonderful. Everything's coming up roses for you."

"Mostly," Park said.

They settled at the dining room table. "What did you and Cam do last night?"

"Watched T.V., played with the dog. Cam revised to his letter to Santa. He said he'd been good since last week, and he'd like it to snow, but Santa would need to bring some boots for Dudley, two pairs, please. He also wants a tattoo for you, if it's in stock."

Madison laughed, sobered, drew designs in the sweat beads on her glass. "This is kind of like therapy, isn't it? Hard to get started on the painful stuff."

"Did you talk to your father?"

"Yes. You've found your family, Park. You're not only my brother. You're my twin brother."

"Your twin," he echoed, dumbfounded. "I'm your twin." He shook his head to clear it. The fact that she was his sister was hard enough to grasp, but that she was his twin felt even more unreal, like a game of make-believe—little children dressed up in clothes that pooled around their feet, strings of beads that hung to their knees, feathered hats that slid down their noses. "No wonder you and I collided like we did. How in the world does one twin get separated from a family?"

Madi's eyes traveled to the thick scar that started at the base of his neck and ran straight down the middle until it disappeared under his shirt. "It was because of your heart problem."

He listened raptly as she told him the story. When she finished, he said, "My God, I have a father, and a whole, huge family."

"Two sisters, two brothers. How did you feel when you found out you were adopted?"

"Shocked, of course. Confused. I didn't understand why my mother hadn't told me."

"Did you ever try to find us?"

"I thought about it, especially after my mother died, and I felt so alone in the world. I made a sort of half-hearted attempt at it, but the leads dead-ended. And I was afraid."

"Of what?"

"Disrupting their lives, rejection, finding out some horror story, like maybe I was the child of rape, or my parents were in prison for some heinous crime. Most kids know they're adopted, but I didn't, so I assumed my mother was protecting me. Anyway, I didn't want a relationship with my bioparents, I just wanted to know who they were and why they gave me up. I loved my adoptive mother and saw her as the real deal."

"It sounds like you were better off—the Cleavers, we are not."

"All families are dysfunctional in some way; I wasn't expecting the perfect family. Imagine that you are all alone in the world. It's a hollow feeling, especially at holiday time. After Claire and I had Nathan, I fantasized about finding my family, so he would have grandparents and aunts and uncles. Tell me about Christmas morning at your house, Madi. Tell me about everything. Were your brothers in scouts, sports, band? Did they serve Mass? Did you go on vacations, picnics? Tell me everything."

He was like a kitchen sponge, trying to soak up a lake. "We weren't a very happy family, Park. Read my chart, if you've forgotten."

It was true, he knew quite a lot about her history, but now he was viewing it from a different perspective. "There must have been some happy times."

"I suppose, when we were very young."

"Will you show me your photo albums?"

"Of course I will. I'll tell you every single thing about our family."

"The odds of us meeting must be a million to one," he mused.

"Actually, it's a wonder we didn't meet long ago. We lived two streets over from you and your mother. We probably passed each other a hundred times. Do you know anything about fraternal twins? Like, do they have the same kind of bond as identical twins?"

"I don't know for sure—I read once that fraternals have a similar intense psychic connection."

"Maybe that explains our instant closeness." Madison paused for a moment, then said, "Park, there's something I need to tell you." She looked at him with sorrow in her denim eyes. "I thought Cam was your son."

In his soft, therapy voice, Park said, "I did, too."

"What made you think that?"

Park shrugged. "His age, I guess. His name. Because he looks so much like me. The hexadactyly. You had access to the sperm, and given your emotional distress when I left, it might have been an irresistible impulse."

"You're not angry?"

"No. But I do want to know how it happened."

She looked down at her hands, picked at a broken nail, bit it off. Couldn't seem to get any more words out, started to hyperventilate.

"Stay with it, Madi. Just tell me."

Madison explained how the sperm ended up in her hands. "Instead of throwing it away, I put it back in my pocket, and I—I just fell right into that rabbit hole without a thought. I needed things to remind me of you—even things you had touched seemed significant. Your signature on my bill, the to-do list on your desk. To have your baby—well, that was a piece of you I could hold in my arms, and keep forever.

"All my life, I've been forced to leave people I love behind. They just seem to evaporate. Every time it happens, it seems worse than the last time. People say what doesn't kill you makes you stronger. Not me. I just get less and less able to cope.

"I wanted to keep you with me, physically. And something of ours, together—a little boy with your green eyes and blonde hair, my whacky sense of humor, our intelligence—was even better. Superficially, it seemed harmless. I never thought you would know, or that it would matter to anyone. Obviously, I didn't think it through."

"I understand."

"I am so sorry I did it. I'll do anything to make it up to you. Anything at all. If you want to report me, file charges, whatever. If you think I should lose my nursing license, and I think I should, then report me to the State Board. I mean it."

"Madi, hush."

"It was a stupid thing to do. I could have hurt myself—I mean, I refused to use the other contaminated specimen for fear that I would hurt my patient."

"Madi, it's okay."

"And Cam and I could have contracted HIV, you don't

have HIV, do you?"

"No," he said.

"Why aren't you mad? You were mad when I took your cufflinks. I stole something a lot worse. Your fertility."

"You took something that was essentially discarded. You wouldn't have taken a good specimen, would you?"

"Of course not. To begin with, there's no way a good specimen meant for storage would have ended up in my pocket."

"So no harm was done. And honestly, Madi, if Cam had turned out to be mine, I would have been happy. He fills up that abyss in me that Nathan left."

"Thank you, Park," she whispered.

"Please don't be hard on yourself. Our brains are set up to do whatever it takes to keep a loved one. So all those feelings— rage, loneliness, obsessive thinking, despair, separation anxiety, depression—are nature's way of compelling us to do whatever it takes to keep the status quo. I understand, it's okay, and there is absolutely no reason for this to go any further than the two of us."

"But it has to. I already explained it to David. And I need to tell Basc."

"Why tell her? All that will do is create a lot of trouble for you. She seems like the kind of person who doesn't know when it's appropriate to bend the rules."

"I just don't want even a nuance of impropriety to reflect on you professionally."

"Does Basc think we had an affair?"

"No, she just thinks you have major boundary issues."

"Fine. I don't care about that."

Madi shook her head. "AA taught me to be completely honest, Park. Unfortunately, I'm still a work in progress, but I'm trying."

"Don't you think that's kind of selfish? What if you lost your license, or were prosecuted? What would happen to Cam?"

"I should have thought about that before I acted," Madi

said dismally. "One of the problems in early recovery is a desire to reconstruct oneself with spotlessly clean components."

"But that doesn't mean to clear your conscience by revealing every mistake you ever made. That's really only acceptable if there is something for the other person to gain."

"I suppose that's true," she said.

Dear Madi, always harder on herself than anyone else. He'd never known anyone who was so willing to own her behavior, and to act on resolutions. If she could do that, the least he could do was reciprocate.

She picked up their empty glasses and took them to the kitchen, Park trailing behind.

"I know how it feels to have something like that hanging over your head," he said. "To be honest, when I left Memphis, that's the way I felt. I wasn't straightforward with you about my feelings, Madi."

She turned and looked at him, surprised.

"I could make excuses for myself by saying I was confused. And I was. Part of me was worried about my professional reputation and my marriage, and part of me was worried that it would make your pain worse, but mainly, I didn't want to deal with it. I just wanted it to be okay for you and for me, and it wasn't. Your reaction to my leaving horrified me. I knew I had caused you unspeakable pain, in the name of helping you.

"I fell in love with you," he said, his voice full of wonder. Madi's eyes widened, and she sucked in her breath, and it took everything he had not to kiss her parted lips. "I love my wife, but with you, the feeling went beyond the ordinary, and it frightened me, so I denied it, even to myself. Maybe it would have been better to tell you. I think you knew it, anyway, but I left you in confusion."

"Yes," she said.

"I am very, very, sorry I hurt you. But the point is, we hurt each other. And there is no need for you to punish yourself any further."

"Okay."

"Promise me you won't tell Basc. There's nothing but more harm to come from that."

"Okay."

They walked out to the front room. "Park, Dad wants to talk to you. Will you call him?"

"Sure."

Madi perched on the recliner, wrote down their father's name and number, handed it to Park. "Do you want to call him from here?"

"No thanks, I think I want to be alone."

"Don't expect a gush of emotion from him. He might come off as distant, but he's really just inarticulate."

"Yes, you've said he's kind of reticent."

"Come back after you've talked to him?"

"Okay. I'm glad we live so close to each other."

She looked away.

"What is it?"

"I don't know how much longer I'll be here. I'm going to marry David. And he wants to move to Utah."

Move to Utah. Park stared at her, too stunned to react. He remembered her describing the same feeling on the day he'd told her he was leaving Memphis. "Congratulations," he choked out, heading for the front door. If he didn't get out of there, he was going to decompensate in front of her.

Madison trailed after him, offering explanations that sounded lame, just as he'd done to her. "It's his home. He just lost his father, and I think he wants to be near his family."

Park kept going, waving goodbye without turning around. He made it back to the rental before he burst into tears, sat there and blubbered like a three-year-old. It was all too much, just too damn much. He couldn't stand being separated from Madi again. He couldn't stand the fact that she was his *sister*. He looked at the heart-shaped, hot pink Post-It note she had given him, with the most important piece of information he'd ever received in his life written with a black calligraphy pen: His father's name, a Memphis number.

He thought about all the times he'd needed this information. How near his real mother had been when his adoptive mother was dying. How his own father, whom Park thought was dead, had sat at their kitchen table many times, pretending to be nothing more than a friend who'd stopped by for a cup of instant coffee.

He didn't know what to call them anymore, his mothers and father, birth and adoptive. From now on they would be Barbara and Mac. And whatever his biological mother's name had been.

How naïve he'd been, thinking he would feel nothing but joy when he found his family. Instead, he was stunned that he'd been deprived of their help when he was losing what he thought was his only parent.

Park was eighteen when Barbara died, old enough to drive, vote, serve in the armed forces, and make funeral arrangements for his mother. He'd gone to the funeral home alone. A very nice lady, armed with a three-pronged black notebook filled with neatly typed funeral plans in protective plastic sleeves, had met him in the lobby. She took him into a freezing room permeated with the nauseating smell of mortuary deodorizer, to discuss what to do with Barbara, who hovered near death in the Baptist Hospital. Next was the casket showroom, lined with coffins of cardboard, mahogany and steel. He'd refused to enter the room and opted for cremation. He simply could not deal with a funeral.

His parents had left him alone in the world rather than reveal their secret. Why? Aside from everything else, he could have had quite a pool of potential bone marrow donors, not to mention a perfect match. And he certainly wouldn't have been in this situation with Madi.

He'd promised to call Mac. But Park was afraid anger would flare from deep inside, a fire that had been kept carefully banked for decades. He just couldn't call Mac right now. In fact, he might not call Mac ever.

Park got a beer and tried to distract himself with the book he'd been working on for a year. But it brought him right back to his own problems, because it was about Madi. He had completed the part that was written from the therapist's point of view, and Park had wanted Madi to write the other half from the patient's point of view. But she had already written a fictionalized version of the story, so he would have to abandon his work or revamp it.

He booted his laptop and opened the file that contained her old psychotherapy records, re-reading the story of her life from his new perspective. Their mother, an angry woman full of pride and stubbornness and certainty she was right, who didn't know there was strength in being able to say "I was wrong," and salvation in forgiveness. Their father, who sounded like he had a mild form of autism, instead of being disinterested and rejecting, as his children perceived him. Their older sister, whom Madi worshipped.

And Madi herself, his fascinating twin who read Sartre and Nietzsche and pondered Einstein's theory of relativity in her search for God.

He just couldn't get the idea that she was his sister to gel. Just the night before, he'd decided to pursue her, then decided not to, but now, the overpowering, electrical grip of his love for her intensified. More than ever, he wanted to be in her life and had a right to be, but he felt more like a spy than a suitor or friend. Or a brother.

In the few months he'd been in Houston, he had shifted from the detached love of a therapist for a patient to romantic love for a friend; and now, he was expected to abruptly transform those feelings to sibling love. And she was moving to the opposite end of the country, once again separating them at a critical point in their relationship. He wondered if David had planned it for that very reason.

How he missed the structure and familiarity of his life before he and Claire had moved to Dallas. Before he'd met Madi. Life was fairly predictable, totally boring, and safe. His wife, even if distant and a little cold, had been his ally, and he missed her, too. And he was worried, as well, about her physical and mental health.

Park picked up the phone and dialed his home in Dallas. Claire answered on the first ring.

"Hi, just calling to see how you are," he said.

"I'm packing," she said, her voice hostile.

"Where are you going?"

"Remuda Ranch."

"In Arizona?"

"Yes. Happy, now?"

Happy? How could anyone be happy, with a deluge of news that was just as bad as it was good? Remuda Ranch was an eating disorder treatment center, exactly what Claire needed. But it was hideously expensive, and there were other centers that were cheaper, and just as good. He prayed that her parents were footing the bill, because she would probably lose her job, which meant no income or medical insurance for either of them. But those problems paled beside the fact that Claire was in imminent danger of dying from her anorexia.

"Relieved," he said. "I've been very worried about you."

"Well, you have your new girl to comfort you."

Park sighed. Now was definitely not the time to share his news about Madi. "When are you leaving?"

"In a few minutes. Have you found employment in Houston? You'll need it. I'm going to be gone for a couple of months, and I quit my job."

He almost laughed. It was getting to the point where it would take less time to list what was right in his life than what was wrong. "What about the apartment?"

"Mother and Daddy will take care of that until I'm out of

Remuda. After that, I don't know."

"Call me when you can, will you please? I know you have a rough road ahead."

"Maybe."

"We still have business to take care of, even if you don't want to talk about our relationship or your health."

"I probably won't be allowed to call for a couple of weeks."

"I know."

She reluctantly took his cell phone number, and ended the conversation. Park tried to think of someone he could call, a friend with whom he could share this pain. But there wasn't anyone, he realized. He'd had friends in Memphis five years ago, but like Madi said, all they talked about was their jobs, their kids, and sports. That was one of the reasons he'd immediately bonded with her—she was one of the few people in the world who liked to talk about the same things he did.

In the depths of her pain, Madi had once told him, "I need to talk to my therapist about my problem—but my therapist *is* the problem." Now he was experiencing the same feeling. He wanted to talk to her about his problems—but she was one of them. Or he wanted to talk to Claire—and she was the other.

Frustrated, lonely, and angry, he put on his sneakers, grabbed two beers, opened one and stuck the other in his pocket, and headed out the door.

Maybe he could run off a little of his agitation.

CHAPTER TEN

Shock waves rolled through Madison's family. The phone rang constantly, everyone calling back and forth, comparing notes. Finding another sibling was like trying to fit another piece into a jigsaw puzzle that was already complete. Madison talked to her older children, Emma and Dane, as well as her sister and older brother, and her father called again, to see why Park hadn't called.

That was odd. Park had seemed prepared to call their father when he left. She hoped he was all right, tried to think how she would feel if she were over there in that grim house by herself. She decided to get Cam from school, then check on Park.

On the way to Cam's school, she pondered Park's statement, "I fell in love with you." How she would have loved to hear those words when they were in Memphis. Now, all she could think was, "You're too late." She loved him, but she couldn't trust him; the feeling that he had her back 100% of the time was lost the day he had told her he was leaving Memphis. Even if things had changed so they could have a real relationship, she would never be able to trust him not to abandon her. Consequently, she had chosen David, who had always been there, quietly, solidly.

Cam was watching for her at the front windows of the school, his face blotchy and streaked with tears. She listened to a long tale of woe about a broken red crayon.

When he wound down, she said, "Cam, David is home from the hospital. He has big white bandage on his head, but you don't need to worry, he just has a cut on his forehead."

"Is he all red where he caught on fire?"

"What? David didn't catch on fire."

"Uh huh, 'cause the fire trucks came to put him out."

Madison bit her lip to keep from laughing. "No they didn't, honey. Fire trucks come when someone is hurt because they have a person trained to help, and they can get there faster than anyone else."

"Oh. I was scared all night. I'm glad David's not hurt bad, 'cause I love him. I wish he could be with us every single day."

"Well, I think he will be, soon."

"What do you mean?"

"David and I are going to get married."

"Yipee! Is he gonna 'dopt me?"

Madison really hadn't intended to tell Cam that David was his father until she'd had a chance to think about how to explain it. But since Cam had brought it up, she said, "He doesn't need to adopt you."

"Why not?"

"Because I just found out that you weren't made from the cell I got from California Cryo, like I thought." So much for rigorous honesty . . . it just seemed impossible, where Cam was concerned.

"I wasn't?"

"No. I'd forgotten that David had also given me a cell. You were made from David's cell."

She held her breath, dreading the questions that were sure to follow, but Cam was quiet. In the rearview mirror, she could see him staring out the window, a big grin on his face.

"Do you know what that means?" she asked.

"It means David is my dad. I got a dad, like everybody

else."

"Are you happy?"

"'Course. Me 'n David can build the tree house every day when he comes home from work, and he said if Santa brings me a bike he'll teach me to ride it, and we can go fishing every single day . . ."

The list went on and on. Madison knew Cam loved David, but she hadn't realized how much his presence filled up Cam's life, as well as hers. More than ever, she knew this marriage was the right thing to do.

When they got home, Cam raced into the house. David was on the daybed, watching TV.

"Hey, Spike," he said.

Cam studied David's bandage. "You didn't look both ways, that's why you wrecked. And you didn't wear your brain bucket, that's why you got a bad head bonk. Do I still gotta call you David?"

David gave Madison a lopsided smile, clearly pleased that she'd wasted no time telling Cam the news. "What do you want to call me?"

"Dad."

"Dad it is, then."

Madison left them alone to bond in their new format, and walked over to Park's house. He was sitting on the front porch, staring at the bayou.

"Are you okay?" she asked.

"I'm just trying to absorb it all. It feels totally surreal."

"Yeah, I know what you mean. Everyone is calling. They all want to meet you. Are you going to call Dad?"

Park looked away from her. "I'm not ready to talk to him, or anyone, yet. I don't feel connected, and don't really know if I even want to. I mean, I want to meet my family eventually, but I have a lot of processing to do before then."

"Of course you do," Madison said. "And you don't have to

talk to anyone until you're good and ready." She looked at her watch. "It's almost dinner time. Come eat with us. I'll get my scrapbooks out and take you on a family journey."

"Okay," Park said.

By five p.m., Madison, Park, and Cam were settled at the dining room table, eating lasagna and salad. David had taken a pain pill, and was asleep. After dinner, Park leafed through Madison's library of scrapbooks; it was slow going, with him demanding detailed explanations along the way.

"This is your paternal grandfather," Madison said, showing him a black and white photograph of a thin, elderly man sitting at a baby grand piano. "He and our grandmother were classical pianists, and Grandad was a classical composer. We have a book of his music."

"I'd like to play it sometime," Park said.

"You play the piano?"

"Since I was five."

"Me, too. You're welcome to use mine anytime."

She turned the page to a shot of their family on a Christmas day. Their sister and older brother were playing Monopoly, and Madison, who looked like she was about six or seven at the time, was on, the sofa, nose in a book.

"Why am I not surprised?" Park said, laughing. "What are you reading, the *Theory of Relativity*?"

"Nah. Probably *Cherry Ames, Student Nurse*, or whatever kind of nurse she was that day. The girl had more jobs than Orville Redenbacher has popcorn kernels."

Cam walked around the table and handed Park a black and white photo of Madison and her siblings as small children, lined up in a row, according to height. They were all dressed in cowboy outfits.

Park looked at her, a stricken expression on his face. "Your outfits match the one Mac bought me."

"And he took your picture, the one we looked at earlier, to

complete the set, I guess."

Madison pulled her Central High School yearbooks from the bottom of the pile. She and Park had been in the same class their junior and senior years. As they turned the pages, laughing at their formal pictures and sharing memories of school events, they found a couple of candid shots that they were in together, one at an assembly, one at a football game.

"Amazing," he said. "We were right in the same room." He opened an older scrapbook to a picture of a laughing blonde holding up a pumpkin pie with an egg cooked in the middle, yolk intact.

"That's Mom," Madison said. "Her name was Meredith. That picture was taken on Thanksgiving. Bree and I used to cook dinner for the whole family at her house, since it was the biggest. We'd get the turkey in around noon, then start drinking Irish coffee and playing chess. We'd be four sails to the wind by the time everyone got there for dinner. I guess the Irish in the coffee had already kicked in when I made that pie, and I didn't get the eggs stirred in good."

"Meredith seemed to enjoy your antics."

"Yeah," Madison said, "I guess she did. She loved to laugh. Underneath her high school graduation photo they wrote, 'A laugh is worth a groan in any market.' She wasn't witty, but she loved people who were."

"Then she must have adored you," Park said softly.

"It's hard to remember the good things. I know my mother loved me. All I ever wanted her to do was—" She stopped and glanced at Cam. "Never mind. Little pitchers . . ."

"Little pictures have big ears," said Cam.

"And a big mouth," Madison added.

"The dentist says I have a little mouth."

"Well, he should spend a whole day with you, Mister." She looked at her watch. "It's time for you to get your jammies on." Whining, Cam went off to his room.

The era of the scrapbooks gradually changed, going through Madison's early marriage, and then David started appearing in the photos. Park turned the page, and there were pictures of New Year's Eve years ago, with David kissing Madison. He closed the album and headed for the front door.

Madison followed, glossing over his discomfort. "I was thinking it might be nice if we did some traditional family holiday things."

"Like what?"

"We could put the Christmas tree up, like our family always did the weekend after Thanksgiving, and we could cook some of the traditional things. I have my—I mean our—grandfather's recipes for Christmas candy. Stuff like that."

Park smiled, his eyes full of gratitude. "I'd like that very much."

"Okay, tomorrow morning, say at nine? We'll start by getting the Christmas decorations out."

"You got it. Good night."

Madison put Cam to bed and closed up the house for the night. David was asleep when she got in bed, an open magazine face down on his chest. She put the magazine on the bedside table, turned out the light, and fell asleep to visions of an old-fashioned family Christmas dancing in her head.

* * *

In the morning, Park lugged three boxes of Christmas decorations down from the attic, and he, Madison, Cam, and, of course, Dudley sat in the middle of the living room floor, examining each decoration as it was taken from its tissue-paper wrapping. Cam gave Park a running account of the origin of each item.

Madison was dissatisfied with the collection, and decided they needed to go to the Christmas Superstore. While Cam and Park put on their jackets, she went to the bedroom to tell David where they were going.

"Do you want to go with us?"

"It's too early to put the tree up. We do that in mid-December."

"Well, we're going to do it in late November this year."

"Whatever," he said. "Anyway, my head hurts."

"David, I'm worried about you. If you're not up out of the bed when I get home, you're going to the E.R."

"No, I'm not."

Cam came into the room. "Dad, are you going with us? You promised to buy me a Rudolph to put in the front yard."

"Take my Visa and get that for him, please? And whatever else you guys want."

"Thanks, but I don't need the Visa. I seem to have a large sum of money in my account that I didn't put there."

"Come on, Mom," Cam whined. "We'll get good stuff if Dad buys it."

"Not to worry, we'll get good stuff. Go get in the car. I'll be there in a minute." She turned back to David. "So, what's the money for?"

"I just thought Park might need some help. Is he going to be able to pay his rent?"

"I don't know."

"Don't you think you need to find out? Even if Baylor hires him, it will be a while before he gets a paycheck. We need to take care of it."

Madison kissed him, her heart overflowing with love. "Thank you, David."

Madison, Park, and Cam spent the afternoon happily weighing the merits of various Christmas decorations. To her delight, she found some old-fashioned bubble lights, exactly like those their family had when she was little. Tents with live trees had already been set up at the Baytown Mall, and they picked out the perfect tree.

"Did you ever cut down your own tree?" Park asked.

Madison laughed. "Now there's an idea that's much more romantic than practical. When we lived in Denver, Dad drove us up into the mountains to cut down a tree. It was freezing, our boots filled up with snow, and he like to never got the tree cut down. Then it was full of bugs."

"Well, we'll skip that, then."

"We don't got any mountains in Texas, anyway," Cam added.

"We don't *have* any mountains in Texas," Madison corrected.

Cam looked at her like she was crazy. "That's what I said."

By the time they headed home, a cold front had moved in, and dark clouds filled the sky. Park wrestled the tree into the house and set it up in the holder, while Madison put frozen pizza in the oven, made hot chocolate, and put on some Christmas music. The room was chilly, and she turned on the electric fireplace.

David had showered; he sat up for a while, then lay down on the daybed. Madison tried to include him in the conversation, but received only monosyllabic answers. If he didn't perk up by tomorrow, she was going to call his doctor. It seemed like he should be up and about by now.

They ate pizza, then decorated the tree. Park put the bubble lights on, and Cam added the ornaments and icicles, all of which went on the lower branches. When they were finished, Park hoisted Cam up to put the angel on top.

Cam, exhausted by his day, crawled up beside David, and both of them fell asleep. Madison and Park sat on the floor next to each other and tidied up the boxes and litter. Outside, a gust of wind rattled the windows and pelted them with rain.

Madison felt a deep sense of contentment. She hoped Park would feel the same, once he had worked through his feelings about his newly discovered family.

"What's the very first thing you can remember?" Park asked.

"Standing on the steps of an elementary school, howling with rage because my sister got to go in but I didn't. You?"

"A needle being stuck in my arm. I spent a lot of time in hospitals when I was a kid, and at home in an oxygen tent. I learned to read to entertain myself, like you. I developed an interest in history, so after I blew through the Hardy Boys, I read all the history books I could get my hands on, as well as the whole Encyclopedia Britannica."

"I always envied families that had encyclopedias. All we had was an ancient set of Groliers that weren't good for much. Were you in the Honor Society?"

"Of course. Weren't you?"

"Of course."

"What's your favorite color?"

"Puce," she said.

Park chortled. "That's not a color."

"It most certainly is. Do you cheat at Monopoly?"

"Nope. But I must confess I cheat when I'm trying to finish the New York Times crossword on Sunday."

"Everyone cheats on that," Madison said. "What was your favorite thing to do when you were a teenager?"

"Ballroom dancing."

"Seriously? You didn't tell me you're a ballroom dancer when we were playing seven sevens at Anderson. Can you teach me the quickstep? No, the paso doble."

"Sorry, not enough room in here. How about a waltz?"

"Okay." Madison got up and put on Chris Botti's trumpet solos. By the time the second song came on, they were dancing smoothly.

"I always think of you when I hear this song," she said, as a haunting melody ribboned through dark room, lit only by the fire and the tree.

"I'll never forget the day I met you," he replied. "I thought you were the most exotic creature, in your dinosaur robe and dust mop slippers, hospitalized for clinical depression and still able to debate the existence of God. Oh, what a girl."

He pulled her closer and she felt the forbidden electricity leap between them. They slowed until they were barely moving. Madison felt like she was inside the music, in that special place she used to go in therapy, fused to Park's soul.

It was a bittersweet feeling. She put her head on Park's shoulder and closed her eyes, allowing herself to feel the full blast of her love for him one last time. She knew she had to push him away; being around each other would only keep sucking them into that dangerous vortex of impossible love. It had to stop. He was her brother, and anyway, she had chosen David.

When she opened her eyes, David was awake, watching them. She broke away from Park and said, "I'm tired. Let's call it a day."

David carried Cam to bed. Park lingered at the door, reluctant to end their evening. She finally got him to leave by promising him waffles for breakfast. By the time she locked up the house, David was already in bed, looking despondent. She crawled in beside him. "What's wrong? Are you in pain?"

"Just the same headache."

"Then what is it?"

"I wish you could have seen your face when you were dancing with him. I'll never, ever be that close to you. I want my wife to be 100% mine, and you're still in love with him."

"David, he's my brother!"

"That doesn't make any difference, and until you figure out what you want, I think we better put us on hold."

"No! We don't need to do that. I know what I want, and I want you. We all need other people in our lives. Park was the first person who instinctively understood me and allowed me to be myself. He knew everything about me, and he still liked me. And I came to love him for that. It's not a sexual feeling, David. In fact, I used to tell Park that if I could write the script for the future, I wouldn't know what to write. And part of that was the issue of not being able to completely and permanently cross those boundaries between therapist and patient. Now those boundaries will definitely never be crossed, so you don't need to worry about that."

"Don't you think I understand you?"

"Not really. I think you like me and you think I'm funny and smart, but you don't really *get* me. So I don't look to you for that sort of stuff."

"That's what makes me feel left out, Madison, pushed away, excluded from your two-member club."

"I'm sorry you feel that way, but don't you think that's something we all experience to some degree? There's no one person who can fill all your needs. How do you think I feel in the staff meeting at work? I have a basic understanding of what the doctors are talking about, but when you guys get deep into biochemistry and statistics, I'm completely lost, and you're in your element. How would you like it if you had no one to talk to about those things? And you get on the phone to Utah and discuss wine. Do you think I know what a 'smooth vanilla finish' is, or 'bright cherry overtones?' Or will ever know?"

"But that doesn't involve my heart, Madison. Only my brain."

"David, he's not a rival. He's more like the father I always wanted."

"Or a good shrink, who only takes care of the wounded part of you? Like Xylocaine on a burn?"

She looked away, surprised at his perception. Perhaps she had underestimated David, for he was exactly right. That was what made the difference; she only knew the Park who took care of the wounded part of her. The rest of him, she was just beginning to know. "Yes," she said. "Would you deprive me of that?"

"Maybe," David said in a low voice. "It scares me, your bond to him."

She leaned over, looked him squarely in the eye. "Don't be

scared. I love you, David Thorpe, and I am going to marry you and we are going to live happily ever after with our little boy. Park is not going to move into our daily lives on a permanent basis. I'm just trying to support him until he can get the training wheels off his life, and ride by himself again. You're a decent man, David. Help me do that."

"I'll try. It's just hard. He has his eyes on you every second he's with you, like he's memorizing you, pixel by pixel. Or he has his hand on your shoulder, your arm, your hair. I don't like it, and I don't care who he is. I wouldn't touch his wife like that."

"You're right, that's inappropriate. I'll talk to him."

David pulled her into his arms and kissed her, and she leaned into that special place that excluded Park. "Madison, I want to move to Utah."

"I know you do. Let's go. We can always come back if it doesn't work out, can't we?"

"We can."

She knew it was the right thing to do, but still, she felt a deep stab of pain at being so far away from Park.

CHAPTER ELEVEN

December raced by in a flurry of activity, Christmas shopping, baking, parties. Park, David, and Cam decorated the house and front yard, putting up so many lights that Madison could see the house glowing a block away when it was dark. Madison made the old family favorites, mint taffy and carrot cookies and popcorn balls with red and green food coloring in the syrup, and their mother's cinnamon rolls for Christmas morning.

Park started work full time at Baylor in mid-December. His first project was to create a support program for couples struggling with infertility. The department chairman was impressed with the work, and planned to offer the program city wide.

Park's blood count made a slow but steady climb back to normal. Color returned to his normally pink cheeks, and his energy level improved. In February, he was discharged from the care of M.D. Anderson, except for the occasional follow-up visit.

Madison and David were married in a quiet ceremony in March, attended by Basc, Park, and Cam. Once David had a formal commitment from Madison, he was less intolerant of Park, and the tension eased.

One month later, on a warm spring day, Park and Madison said goodbye again.

They stood on her front porch, their roles completely reversed this time—she leaving for a new life, he left behind with a broken heart.

Park remembered the analogy she'd used when he'd left her in Memphis—that she felt like she had a rock inside, a little bit bigger than she was—and now he knew that physical feeling. He crushed Madi against him, one hand in her cool, silky hair; closed his eyes, breathing in her clean-cotton scent. He tried to muster his shrinkly reticence, but it took every fiber of his will to keep from screaming, "Don't leave me!" She'd once said those exact words to him.

She handed him her house keys, the last order of business. The house was convenient to Park's job, and they'd worked out a lease-purchase agreement.

"I labeled the keys for you and wrote down the alarm code; remember, you only have 15 seconds to get in or out before it goes off. And don't forget to water the foundation of the house, or it will crack."

She stopped and pressed her head against his chest. "I can't do this."

"Not to worry, Madi. We'll see each other again. After all, we're family now."

But the fact that she was his sister still felt unreal. Even a trip to Memphis to meet his father and siblings hadn't helped it solidify.

In the end, Madison left him the way she had the first time, ripping herself away without another word. She ran to the cab where David, Cam, and Dudley waited. As they drove away, she craned her neck to look at Park, her agonized expression searing his heart.

He remembered her sitting in his Memphis office right before he left, crying pitifully and saying, "I'm going to feel like this for a long, long time . . ." and he knew what she meant.

What did the textbooks say about this? Redirect your attention to something else. That was it. That was the ticket.

Park pawed listlessly through the kitchen cabinets, but couldn't find anything he wanted to eat. He grabbed a longneck, felt the icy sweat on the bottle, imagined the bite of the cold beer. Back when Madi was battling her alcoholism, he'd ordered her to call him when she craved a drink. He'd denied his own problem and pretended to know how to handle hers. What a joke.

He put the bottle back, took it out again, opened it. Like Scarlett O'Hara, he would think about that problem tomorrow. He would finish these two six packs, then start sobering up. He laughed bitterly; it was the same old resolution, to face his demons on Monday. Some shrink he was.

He turned on the T.V. and surfed for a while, unable to focus. On the end table, like a rabid dog he was trying to ignore, was Madi's *Alcoholics Anonymous* "Big Book". It was a well-loved book that had gone through several owners, with pages yellow with age and the binding falling apart; the book was highlighted in various colors of markers, and there were annotations in pencil and ball point and fountain pen in various scripts, some of it Madi's.

Park read for a while, his mood darkening. He'd hoped AA would help him, but he didn't see himself in this book; he had not tornadoed through other peoples' lives, as a general rule, Madi's being the exception. What he did need to do was find a shrink and get to work on his issues about Claire, Nathan, Madi, and his newly-discovered family.

He tossed the book aside and picked up the other thing he was trying to ignore, a wooden box his father had given him. He knew that inside on the hinged lid, two words were wood burned: For Park.

The box was filled with mementos that his biological parents had saved for him. There must have been a hundred letters from his mother, written specifically to him. Some on different kinds of formal stationary, sealed, with his name on the envelope; some on folded typing paper. Others on scraps of paper—the backs of grocery lists, children's homework assignments, bills, letters from friends. There were sealed birthday cards for every single year up to the year of Meredith's death.

Months after he'd received the box, he still hadn't read any of the letters. Happiness and resentment were swirled and fused in him like the glass Claire created with her torch. Park didn't know what he was waiting for, but it seemed like a day would come when it seemed right to read them.

He abandoned the box and booted his laptop, pulling up Madi's manuscript. It was finished except for the last chapter, which neither of them had been able to write, as if completing the book would neatly sum up their relationship and end the need for endless ruminations on the past. *Negotiations and Love Songs*, how clever was that title? Not only were they often confused, but sometimes even a professional couldn't tell the difference. He had tried to negotiate a way for Madi to remain his patient and think of their relationship as a way to gain acceptance and understanding, and she had mistaken his actions for love. By the time she realized this, he had realized he really did love her, but she was lost to him. And a good thing that was, considering their true relationship as siblings.

Again, Park wasn't staying on task, and he spent the rest of the afternoon trying to erase Madi from his new home. Her furniture had been shipped to Utah yesterday; she'd left him a bed, recliner, the T.V. and her piano, and he would gradually add other pieces to the empty rooms.

He made a trip to Home Depot to buy wall primer and paint, and then started on the lavender living room walls, frantic to change the things that would stimulate memories of her. By noon the priming was complete, and he started a layer of off-white paint.

By sundown, however, he admitted that nothing short of an exorcism would erase her. She had permanently seeped into the walls and woodwork of his home and his psyche.

As soon as it was dark, Park went to bed, but sleep eluded him. He kept seeing himself and Basc standing up for David and Madi at their wedding; the way David looked at Madi, his eyes following her as she left a room. He imagined Madi on the plane, flying over the rusty crags of the Grand Canyon at sunset, David smiling at her, anticipating their happy future.

Park consoled himself with Madi's philosophy that only the toughest souls come to this world. It's a hard place to be, she said, and only the most stalwart can tolerate it and continue growing until the moment of death. Happiness was dished out in tiny increments, just enough to keep the hope of a satisfying life alive. Just enough to keep us here. He thought about the night he and Madi had spent on the daybed after his first chemo treatment, how he had almost kissed her. What an awful mistake it would have been. Perhaps nothing in the universe should be forced. Once again, he longed for Claire, for his old, flavorless life.

She was still in the hospital last week when he'd called. She had refused to talk to him, but according to her parents, she was making progress. Park had been writing her long letters explaining and exploring the events of the past few months. Not in hopes of a reconciliation, but perhaps to help them sort out their problems. He had no idea if she had read the letters.

The doorbell rang. He slid into his jeans and ran for the door, insanely hoping Madi had come back. Instead, to his surprise, he found Claire, white-blonde hair loose on her shoulders, face filled out, eyes clear. Most surprising of all, she wore an old college sweatshirt of his over paint-splattered jeans, this wife of his who wore designer sweats to clean the bathroom.

"Claire! Come in! When did you get out of the hospital?"

"Today."

"You look wonderful."

"Thanks. Can we sit down somewhere? I really need to talk to you."

He gave her the one chair in the room, and then perched on the end table.

"I've been reading your letters and thinking a lot about what happened to us," Claire said. "You said you needed to own up to the fact that you had an emotional affair with Madison before you found out you are related. That matters, Park. That you admitted it, I mean. Now we can talk about it, instead of trying to climb over your denial."

Park hung his head and said, "Yes."

"Now for me—I came to apologize for treating you so badly, and—and to ask your forgiveness." The words came out stiffly, and Park knew the apology had cost her dearly. "I abandoned you because I thought you were going to die. You know I don't do death. I can't handle it, just the thought of it makes me feel like I'm losing my mind. I panic, I freak. "

"I wish you had told me that years ago."

"I wish I had, too. The irony of it is that I came within an inch of death while I was running away from it. It made me realize I didn't want to die, I just wanted the pain to stop. I remembered a lot of things you said over the years, in particular, attacking a resistant problem from all angles. I've been working hard in therapy, taking antidepressants, and working a twelve-step program."

"That's fantastic."

"I have a long way to go. But I just wanted to tell you that I love you, and I miss you, and all the stuff—the house, the cars, the money—is meaningless without you. I blamed you for Nathan's death because it was the only thing that made sense, and I couldn't live in a world that didn't make sense. I spent the last twenty years running from that fear. I've been such a bitch. You probably hate me."

"Actually, I was lying in bed wishing I could go home to you."

"Then come home, Park. I want to put us back together. I want go back to school, get a degree in counseling. Help other people with SIDS babies. Do something with my life other than spend money and look like a trophy wife."

This was the Claire he had lost the day Nathan died. His wife, his life partner. Was it possible to be in love with more than one person at a time? People loved parents, children, and friends simultaneously. Where a significant other was concerned, perhaps it was a matter of choice; and every choice excluded other options. We negotiate whom we love.

Now he knew how Madi's book should end.

"Why don't you come here?" Park said. "Madison and David are married and have moved to Utah, and they're helping me buy this house. I have a good job now, and I'm well. There are lots of colleges here."

"I can't believe you're willing to forgive me, after the way I've treated you."

"Everyone gets hurt in life, Claire. I don't get to be the one who doesn't have pain. And I hurt you, too."

"What about Madison? Do you love her?"

Unwilling to restart his relationship with a lie, Park said, "I do love her, Claire. It happens occasionally, with shrinks. I put the feeling away, knowing the intensity would fade in time. It never would have gone anywhere if you hadn't detected it and reacted the way you did. I'm not blaming you—I'm the one who felt the need to reconnect with Madi, and if I hadn't done that, you wouldn't have had anything to react to. But most important of all, I think the immediate closeness that both Madison and I felt has its roots in the fact that we're twins. So when the reality of that sinks in, I expect those feelings to settle where they belong—the closeness and love of siblings. Can you live with that?"

"I can, if I think you still love me too."

"This Claire," he said softly, "I never stopped loving. Welcome home."

That night, Park and Claire slept in the bed Madi had left for him, the fragrance of the freshly washed quilt and linens surrounding them. Tomorrow, he would write the final chapter of her book. Park wrapped his arm around his wife and closed his eyes, falling into a deep, contented sleep.

ABOUT THE AUTHOR

I so clearly remember when, as a small child, I first *got it*. All those letters under the pictures of Dick and Jane made *words*, and words made *stories* I could read all by myself! When I was seven, my big sister got tired of me tagging along after her and her friends. She shoved a Nancy Drew book in my hands and said, "Here. Read this. It's a good book."

I'm sure she didn't really think she could get rid of me so easily, but as she made her escape, I opened the book and thought, "I can't read this. It doesn't have any pictures. Oh well, she said it was good, so I'll try." I settled down and concentrated hard on figuring out the words, and entered a world of magic. After I read all her Nancy Drews and all my brother's Hardy Boys, oh heaven, I discovered Cherry Ames, who had so many kinds of nursing jobs, she couldn't have been employed at any one place for more than six months at a time.

I already knew, at age eleven, that I was going to be nurse. I decided that after I had a few years of experience, I would write stories about nurses.

You may know how it is—your grandmother says you write a good letter, your high school English teacher says you write a good paper, and everyone says you should write because you read so much. With 15 years of nursing under my belt, I was ready!

I finally was able to afford a typewriter and a desk. I sat down, rolled a piece of paper in, put my hands on the keys, and literally waited for the book to come out. Yes, indeed, I laugh every time I think about that!

Eventually, however, a book did come out. I marketed it for a while, which was very discouraging. In those days, I'd send out a pristine 350 page paper manuscript, and three or four months later, come home to find it thrown on the doormat, ratty and coffee-stained. It took about a year to send it out four times, and no luck. A very nice editor from St. Martin's Press informed me that it wasn't my writing—there just wasn't a market for medical stories.

Well, it seemed to me that the successful medical writers had fancy titles, like MD or PhD, so off I went to the university to get some more education. I accidentally enrolled in a senior fiction writer's boot camp, thinly disguised as a creative writing class. I had to produce short stories, and my professor and classmates laughed at me until I cried. First I had to learn about sentimentality; next I had to unlearn my vocabulary; and horror of horrors, I learned that if you don't understand what I write, it's my fault, not yours! I wouldn't show my first novel to anyone on a bet, but it is slated to go through the word processor a few more times.

In my 45-year nursing career, I've been privileged to work in the operating room, helping pioneer liver and pancreas transplantation and general surgery laparoscopy. I spent ten years in reproductive endocrinology research, and for the last ten years have been a legal nurse consultant, currently working half-time at home in Cordova, TN, a suburb of Memphis. I have a daughter, a son, three delightful grandchildren, two granddogs, and three grand cats.

For down time, I have many hobbies, but my favorites are reading, writing, quilting, scrapbooking, doll making, and teaching all those things to my little grandchildren, who whine when it's time to leave "Granny SuSu's" house. I would too, if I were my grandmother!

Right now, it's time to thaw out poor old Frozen Frank and get his story ready to publish!

I hope you enjoyed *Negotiations and Love Songs.* I miss Madison, Park, David, and most of all, Cam and the trundle-tail!

Happy reading,

Suzi

EXCERPT FROM

ATTIC OPERATIONS

A MEDICAL THRILLER
BY SUZI LINDSAY
COMING IN MAY, 2014!

April, 1988

The nurse sighed with relief as she and Frank boarded the old freight elevator. Apparently she hadn't been recognized, and they'd made it through the teeming Emergency Room waiting area without any of the hospital employees stopping them. Leaving her to wrestle with the leaden horizontal elevator doors, Frank stuck his hands in his pockets and shifted from one foot to the other. By the time they jerked to a stop on the fifth floor, sweat beaded his upper lip and glistened through his crew cut.

They emerged in a hallway illuminated only by moonlight, which barely penetrated a small, dirty window. To the left, a plywood wall sealed the 200-year-old east annex, which was scheduled for demolition in a few months. Ignoring the prominently displayed "DANGER—NO ADMITTANCE" sign, the nurse pried a panel loose, and they squeezed around the barricade.

"Hey," Frank said, "where are we going? You said my surgery would be done in an operating room."

With a grunt, the nurse pulled the panel back in place. "It will be, Frank, but I can't exactly take you through the front door and sign you up in Admissions, now can I?"

Wiping her hands on the seat of her beige double-knit pants, she set off down the dark hall at a fast clip, glancing over her shoulder to make sure he followed. She saw him wobble a little as his foot found one of the areas where the linoleum sank into the termite-eaten subfloor.

"I don't like this at all," Frank said. "Something funny is going on here."

"What's funny is that you don't realize you're in this way too deep to back out now." She led him into the vestibule of the old hospital chapel, its swinging doors screeching on their hinges, and up a narrow, winding staircase that creaked with every step. On the landing, a votive light at the foot of a life-sized plaster statue of Christ threw huge, flickering shadows on the walls.

They emerged in an eaves room jammed with outdated equipment, carelessly packed boxes of supplies in yellowing paper, and trays of old surgical instruments. A mobile surgical spotlight cast a yellow glow on a wooden table covered with a sheet. At the head of the table was an antiquated anesthesia machine; to one side were a three-tiered console with new equipment, and another table with neatly arranged instruments and supplies.

Frank cased the room, his respirations shallow and fast. "Are you crazy? This isn't an operating room—it's an *attic*."

"It's an *attic* operating room, okay? Good enough for a ten minute procedure. Just relax. It's not like I have to make a big incision, or anything." She flipped him a hospital gown. "Hurry up and get undressed."

Frank caught the gown and took a step back toward the stairs, his eyes riveted to hers.

"Do you want a million bucks, or not?" she said menacingly.

He hesitated, then turned away, peeled off his clothes, and put on the skimpy hospital johnny. She thumbed him toward the makeshift operating table. "Lie down."

Frank reluctantly settled on the hard table, his eyes darting around the room.

A bulky man, hair and face covered with surgical cap and

mask, lumbered into the room and barked an order. "Medical history."

Bristling at his tone, the nurse answered in a clipped voice. "23-year-old, weight 81 kilograms, height 6'2". No known drug allergies. General anesthesia without complications at age ten for tonsillectomy. No medications. Nothing to eat or drink since 8 p.m. That's eight hours."

"Anything abnormal on his physical exam?"

"No—I would have told you, wouldn't I?"

"Don't give me any shit. Get an IV started." Without speaking to Frank, he walked to the head of the table and began taking medications out of a portable red toolbox.

"Who is he?" Frank asked.

"Don't worry about it," the nurse said.

"I feel like I can't breathe," Frank said, trying to sit up.

The nurse pushed him down and applied a tourniquet to his forearm, a little tighter than necessary, and slid a needle into the bulging vein on his hand. "Quit whining, Frank. You'll be in Baghdad by Monday with your big, fat bankroll."

"You better make sure I come out of this okay," he said, watching her remove the tourniquet and connect the IV fluids, "or you'll be sorry."

The doctor fit a mask over Frank's nose and mouth and strapped it down, while the nurse taped the IV catheter to his hand and slowed the drip rate. "Really? Why's that?"

In rapid sequence, the doctor injected a dose of sodium Pentothal, a muscle relaxant, and a short-acting narcotic.

"Because," Frank said, his voice muffled by the mask, "I wrote a letter to . . . to be opened if anything happened . . ." His eyes lost focus; one arm slid off the table and hung at his side. The doctor ran his index finger lightly over Frank's eyelashes; there was no reaction. He tipped Frank's head back, squeezed the bag on the anesthesia machine several times, took the mask off, and deftly inserted a breathing tube.

"Do you think he really left a letter somewhere?" the doctor asked as he hooked the tube to a ventilator that would breathe for Frank, and adjusted the anesthesia gasses to keep him asleep.

"Nah, he was bluffing. He tried to chicken out on me on the way in." She covered her curly blonde wig with a surgical cap and tied on a mask. "You should have seen his face when we got off the elevator. He was terrified."

From a zipped pocket in her cracked black patent leather handbag, she took a handful of fountain pen cartridges and dropped them into a bowl of disinfectant. The doctor peered into the bowl. "Are you sure you cleaned all the ink out of those things before you sealed the film in them?"

Ignoring him, she painted Frank's abdomen with brownish-orange antiseptic, donned sterile gown and gloves, and backed up to the doctor. "Tie me up," she said, and he snapped the neck of her gown shut and tied the strings at her waist.

After the nurse squared off Frank's mid-section with sterile paper drapes, she took a knife from the instrument table and made a half-inch, semicircular incision at the lower edge of his navel. As she plunged a six-inch needle into Frank's belly through the incision, the doctor asked, "Are you sure you know what you're doing?"

She hooked a silicone hose to the needle. "Of course I do. I've watched it done in the dog lab a couple of times."

"And called it experience. Spoken like a true overachieving nurse."

She threw the free end of the hose off the sterile field, narrowly missing his face. "Just hook this up to the insufflator." His continual checking and re-checking wore on her nerves. What was wrong with him? They had gone over the plan ad nauseam—he would put Frank to sleep, she would put the cartridges in his abdomen, and when Frank shipped out to Baghdad, another doctor would take them out. Simple. What could go wrong?

She pointed to the connection on the machine that would

force carbon dioxide gas into Frank's belly, pushing his abdominal wall away from his internal organs so they wouldn't be injured when she put in the nail-like trocar. The doctor connected it and turned the gas on. For a several minutes, nothing happened. He drummed his fingers of the softly sighing ventilator. "How long is it supposed to take to get enough gas in?"

The nurse frowned. "I don't really know. Maybe the needle is in the wrong place."

"I thought you knew how to do this."

She yanked the needle out and shoved it in his face. A drop of blood splattered on Frank's forehead. "If you're such an expert, you do it."

"Okay, okay. Don't get your panties in a wad." He turned his back to her and fiddled with his machinery.

She reinserted the needle, advancing it three inches instead of four. This time, Frank's abdomen slowly expanded until he appeared six months pregnant. When the digital readout on the insufflator registered three liters of gas delivered, she pulled the needle out. Tapping on Frank's belly, which sounded like a drum, she said, "Perfect."

The nurse picked up a four-inch long hollow plastic tube the diameter of her thumb, into which she inserted a trocar that resembled a huge aluminum nail. Its razor-sharp triangular point protruded from the end of the tube as it slid into place with a decisive click. Holding the assembled instrument at an angle toward Frank's groin, she worked its tip into the incision, thrust it deep inside his belly, and pulled the trocar out, leaving the plastic tube.

"Nothing to it," she said, looking up with a smugness that turned to alarm when she saw the doctor frantically drawing up drugs and pushing them into Frank's I.V. "What's wrong?"

"I don't know. Blood pressure's gone. Can't ventilate him."

The nurse looked at the EKG monitor. Frank's heart rate steadily accelerated. 160. 170. 180. "Shit, he's going to fibrillate!"

As soon as the words were out of her mouth, the regular pattern on the monitor changed to the coarse, spiky waves of ventricular fibrillation. On her arms and the back of her neck, the fine hair stood up. They were using a monitor she had resurrected from a corner of the attic. It had no defibrillator to shock the heart back to its regular rhythm. The only one available was in the real O.R., three crammed storage rooms and a long hall away. It would take too long to get the machine.

It would be too late.

With a meaty fist, the doctor delivered a single blow to the middle of Frank's chest. The EKG fluctuated wildly, then settled to a flat line. Grabbing a pre-filled syringe of intracardiac adrenalin, he attached a six-inch needle and plunged it into Frank's chest, straight into the heart, and injected the medicine. "Pump his chest!" he screamed as he pulled the needle out.

Heart pounding as if she, too might fibrillate, the nurse located the tip of Frank's sternum, placed the heels of her hands just above it, and began compressions to the silent count of one, one-thousand, two, one-thousand, three, one-thousand . . .

After an estimated minute, she stopped to check for a pulse, and feeling none, resumed compressions for what seemed an eternity. Again she paused. Still, there was nothing but a flat line on the monitor, which filled the room with the dreaded continuous hum that indicated cardiac death.

"Did you try isuprel?" she gasped.

"Of course I did. I've given him every damn thing I have. We might as well give up; he's dead."

"Give up? Are you crazy? We need him!" She pushed harder and harder on Frank's bony chest, feeling a sickening crunch as she sheared a couple of ribs off his breastbone. "Come on Frank," she panted. Sweat stung her eyes and made her neck itch unbearably.

Frank's face was a waxy bluish-white; his eyes, corneas shriveled and opaque, were fixed on the peaked ceiling. The doctor turned off the monitor and ventilator. Forcefully, he chunked needles and empty glass medication vials into a plastic bowl on the instrument table.

The nurse delivered one last, vicious blow to Frank's chest. "Damn you, I knew you'd screw me up." She ripped off her cap, wig, and gown, and collapsed on a dusty carton of books, wiping her sweaty face on her arm. "What are we going to do now?"

The doctor slammed the lid of his toolbox. "*We* are going to dispose of the body, then my part of the bargain is over. *You* are going to return equipment and clean up this mess so no one will ever know we were here. And I suppose you ought to call your friend Max Gordon and give him some explanation for Frank not showing up. Not to mention scrounging up another courier."

"The day shift will start arriving at 6:30. I'll never get it all done by myself. Can't you at least help me move equipment back to the O.R.?"

"I told you the only thing I'd do is put him to sleep."

"Yeah, well you put him to sleep, all right. What did you do to him, anyway?"

"I didn't do anything to him. All of a sudden, I couldn't ventilate him, and his pressure tanked. Could've been a reaction to the anesthetic. Or maybe he had asthma."

"Asthma?" Frank *had* mentioned asthma; he'd lied about it to get into the Marine Corps. "Why would that be important?"

"Because anesthesia agents can aggravate it and cause intractable bronchospasm." His eyes narrowed. "Did you forget to tell me something?"

She walked to the instrument table, put on another pair of gloves, opened a suture, and loaded it onto a needle holder. "Of course not," she said thinly. She released the gas from Frank's abdomen, pulled the plastic tube out, and put two stitches in the oozing wound. "We have to figure out what to do with him. Maybe we could stick him in that old chest freezer down on five, next to the elevator. You know, the one they used for placenta storage, years ago? It'll be months before anyone discovers the body."

"At least he won't stink until you can think of something better," the doctor replied. "With luck, the demolition crew will dispose of the freezer without opening it."

The nurse wrapped Frank in the sheet on which he lay, while the doctor tore long strips from old green O.R. sheets that were being used for dust covers for machinery. They bound the unwieldy corpse tightly around the neck, chest, and ankles, then lowered it to the floor and dragged it through the storage rooms to the staircase by the freight elevator. As they dragged Frank's stiffening body down the stairs, his head thumped on each step like a runaway basketball.

In the narrow room beside the elevator on five, they heaved Frank's body into the old chest freezer, flexing his legs to make it fit. The nurse plugged in the macabre coffin.

It hummed contentedly.